LONGARM ACI

Longarm got to guess a heap about the message Sergeant Foster had sent him. The infernal letter had advised him the matter was too delicate to confide to paper but intimated there might be a matter of vital importance to both Canada and U.S. of A.

Foster was a good old boy who'd looked the other way when a lawman without a royal warrant from south of the border chased an outlaw across the same. So at face value, Longarm had guessed that Foster was likely after somebody both countries wanted pretty bad.

Longarm wondered why he hadn't just come south to gather up the son of a bitch. That was the way Longarm had always invaded Canada.

"About this mysterious town of Natova?" asked Longarm.

Foster said, "It seems Natova is a sort of mountain resort for gentlemen of fortune who need to cool off a bit after a jail break or the sort of robbery that gets one's name in the newspapers. From the way our informants described it, Natova seems to rather resemble that resort for wicked boys described in that tale about Pinocchio. Wine, women, and games of chance, as long as one's money holds out."

"How long did you say all this has been going on?"

Foster answered simply, "We don't know. We don't want it to go on much longer. Are you in?"

Longarm said, "I reckon."

TABOR EVANS

LONGARM

AND THE UNDER-COVER MOUNTIE

JOVE BOOKS, NEW YORK

THE BERKLEY PUBLISHING GROUP
Published by the Penguin Group
Penguin Group (USA) Inc.
375 Hudson Street, New York, New York 10014, USA
Penguin Group (Canada), 90 Eglinton Avenue East, Suite 700, Toronto, Ontario M4P 2Y3, Canada
(a division of Pearson Penguin Canada Inc.)
Penguin Books Ltd., 80 Strand, London WC2R 0RL, England
Penguin Group Ireland, 25 St. Stephen's Green, Dublin 2, Ireland (a division of Penguin Books Ltd.)
Penguin Group (Australia), 250 Camberwell Road, Camberwell, Victoria 3124, Australia
(a division of Pearson Australia Group Pty. Ltd.)
Penguin Books India Pvt. Ltd., 11 Community Centre, Panchsheel Park, New Delhi—110 017, India
Penguin Group (NZ), Cnr. Airborne and Rosedale Roads, Albany, Auckland 1310, New Zealand
(a division of Pearson New Zealand Ltd.)
Penguin Books (South Africa) (Pty.) Ltd., 24 Sturdee Avenue, Rosebank, Johannesburg 2196,
South Africa

Penguin Books Ltd., Registered Offices: 80 Strand, London WC2R 0RL, England

LONGARM AND THE UNDERCOVER MOUNTIE

A Jove Book / published by arrangement with the author

PRINTING HISTORY
Jove edition / December 2005

For information, address: The Berkley Publishing Group,
a division of Penguin Group (USA) Inc.,
375 Hudson Street, New York, New York 10014.

ISBN: 0-515-14017-1

JOVE®
Jove Books are published by The Berkley Publishing Group,
a division of Penguin Group (USA) Inc.,
375 Hudson Street, New York, New York 10014.
JOVE is a registered trademark of Penguin Group (USA) Inc.
The "J" design is a trademark belonging to Penguin Group (USA) Inc.

PRINTED IN THE UNITED STATES OF AMERICA

10 9 8 7 6 5 4 3 2 1

Chapter 1

Men of good will on both sides of the Canadian border were forced to walk on eggs during the administrations of President Rutherford B. Hayes and Sir John MacDonald, the prime minister Queen Victoria kept refusing as he begged and pleaded for permission to declare war on the Bloody Yanks.

Aside from his traditional views that God was British and that any parts of the globe not colored Imperial Pink were an oversight, Sir John was particularly annoyed that particular summer about the half breed Canadian rebel, Louis Riel, openly teaching school in Montana Territory, just out of reach of the Mounties.

He wasn't thrilled by Fenian songs sung in many an Irish American neighborhood saloon, either.

President Hayes was just as vexed by all those Arapaho, Cheyenne and Lakota who'd won at Little Bighorn openly hunting buffalo and waving scalps on Canadian prairie denied to the U.S. Cav, and, after that, they just plain didn't like each other.

But more practical men charged with upholding law and order still had to try, and fortunately the Piegan or Blackfoot Nation extended north and south of the border along the eastward slopes of the Rocky Mountains and an *Aghsee* lawman trusted by the Piegan on one side of the border could get word to one on friendly terms with the Piegan on the other, no matter what they might have heard from Ottawa or Washington.

Thus it came to pass that on a sunny Sunday afternoon in June a man riding tall in the saddle reined his horse in by a lonely graveyard on a windy hill with a big bouquet of store-bought roses in his free hand. For nobody could fault a Deputy U.S. Marshal for paying respects to a lady who'd once said she loved him, and the lawman who'd ridden out from the rail-head on a hired chestnut gelding meant what he said as he dropped to one knee in the grass by her grave marker to place the red roses in the fair-sized mason jar along with the wilted blue cornflowers already there.

He said, "Howdy, Miss Sally. I see them Indian kids I asked have been doing right by you. But, seeing I was up this way, unofficial, I figured a few more flowers wouldn't hurt."

Longarm, or Custis Long, as Roping Sally had known him, looked away and swallowed as he got a better grip on his feelings. He'd known as he'd dismounted he was fixing to blubber up if he didn't watch it. For Roping Sally had been pretty as a picture; she'd sat her pony like a queen, roped better than anyone else he'd ever come across, and it just wasn't fair.

He didn't turn as he heard the soft swish of dark moccasins coming through the graveyard grass behind him.

He'd been expecting to hear it. You never heard a Piegan coming if he was sneaking up on you.

Longarm went on arranging the flowers in the mason jar until a voice that surprised him said, "If you are the *Otokansaki* they call *Ochist Innya* I think you should come with me. If you are not *Ochist Innya* forget what I just said."

He turned to smile up at the Indian gal standing there. It was easy to smile at any gal that handsome. She looked to be somewhere in her twenties and at least a quarter white, or *Otokansaki* as they put it in her own native tongue. She was dressed more in accordance with Late Victorian fashion than your average so-called Blackfoot. She walked in moccasins and he doubted she had on a corset and stays, but her mail order summer frock had been ordered in her size, not handed down, and she filled its blue polka dots just right.

The Algonquin dialects were the most familiar to the white ear, having been recorded earliest as "Indian talk." But Longarm had to think as he decided *Innya* meant *long* whilst *ochist* meant *arm*, unless it went the other way. Algonquin words such as *makasin*, *moos* or *wampompeg* were easier.

He knew better than to call her a squaw; she was an *Ahkequiain* or a young and pretty gal in her own lingo. He got to his feet and tipped his hat brim to her as he tried, "*Niston Ochist Innya. How ne tukka*?"

She looked pained and asked, "Are you crazy? I speak English and if you think you make any sense in Piegan, you do not. Call me Maria. That is the name the black robes gave me at the mission school. You would not be able to say my Piegan name if I said it eleven times. They told me you would be wearing a brown tweed suit. I see you rode out here in blue denim. That is the only reason I asked who you were in Piegan."

Longarm gravely replied, "I figured as much Miss Maria. I ain't got on the duds I wear on duty because I ain't supposed to be on duty up this way. I ride for the Denver District Court and to tell the truth I hope nobody from the U.S. Marshal's office in Helena knows I'm up this way."

The pretty but sort of snotty Maria tossed her head and replied, "Hear me. They don't. The red coat you are to meet is not in uniform, either. Are you coming with me or do you want to weep over the *ourcar* of a woman I heard described as fat?"

Longarm bit his tongue before it could tell the petite snip to go fuck herself. He hadn't come all this way to *guess* where Crown Sergeant Foster of the Northwest Mounted Police might be holed up south of the border. So he contented himself to observe, as he followed Maria out to the two ponies tethered by the graveyard gate, "Miss Roping Sally was a good-sized gal. But there wasn't much lard on her athletic frame and if there had been it ain't polite to mean-mouth a lady who was killed as she was trying to help your nation."

The Indian girl gathered her grounded reins and mounted her own paint, saddled center-fire so's she had to ride astride with more of her legs on display than late Victorian fashion dictated.

Longarm tethered the mount he hadn't known that long. As he untied the half hitch around the gate post Maria declared, "You are right. I do not know why I spoke ill of the dead just now. I never knew your Roping Sally. But they told me why boys still put fresh flowers on her *ourcar*. You were the one who killed the *Wendigo*, the *Cristeccom sah* who murdered Roping Sally, *ah*?"

Mounting taller beside her, Longarm said, "Wasn't no evil spirits as killed Roping Sally and all them others on your reservation. That so-called *Wendigo* was a hired assassin acting spooky for a plain old land grabber. He wound up dead, too. But that was then and this is now and so where on your reservation might Crown Sergeant Foster be holed up?"

She reined her paint out to the wagon trace as she told him, "Your red coat dressed like a ranch hand has been staying at a hotel over in Great Falls. He crossed the border up by Sweetgrass. He has told everyone in Great Falls he came up the Missouri on a steamboat because he is from Texas, if anyone must know."

Longarm blinked and observed, "Great Falls would be going on sixty miles by crow if we were riding crows and it's already well past noon."

She said, "*Aghsee*, anybody following us at a distance will lose sight of us at sunset and we are not heading directly for Great Falls until after dark. The red coat waiting for you in Great Falls is worried about people on this side of the border knowing why so many call you the man with long arms."

As they rode side by side at a walk, Longarm frowned and said, "He must be. Might you know what this is all about, Miss Maria?"

She answered, simply, "*Sah*. None of us asked him. Our kinsmen to the north know Crown Sergeant Foster talks straight with a good heart. We know you to be the same sort of *Otokansaki Aghsee*. So we know nothing bad will happen to us when the two of you meet to . . . do something to somebody else. That is all we need to know. When people know things they do not need to know other people might find out about it. When we top the rise ahead I think we should lope down the far side and watch from the next rise to see if anybody raises any dust on this side."

Longarm said, "I'm game. But let's study some on your proposed cross-country jaunt with neither canteen water nor bedrolls, Miss Maria. Never expecting such travel plans, I only hired this livery nag and bare saddle for the afternoon. I figured anybody meeting me back yonder would have a closer destination in mind."

She nodded and replied, "That was why you were told to wait for somebody like me so close to the railhead. Should anybody ask, you rode out to that dead girl's *ourcar* with red roses and no trail supplies. When you don't return by sundown, anyone who cares may think you are somewhere out this way, meaning to come back in the morning. *Pokaaah*!"

So then they were tearing down the slope at a dead run, with Maria laughing and light in the saddle as her long black hair streamed out in back of her. So Longarm laughed, too, and decided, "Well, it remains to be seen how well she can *rope*."

He warned himself not to consider other ways Maria might compare with the late Roping Sally. He got along tolerable with Indians by not jumping to conclusions about natural gals inclined to show more flesh and feelings than your average white dance-hall gal. For many an old white boy had wound up prematurely bald after mistaking a flash of tawny flesh for an invitation to feel it up.

They reined in atop the next grassy rise of the rolling shortgrass prairie, still green that early in June. The dust the two of them had stirred up hung hazy in the draw they'd just loped across. But no other dust hung above the trail behind them. So Maria suggested they cover some ground the sensible way, trotting downslope and walking upslope at a mile-eating but not too comfortable pace.

The spine of a horse and the crotch of a human being had not evolved to move together in that rhythm. Not the crotch of a *male* member of the human race, least ways. Longarm had long suspected the attachment so many young gals felt to their precious ponies might have something to do with the way saddle leather pounded a body betwixt spread thighs at a trot. Others suspecting the same had designed and decreed side saddles for young ladies. They were more inclined to simply spank young rumps than they might be to arouse turgid privates. But all a mere male got out of an infernal pony trot was bruised balls if he didn't stand in the stirrups just right.

This was no doubt the reason so many young gents tended to gallop by as ladies rode at a steady trot. At a gallop a man's crotch stayed with the saddle, as comfortably as in a rocking chair, and it was a crying shame horses couldn't hold that pace for more than four to five miles or so.

Since they couldn't, Longarm spent a heap of time standing in the stirrups that afternoon as he tried to figure out where Maria might be leading him.

She'd allowed they were headed for Great Falls. But unless his own mental map was badly flawed they were trending too far to the east for the last important town up an increasingly shallow Big Muddy.

They broke trail for a leg stretch and some grazing every hour or more. By the second break Longarm was pretty certain nobody could be following them. Maria still couldn't tell him why in thunder anybody might be *wanting* to follow them.

Since Maria couldn't tell him, Longarm got to guess a heap about the message Sergeant Foster had sent him by way of a letter with the return address of his other pal, Crow Tears of the Indian Police, postmarked the Blackfoot Reservation up this way.

The infernal letter had advised him the matter was too delicate to confide to paper but intimated there might be a matter of vital importance to both Canada and the U.S. of A. Leaving Longarm to read betwixt some lines, Foster had coyly gone on to ask if Longarm might recall the time the two of them had shared mutual interests about sporting events.

Longarm had never played poker with Crown Sergeant Foster, and the first time they'd met they'd had a swell fight about jurisdiction. But Foster was a good old boy who'd looked the other way when a lawman without a royal warrant from south of the border had chased an outlaw or more across the same. So at face value, Longarm had guessed and his boss, the canny Marshal Billy Vail, had agreed Foster was likely after somebody both countries wanted pretty bad.

So here he was, on officiously unpaid leave to lay roses on the grave of a lost love, and if President Hayes and his Lemonade Lucy never heard a thing about it, they were no more likely than Sir John MacDonald to kick up a fuss.

Longarm was still working on why Foster hadn't just come south without his red coat and gold stripes to gather up the son of a bitch. That was the way Longarm had always invaded Canada.

Not being able to talk about Crown Sergeant Foster or international skulduggery, Longarm and Maria perforce got to know one another better with nothing better to jaw about as their shadows kept getting longer out ahead of them. Before sundown he'd learned how, as he'd expected, a part-white mission-educated gal had developed that defensive chip on her trim shoulder, teased by assholes on both sides of her family tree as they'd found it hard to decide what to make of a gal who wasn't all that sure about her ownself.

The Black Robes who'd educated her about the world outside her proud but stay-at-home nation had taught her no man who respected her would expect her to abide other women in bed with them. Traditional Blackfoot, divided as they might be into Piegan, Kainah or Siksika bands, practiced polygamy in a manner to shock a rich Mormon elder. Blackfoot braves were distinguished by how many ponies and wives they could handle, and friends as well as enemies allowed they wore no breechclouts and let it all hang out in order to show it hard day or night. Longarm said he followed her drift when Maria allowed she was holding out for a Christian Blackfoot. He'd heard there were such critters, and, meanwhile, there went any plans a man might have made in the company of a pretty little thing with bare legs hanging out from mid-thigh down.

Longarm had no idea where they might be headed as the sky before them got ever more purple and the green grass all around turned to charcoal.

A distant light winked on near the horizon as somebody lit a lamp in a far-off window. It was off to their east, out of their way. Or so it seemed until the sky ahead got starry and Maria headed them toward that brighter lamplight. When he asked her who might live yonder Maria said he had no need to know and that seemed fair. Whites and Indians sometimes lived together. Indians got to live alone off the reservation as long as they behaved themselves. As they rode in, a yard dog commenced to bark and then it stopped as if somebody had told it to. Nobody was out in the dooryard as they reined in. But two ponies were tethered to a hitch rail as if waiting on their riders. Maria said, "The people here will take your livery nag back to town and claim your deposit. We will ride south on these fresh ponies."

As they dismounted in the tricky light Longarm could see that the unshod Indian ponies had been heavily saddled with water bags, feed sacks and no doubt other trail supplies. He nodded in approval and offered Maria a boost as she mounted her more awkwardly laden buckskin. As he untethered the roan meant for his own larger frame he saw it packed even more feed and water, but lacked the bedroll Maria had behind the cantle of her own saddle.

So he started to ask how they'd manage if they had to camp out on the open range a piece.

Then he wondered why any man would ever want to ask a dumb question like that one.

Chapter 2

In spite of her education, Maria told time Indian style, or the way everybody had before the Industrial Revolution got time going, back in the late 1600s, with the first crude steam engines and stagecoaches set to come and go on schedule. Up until then country folk, red or white, had gone by the way things *felt*. Going to bed when you were tired, getting up when you felt rested, and going about what needed to be done when it needed to be done worked well enough and felt a lot better than moving along to ticking clockwork whether you felt like it or not. So Maria called for trail breaks when she sensed her pert rump or her Indian pony needed one and Longarm didn't argue, even though it sure beat all how a man raised to tell time by wall clocks or pocket watches got to where he could feel about what time it was without looking.

So he knew that in her case it wasn't true what they said about lazy redskins because she called trail brakes more than an hour apart and said it was midnight around a quarter to one. Longarm had checked by fishing out his pocket watch whilst lighting a three-for-a-nickle cheroot.

Maria allowed that in either case it was time to water and fodder the ponies more seriously and unsaddle them to air their hides as she and Longarm treated themselves to square meals, seated atop a grassy rise with the ponies tethered downwind.

They dined on jerked beef and trading-post sea biscuits, washed down by tomato preserves, so they didn't need to risk a fire. Maria had no call to warn Longarm about his smoking. She'd already seen that he kept the lit end of his cheroot safely cupped in his big fist. She seemed surprised when he asked her if she cared for a smoke.

She confessed, "I have liked to smoke ever since the Black Robes told me nice mission girls did not smoke. I have dipped snuff, in private, too. But, hear me, I am a woman and you are a man!"

Longarm chuckled and replied, "I never would have noticed. Do I look like an . . . *Ahecoo-ah nin nah* to you, Miss Maria? Did I tell you how many gals I've shared a smoke with, you'd think I was bragging."

She demurely suggested they grub up whilst she thought about that. So they did. As they perforce chewed reflectively on jerked beef, they had plenty of time for conversation. It hurt when you ate sea biscuits and jerked beef too fast.

Halfway through their meal she soberly asked whether he'd smoked with Roping Sally before those land-grabbers killed her.

Longarm looked away and said, "More than once. We wasn't bound by your tribal traditions. Albeit, being a lady, old Sal never smoked in public or entered no saloon."

Maria softly replied, "Some of our men who knew her say she was very beautiful, no pony could buck her off and she was brave as any man. They told me that when you found her mangled body out on the prairie you did not try to hide the tears in your eyes. Her *Ah-een* must feel very proud when she boasts of this in the *mo-ees* of *Kee-pe-tah-tee*. The other ghosts must envy her. You are an important man yet you wept for her, as if she had been important, too!"

Longarm grimaced and said, "Everybody is important, to somebody. Can we change the subject, Miss Maria? Like I told you earlier, that was then and this is now."

She said, "I am sorry. I keep forgetting. At the mission school the Black Robes would go on and on about bad things that happened to their kind far away and more than *ee-sooy-perug* summers ago. But men who can *remember* bad things do not enjoy talking about them as much. When I was little I asked my father if he remembered our shining times when we were feared by all the other nations. He raised his hand as if to slap me and went outside, and it was snowing, and my mother told me not to ask questions that hurt brave men to remember."

Longarm went on chewing. He had no call to say he followed her drift. They both knew how, in their day, her flashily dressed and oversized kin had terrorized everybody who'd come anywhere's near them. With the U.S. Cav conceding it had been fortunate as hell that the so-called Blackfoot had been less inclined to roam than say Arapaho, Cheyenne or Lakota. Because pound for pound the Blackfoot had been one fighting son of a bitch.

They'd been whupped down, of course. Smarter as well as tougher than some more notorious nations, the Piegan south of the border and Siksika north of the border had hammered out treaties early, whilst they could still get halfway fair terms, and never given anybody in the Indian Ring an excuse to tear their original deals up.

That had doubtless meant many a born hero swallowing

his pride as he perforce took shit off Indian agents who'd gotten their notions about Indians in front of cigar stores back east. But as those land-grabbers had found out a spell back, Maria's kin were too slick to panic into a reservation jump or scalp dance.

White men who knew them knew they'd be more notorious than Sitting Bull's Lakota Confederacy had they lost their self-control.

But they hadn't. They were one of the smartest self-governing Indian nations and Crown Sergeant Foster had known what he was up to, whatever he was up to, by enlisting Canadian Siksika to work off the record with American Piegan. With any luck, the rascals they were after would have no idea what was up.

Longarm was halfway to Great Falls and *he* had no idea what was up.

Washing down the last of the gritty but filling sea biscuit with the much sweeter tomato preserves, Longarm fished out a couple of cheroots and lit them both with the same screened match before he told Maria, handing her one, "This ought to calm our innards down, Miss Maria. Ah, what time were you figuring on turning in, tonight?"

She took the cheroot, saying, "We still have much of this *skaynatsee* night with no *coque-ahtose* ahead of us. I think we should sleep after it is light and go on into Great Falls after it is dark again."

Longarm said, "If you say so. I don't know where we are. Might that *coque-ahtose* stand for moonlight, Miss Maria?"

She said, "*Ah.* If we ride on as soon as we have smoked there is this place my people used to hide in, north of Great Falls. Nobody, not even my own people, camp there now."

She took a drag on her cheroot and marveled, "This is very very sweet *pistacan*! Do you pay a lot for it?"

He said, "If *pistacan* means tobacco, it ain't considered all that fancy by my kind."

She took a thoughtful drag and replied, "I'm sorry I keep falling back into the tongue of my elders, too. I'm not trying to confuse you. I don't usually do so when talking to your kind. I think it may be just because I keep forgetting we are not the same kind. I do not feel as . . . stiff around you as I do around most of you *Otokansaki*."

She laughed and said, "There, I've done it again.

He allowed he didn't mind and said he found her comfortable company as well.

She didn't answer for a time. When she did she asked, "As comfortable as you felt with that dead woman they called Roping Sally?"

He thought some before he declared, "How do you compare apples to oranges? We've just now met. Me and Roping Sally . . . knew each other a spell before them land-grabbers killed her."

"Were you going to marry her?" Maria asked.

Longarm took less time to answer, "Can't truthfully say. They killed her before that first glow could wear off. Old Sally never got around to suggesting I shave my mustache, ask for a raise or quit smoking. So I will never get to wonder what I could have been thinking when first I kissed her. I'll always remember her as young and pretty with a whole lot of . . . kissing stolen from the two of us."

He took a drag, blew a thoughtful smoke ring and added, "The Vikings held it was best to go down fighting in your prime so's the world would always remember you that way. This kindly old philosopher once wrote, in French, of course, that all great love stories end in tragedy or farce, and tragedy left sweeter memories of lost love. Knew this old boy, one time, who'd been happily married to the same childhood sweetheart for going on twenty years before he discovered she'd been whoring on the side all that time for pin money. He said he resented all those wasted years more than he bitterized about a woman who meant nothing at all to him in his middle age."

She said, "Oh, the poor man! When did he tell you such a sad story, ah . . . Custis?"

Longarm replied, "Night before we hung him. I was stuck with the death-watch detail that night. Seems he shot up six others along with his wife in the house of ill repute he found her working in."

"Are you mocking me?" Maria demanded.

To which he could only reply, "Wish I was. I got to feeling for that poor old boy by the time I had to walk him out to the gallows. It hit me later he'd have lived longer with sweeter memories if a bride he still recalled as mighty lively had died on their honeymoon."

Maria said, "I still think you are mocking me. Finish your smoke. We still have a long way to ride."

He said he smoked in the saddle just fine and rose to help her to her own black-moccasined feet. She protested that she could saddle her own pony but he insisted on doing it for her, the heavily laden stock saddle weighing more than she did, if he was any judge of she-male curvature.

They rode on and on, leaving few if any tracks in the greenup grass with their unshod ponies. He'd figured early on they'd been outfitted with Indian ponies ridden white with such details in mind.

Riding by the dark of the moon, despite all those stars above, with the Milky Way brighter than at lower altitudes, they had to trust to the better night vision of their mounts as they loped some through mostly barren foothills in the dry rain shadow of the Rockies. So it was just as well they were both good riders, as their saddles twisted in surprising directions from time to time.

They broke trail every four or five miles but only for a few minutes before riding on. It had gotten mighty tedious by the time the sky got pearly off to the east.

Just about the time Longarm could make things out all around them Maria pointed out a fuzzy darkness to the south and said, "We made it. Lope with me for that wooded draw before the sun comes up!"

So he did and as the sky above got too blue for the stars to show, he found they were down in an eastarn winding draw where box elders, cottonwoods and crack willows formed close ranks along the banks of a sandy dried-out streambed. Maria suggested they make camp a tad higher, on the still wooded slope, to avoid flash flooding. Longarm was too polite to say she'd insulted an experienced High Plains rider.

He unsaddled both broncs as Maria removed their bits and tethered them to cottonwoods with rope hackamores. She filled their leather nose bags with plenty of water before offering either cracked corn, or even letting them browse cottonwood leaves—for a jaded pony was sure to bloat its fool self if you let it have its fill of dry fodder before you added water to the mixture in its gut.

Having seen to their ponies first, the two experienced riders made a fireless camp in a nearby grove of box elders, which were really a form of dwarf maple that didn't need as much ground water to get by on.

Maria spread the one bedroll so's they could set on the top canvas tarp as they shared more jerked beef and sea biscuits. It didn't take much of either to satisfy one's gut growls. That was how come they made good trail supplies. Slurpy tomato preserves, seeing the canners had sweetened them some with sugar, were more satisfying than lemonade to a hungry camper, even though both left a body craving coffee you couldn't manage without a fire.

Nobody on the dodge made a campfire in broad daylight. You could hide a night fire in a hollow. But rising smoke against a cloudless sky could be seen for many a mile.

Maria turned down Longarm's offer of an after-breakfast cheroot with a yawn and asked, "*Cho hetta key tesistico*?"

Then she blushed becomingly and said, "There I go again. It seemed so much easier to ask if you were tired as I would have asked one of my own kind!"

Longarm followed her drift, but contented himself with allowing he did feel sort of tuckered, now that she mentioned it.

So Maria commenced to undress as if they were old pals. As she shucked the mail-order frock off over her head he saw he'd been right about her not having a corset or a stitch of anything else under it. The way her tawny hide covered her trim young figure was still a delightful surprise. He'd been undressing her with his eyes since first he'd laid eyes on her and he still saw his imagination had been somewhat limited.

That was likely what made French postcards so popular. Nothing a man could picture in his mind looked as inspiring as a bare-assed gal the first time you saw her bare ass.

Longarm started to ask a dumb question. Then, since Maria was getting between the white Hudson Bay blankets sandwiched betwixt the top and bottom canvas tarps, Longarm just shucked his own duds, taking longer, and slid in beside her.

He was still coiling his gun rig to tuck his .44-40 in the crown of his coffee-black Stetson, handy to their heads, when Maria grabbed hold of all he had to offer and gasped, "*Aghsee*! This is more than I expected! *Pohka a potey*!"

So he did, figuring she couldn't be asking him to go away, and as he entered her he could tell from the way she rose to the occasion he was in the company of another experienced rider.

So a good time was had by all in the shade of those box elders as the sun rose ever higher. The sun couldn't get at them on the north slope of the timbered draw, but Maria sure looked pretty when she got on top with the bedding cast aside and bitty pinpoints of sunlight dancing along her tawny curves whilst she moved up and down, a heap.

Longarm never asked where a gal holding out for an assimilated husband might have learned to screw so fine. She'd said she objected to sharing a man with other women. She'd never said she was a one-man woman. And so, since he wasn't exactly a one-woman man, they just enjoyed one another for such time as they might have, without discussion of the past or the future. Of course Longarm couldn't help hoping that, when the future got there, she'd be a better sport about it than some gals of various shades he'd met up with in the past.

He was really worried by the time she was willing to try for some shut-eye. For whether she meant all those mysterious Blackfoot phrases or just hadn't been getting any lately, the little breed he barely knew a thing about was all agush with passion and love juice as she did most of the work that morning.

She did more that afternoon, once they woke up and ate some more. She reminded him of one of those Greek statues, only more so, as she rose in all her naked glory to move the ponies to fresh browse and water them some more.

The afternoon was lazed away in alternate catnaps and bouts of a more exciting nature. Then it was getting on towards dusk, and they had to get up and get dressed and ride on, and then on some more, until they topped a rise to spy a necklace of lamplight ahead and Maria reined in to tell him, "That is Great Falls. Your friend from the north has checked in to the Pronghorn Hotel near the river. Leave that pony and its gear in the municipal corral."

So Longarm heeled his mount on down the far slope. He'd only gone a ways when he noticed he seemed to be riding alone. He neither reined in nor turned in the saddle to look back. Things happened that way, now and again, when a man with a tumbleweed job met up with the right sort of gal.

Chapter 3

The Great Falls were where the Missouri and Sun rivers wrestled on the front steps of the Rockies. So they were as far upstream as even the bitty shallow-draft sternwheelers plying the upper reaches of the Big Muddy could manage, and passengers and freight bound for Fort Shaw or less serious settlements to the west had to be unloaded to travel the harder ways along wagon traces or pack-train trails.

The modest town that had mushroomed around an original trading post by a steamboat landing consisted of a few frame and more log structures lining the few unpaved and uncertainly laid out streets. It rained too often for 'dobe, that far north, and fired bricks cost too much to ship that far upstream.

Longarm had no trouble finding the municipal corral, where he parted with his borrowed Indian pony friendly, tipping the hostlers to make sure it was rubbed down and watered good.

Finding his way to the Pronghorn Hotel was no tougher.

The whole town was less than a rifle shot across. Great Falls was neither a cow town nor a mining camp. So such business as took place in such a transfer point on the map tended to make for steady jobs at modest pay, leaving the dirt-paved streets fairly free of the whores, gamblers or trouble in general one found in places such as Dodge or Deadwood.

Longarm never asked for Crown Sergeant Foster of the Northwest Mounted Police at the hotel desk. He never even went to the desk. He went into the taproom off the lobby, ordered a scuttle of beer, and took it over to a table in a far corner so's he could sit with his back to chinked logs.

Longarm half-filled one of the steins that went with the scuttle and leaned back to light a smoke, not knowing how long he'd be there. But Foster had been keeping an eye on the corral from his window up the stairs and joined Longarm within minutes.

Longarm managed not to laugh. It wasn't easy. For it sure beat all how military a man could look in blue jeans and a hickory shirt if he put his mind to it. Crown Sergeant Foster had always seemed more human in appearance, walking like so in his scarlet tunic and gold stripes. That new pearl Stetson was worn Mountie style as well and Longarm could have sworn Foster had a ramrod up his ass as he sat stiffly down across the table from him to say, "Howdy. Don't I know y'all from somewheres? I'd be Dusty Rhodes from San Antonio and I could swear I've seen your ugly face somewheres afore."

Seeing there was nobody else close enough to matter, Longarm smiled thinly and replied, "Pleased to meet you, Dusty. I usually answer to Buck Crawford when I'm working undercover and it serves Reporter Crawford of the *Denver Post* right when I do something famous. But that

hat ain't right for Texas and it's best not to go for an accent when you ain't all that familiar with it."

He poured Foster a beer as he continued. "You don't need to worry about accents out here in our west. Ain't that many been raised out our way, yet, compared to all the others crowding in from all over. The late Alexander McSween of Lincoln County and the Masterson brothers of Dodge all grew up in Canada. The notorious Thompson brothers hail from Yorkshire, whilst that tiny terror, Luke Short, cut his teeth and likely his first throat in New Jersey, which he pronounces 'Joisey.' "

He took the cheroot from his mouth to sip some suds before he added in a thoughtful tone, "They say Billy the Kid's from New York and the mighty tough Deputy Chris Madsen riding out of Fort Smith arrests out-laws with a thick Scandhoovian accent. So for Gawd's sake drop that fake Texas accent as sounds more mintrel show than Texas, if you know what you're doing."

"I'm just trying to sound like y'all," the Canadian protested.

Longarm snorted in disgust and insisted, "You ain't even warm. To begin with, it's a dead giveaway when anybody born north of the Mason-Dixon line uses y'all all wrong. Y'all is used as a plural, the way a Mexican uses *ustedes* or a New Englander says "all of you." When a Southern is talking to one person he says 'you' like anybody else. "Y'all come" is an invite extended to all of you. You and anybody else you might care to bring along, see?"

Foster smiled sheepishly and said, "I stand corrected. Did I forget to tell you I arrived in San Antonio from Nova Scotia?"

Longarm said, "You must not have been there long. Folk who know the place better call it San Antone. We'd best say you've been punching cows on the newer range north of the Arkansas. Riders from the north ranger ain't had time to get as set in their ways as Texicans. How come we have to convince everyone up this way we're cowhands, Dusty?"

Foster said, "I was afraid you'd never ask. As you may or may not know, surveyors for our planned Canadian & Pacific Railroad have been scouting for a practical route through our own Rockies and I understand some of you lot have been scouting for a rairoad route out to your own Seattle area?"

Longarm nodded and said, "Great Northern Railroad, if it's ever built. Somebody's fixing to go to jail if it ain't built soon. They've been selling stock in the same for a spell. Is that who you Mounties are after on our side of the border?"

"We've barely room for our own criminals." Foster sniffed, adding in that same annoying tone, "The point I was trying to make is that those perishing, barely explored ranges crossing the imaginary line we've agreed on as our mutual border west of the glaciers of the divide have been barely explored, let along properly mapped."

Longarm demurred. "Oh, I dunno. Many a mountain man must have scouted out that way and the Indian say there's this trail, they call it the Going to the Sun Trail, through the glacier country and beyond."

Foster nodded soberly and said, "That where you come in. You know the Indians south of the border better than I. We've asked friendly Siksika about that route. They say their Blood or Piegan cousins know the country down this way better."

Longarm warned, "Never refer to a Kainah as a Blood. They resent it, same as Shoshone resent us calling 'em Snakes. Kainah means a people with many chiefs. They weren't looking to be called Bloods when they wore red war paint. The Piegan deny that their name means raggedy robes. All of 'em wear black moccasins, talk the same way and stick together against all comers. That about all any white man, including this one, really knows about a truculent and reclusive race."

Foster waved a dismissive hand and said, "Whatever. We're not worried about Indians of any ilk. We're worried about a hidden valley one enters from south of the border if he knows what's good for him."

He sipped some of the suds Longarm had offered and continued. "Some time ago a British subject staggered into one of our outposts south-west of Fort MacLeod, dying of gas gangrene. He'd frozen his hands and feet clawing his way over a glacier somewhere on our side of the border. He was either out of his head or didn't know much about map reading. He was unable to pinpoint the exact location of a settlement called Natova for us. But he claimed he'd escaped from there, the hard way, after being held a prisoner some time."

Longarm brightened and said, "I think *natova* means medicine in Blackfoot."

Foster nodded soberly and said, "It would be *manitou* in the eastern Algonquin dialects. We've been given to understand that the western dialects such as Arapaho, Blackfoot or Cheyenne have drifted apart about as much as say Latin, Italian, Spanish and so on. Siksika we asked say none of them would ever name a settlement Natova for the same reasons none of us would name one, say, Religion. Some white mountain man who fancied he was up on the dialect of his squaw must have named the place."

Longarm said, "Could have been worse. I understand Chicago means Heap Big Stink. How come they were holding that Canadian in such an oddly described place?"

Foster said, "Because he'd wandered into it, from your side of the border, prospecting for color. He says he took it for a rather remote but otherwise ordinary mountain town until he tried to leave. A man he described as a town constable told him he was a material witness in a pending court case and forbade his leaving town. When he insisted he'd just arrived and knew nothing about any local court cases he was warned they might have to lock him up, or worse, if he tried to leave without permission. He suspected they had no jail in Natova. So he never asked what might be worse. He went along with their game until he felt he wasn't being closely watched. He only realized after he'd made a break for it why nobody had felt they had to watch anybody north of the narrow trail he'd followed into the place. It was late last summer, or about as warm as it ever gets in glacier country, and he still wound up with frostbite followed by gangrene."

Longarm whistled softly and sipped more suds to sort his thoughts a tad before he decided, "I'm missing something. If all this happened last year, how come we're talking about it *this* year?"

Foster replied easily, "Two reasons. To begin with, the dying man who staggered out of the Canadian Rockies with a wild story might not have known what he was saying. After that it was too late in the season to contemplate our own exploration of unsurveyed glacier country. But I haven't come to the best part yet."

"There's a better part?" asked Longarm.

Foster nodded and said, "Earlier *this* year, with warm weather coming on, a naughty boy we'd been after for years was picked up in a house of ill repute in Moose Jaw. He hadn't been around Moose Jaw, or anywhere in Canada, as far as we could tell, for some time. So he'd assumed we had given up on him and thought it safe to return to his old haunts."

Longarm nodded soberly and suggested, "Must not have been brung up in Canada. By the way, I've always wondered about that time you stole that dead outlaw's body from me and smuggled it back to Canada. I mean, I wasn't out to cause you any trouble with your superiors, pard."

Foster shrugged and calmly replied, "You didn't. As you knew when you switched bodies on me, the corpse I took back to my own side of the border looked a lot like the outlaw we'd both been after."

"You mean you never told 'em?" Longarm marveled.

To which Foster rather smugly replied, "Why should I have done so? Haven't you heard the Mounties always get their man?"

Longarm laughed and said, "I admire a lawman who can think on his feet. We were talking about this real outlaw you all caught up to Moose Jaw."

Foster nodded and said, "He didn't want to hang for the blood and slaughter in and about that trading post, the poor simp, so he tried to save his neck by offering Queen's evidence. We made him no promises, mind you, but his execution has been put off until we can check out his own wild story."

"About this mysterious town of Natova?" asked Longarm.

Foster said, "His story made more sense to us than the last gasps of that unfortunate frostbitten prospector. According to our murderous youth from Moose Jaw, he'd been hiding out in Natova, snug as a bug in a rug, as he waited for things to cool down back home. He said he'd had to leave, and nobody had tried to stop him, after his money ran out. It seems Natova is operated as a sort of mountain resort for gentlemen of fortune who feel the need to cool off a bit after a jailbreak or the sort of robbery that gets one's name in the newspapers. From the way both our informants described it, Natova seems to rather resemble that resort for wicked boys described in that tale about Pinocchio. Wine, women and games of chance, as long as one's money holds out."

Longarm started to ask an obvious question before he answered it for himself, musing, "Paying customer would have to be free to come and go for the same reasons you don't lock 'em up in whorehouses. Word along the Owlhoot Trail would have to assure some honor among thieves if the place meant to stay in business long enough to matter. But where might this child come in, seeing this mysterious hidden valley seems to be north of the border and patronized by Canadian crooks?"

Foster reached into his hip pocket for a notepad, saying, "Our informant says he was led after dark up to Natova from *south* of the border. For another thing, consider this list of names we got out of our own lovable young thug, the soon-to-be-late Archie Croft."

Longarm set his beer aside to grip his cheroot in his teeth as he perused the Mountie's neatly block-lettered list.

He didn't recall more than half the names he read off from any of the current WANTED fliers he'd been keeping up on. But six of the names went with wanted fliers indeed!

He said, "This gent described as their town law, Constable Philo Brody, could be wanted federal for stopping more than one mail car, if he's the same Philo Brody. If this bird described as a Mayor Levi Ross is the Levi Ross who ran off with that army payroll a spell back I can see how he'd feel more comfortable at higher altitude in a hidden valley that ain't on any map. How long did you say all this has been going on?"

Foster answered simply, "We don't know. We don't want it to go on much longer. Are you in?"

Longarm said, "I reckon. But clarify me some on why we have to work at it so sneaky. I mean, if the outlaw resort is in your jurisdiction . . ."

"With the only approach in *your* jurisdiction." The Mountie cut in, adding in a disgusted tone, "We naturally informed Ottawa as soon as we took the first statement from that dying prospector. Headquarters said they'd have to take it under advisement, seeing there was no way to prove the rumors one way or the other without asking for help from . . . Never mind what they call you lot up in Ottawa."

Longarm grimaced and said, "I follow your drift. Albeit I doubt it was President Hayes himself who called your Sir John a cocksucking Scotchman. But hold on, pard. Are you suggesting just the two of us would be good enough to take on even a small town inhabited by outlaws?"

Foster conceded, "That could be a bit much. My plan is for us to pin the place down on the map, report all those outlaws to both Ottawa and Washington, and let them sort it out. I understand your cavalry has been working with the Mexican Federales against border-raiding Apache these days?"

Longarm nodded thoughtfully and declared, "I reckon anyone who could work something out with El Presidente Diaz might work something out with a cocksucking Scotchman. So I reckon we ought to begin by robbing some poor feather merchants and getting ourselves wanted."

The Mountie in mufti stared owl-eyed across the table as he demanded, "How much of that beer did you have before I got here? Are you aware of the simple fact that I am an officer of the Crown?"

Longarm answered easily, "Up Canada way, you mean.

You ain't got any jurisdiction down this way. You ain't even supposed to be here."

He let that sink in before he continued, "I reckon we ought to get our fool selves wanted down to the mining camps on the far side of Helena. Ain't nothing worth robbing up this way. But hard-rock miners draw three dollars a shift and the average mine payroll is a pisser."

He poured beer in both their steins as he grinned like a mean little kid and added, "Stick with me and we'll end up riding one jump ahead of the Territorial Guard and the meanest Vigilance Committees anybody ever ran from, pard."

Chapter 4

Longarm sensed he'd pushed Foster a tad when the Mountie rose to his own commanding height, sputtering, "I never learn! I thought you were a mental case when first we crossed swords down in your South Pass country that time. But did I listen to my common sense?"

Longarm cut in with, "Aw, sit down, shove a sock in it and hear me out, Sarge. How were you expecting the two of us to get in and out of that robber's roost alive if ever we found it to begin with? A hidden valley is by definition hard to find, you know."

Foster sat back down, still looking confused, as he assayed, "Well, I thought, you being in tighter with the Indians down this way . . ."

Longarm shook his head to point out, "You tell me this Natova is up your side of the border but your own Blackfoot never heard of it. So why should our Blackfoot know, and didn't your Blackfoot think to *ask* 'em?"

Foster nodded but insisted, "We know there's a way in

and out, south of the border. That poor prospector found it, didn't he?"

Longarm snorted, "Prospectors from all over have heard of the gold in them thar hills. Yet only one out of who knows how many stumbled into the place without a guide? We two of us, starting cold, could spend all summer and some summers to follow in a jumble of jagged-ass snow-covered peaks Switzerland can only envy without finding shit, and, after that, we'd have no better excuse than that poor prospector for barging in uninvited."

"So your plan . . . ?" Foster asked.

"Is to get us invited," Longarm replied, adding, "None of them other riders of the Owlhoot Trail could have made their way *un*-invited through such literally strange country. So first we have to establish our fool selves as wanted outlaws on the dodge, anxious as all hell about our own necks with the liquid assets to pay our way. How much money might you have on you this evening, pard?"

Foster stiffly replied, "A little over a hundred quid, in your own gold and silver coinage, of course."

Longarm grimaced and said, "My office sent me out with closer to two hundred. I never brought my well known McClellan saddle or Winchester along, lest some nosey Parker spot me before I knew what I was doing up this way. You?"

Foster said, "I have my own mount, along with its saddle and my own Winchester, stabled out back."

"Is that your usual RIC Webley .445 coyly riding your left hip in that crossdraw rig?" Longarm asked.

When the Canadian nodded, Longarm said, "It can wait until we get down in mining country and help ourselves to some pocket jingle. But we have to arm you more American and, no offense, them standardbred bays you redcoats ride stand out along a hitching rail."

He thought and decided, "Seeing we won't be in business this side of Helena, all I need to spring for, up this way, is a horse and saddle of my own. I vote we spend some time in Helena where we can make some money and outfit ourselves better. We want to show up already rich and famous in the honky tonks of the gold camps further on."

Foster asked, "How do you mean to manage the finances once we get to Helena? Those words about robbing folk were spoken in jest, one hopes?"

Longarm said, "Partly. It was some cardsharp banking a friendly little game I was planning to rob. I know it sounds cruel, but it ain't against our federal laws to fleece a professional fleecer."

Foster laughed incredulously and asked, "You expect to win against a professional cardsharp?"

To which Longarm modestly replied, "Only kind of card players I stand to beat for certain. The old-timers who say you can't cheat an honest man are on the money most every time. It's really tough to figure the hand of an honest young puncher in town for the action. Give me a crooked game of poker, though, and watch my smoke."

Foster said he could hardly wait and asked when they were planning on leaving. Longarm said, "Four in the morning sounds about right. Gives me time for some evening shopping and mayhaps four hours sleep before we haul ass. They say Mr. Edison gets by on four hours' sleep a night and we don't have to think half as hard as we ride out in the wee smalls."

Foster didn't argue that point. He wanted to know why they had to leave town at such an ungodly hour.

Longarm explained, "If nobody sees us going anywheres, nobody can say where we went, or, more important, where we might have come from. Might this be the first time you've worked out of uniform, Sarge?"

He suspected he'd hit a nerve when Foster stiffly suggested Longarm had best get started if he meant to accomplish all he'd just bragged on in the time they had to work with. So Longarm left Foster to finish the beer as he mosied back up to the municipal corral.

It wasn't getting any earlier. But as luck would have it, a rider who'd left his saddle and bridle as well as a fair-to-middling roan gelding had never come back up the river from Fort Peck, as he'd said he might, before the board he owed on a stabled pony added up to more than horse and saddle were likely worth. So they offered the kit and kaboodle to Longarm for fifty dollars, and as long as he was about it, he picked up a Winchester Yellowboy for ten dollars more at a pawn shop he found fixing to close and anxious to get shed of him.

The Yellowboy, so called because of its brass receiver, was the 1866 ancestor of Longarm's somewhat improved and all-steel model 1873. Based on the same B. Tyler Henry patent, the repeating Yellowboy packed the same fifteen rounds, if not as smoothly, in its tubular magazine.

Best of all, it was chambered for the same S&W .44-40 rounds as his double action six-gun. So Longarm felt more ready for action by the time he made it back to the Pronghorn to wrangle another deal.

It was going on eleven and the tap room as well as the lobby stood empty by then. Since there was nobody there but the night clerk, Longarm made an offer he'd made more than once in the past.

As he'd hoped, the night clerk figured what the management never knew would never hurt them. So he agreed to let Longarm turn in upstairs a spell and agreed to wake him before four in the morning without all the fuss of registration or pestering the management with half the usual price for the room.

Hence Longarm was abed before midnight, and, without any company to disturb his sleep, he was ahead of Mr. Edison by the time the night clerk roused him in the wee smalls. He'd slept as well as screwed away the earlier hours of the day before.

Foster seemed to have a tougher time waking up. But he managed, and the two of them were riding south-west toward the territorial capital of Helena before sunrise, in case anybody cared.

It seemed dubious anyone could, seeing neither had advised all that many they'd meant to meet in Great Falls, and nobody in mysterious Natova had any call to worry about either as yet.

Helena lay an easy three days' ride from Great Falls, and they made good time, traveling light as they ate and slept in hill towns along the way instead of making camp. Foster had agreed with Longarm in advance that riders camping alongside a well-traveled trail left more lasting impressions than nondescript cowhands left in beaneries and flophouses in their travels.

Longarm didn't risk a coded wire to his home office down Denver way until he could avail himself of the busier Western Union office in the bustling capital. So that meant they had some time to kill in Helena before they could move on.

They checked into seperate hotels and left their ponies in different liveries. It was important nobody have them down as a hard riding pair before the time came to appear as one. Foster was learning. He thought it was smoothly studied as well as duck-soup simple. Nobody had any call to pay particular attention to one obvious cowhand if he kept to himself and out of trouble in any western town the size of Helena.

So Crown Sergeant Foster kept to himself around his

own hotel whilst Longarm perforce spent more time among the bright lights of Helena after dark, scouting for the action he was interested in.

He found it in a steamboat gothic establishment offering all sorts of sporting events and pleasures, from wetting one's whistle to shooting one's wad, with gambling layouts to tempt every breed of sucker.

Seeing they had the time to work with, Longarm never joined a friendly little game at a corner table his first night in Helena. He bought some chips to hazard at a nearby roulette layout, where he could nurse his limited resources whilst keeping a casual eye on that friendly little game in the corner.

Roulette was a sucker's game but a kindlier one than most. In spite of all the fables to the contrary, it was impractical as well as unnecessary to rig a roulette wheel. The reasons the house had to come out ahead were there in plain sight for all to see. Proving that none were so blind as those who refused to see.

Roulette paid off at thirty-six to one for number bets, two to one for bets on high, low or medium numbers, and even money for odd, even, red or black wagers.

The catch, in plain sight, consisted of the green zero and double zero "house numbers" on opposite sides of the wheel.

Anyone who could count on his fingers could see the odds on any number, even the zero or double zero, stood at thirty-eight to one.

What seemed the odds for odd or even, red or black, were fudged by the house raking in all bets when the ball landed in the green slots with no numbers at all. It was simple as that. The house raked in a slow and steady take whilst paying the winning suckers with the bets of losing suckers. The various "systems" meant to beat the house were as mythical as magnets under the table or other mad scientist's devices the house just didn't need to bother with.

On the bright side, the house take being so modest as well as sure but slow, a man nursing his chips on red or black could stay at the table a good spell before he lost them all. So, knowing he'd lose them all in the end, Longarm invested modestly, bet conservatively and had a good long look at that friendly little game he was really interested in.

Nobody playing poker at another table, including the tinhorn banking the same, had any call to notice a tall stranger on the far side of another table with his eyes shaded by his hat brim.

So by the time he'd been wiped out at roulette that evening, Longarm had the number of the tinhorn dealing dirty at that other table. He drifted to the bar and ordered a needled beer as a nightcap before he mosied home to his own nearby hotel.

He was wondering how he'd fill the hours he'd have to before it would be time to join that friendly little game in the corner. He'd read all the magazines they'd put out that month and he wasn't at all sleepy.

It was only ten thirty by the time he'd made it to his own hired room with that friendly little game figured out.

The familiar type of tinhorn presiding over that friendly little game, a fatherly old fart dressed like a preacher or traveling sales-man, had been dealing a familiar game from the bottom of the deck, as he read each card with that bitty mirror on the inner curve of what he presented to the world as an old class ring, somewhat worn and tarnished by time since his college days.

Reading each card as it was dealt, the fatherly old fart naturally knew what everyone else was holding before the betting started.

Honest poker was more a game of skill than most, with the players guessing when to hold a good hand, when to fold a poor hand, or when a cuss across the table might or might not be bluffing as he raised and then raised some more, despite the high hopes you were holding as you guessed the odds.

When a mechanic already knew what everyone was holding he didn't have to guess. But, like the roulette layout Longarm had been bucking as he watched, the fatherly old fart seemed to prefer winning slow and steady to high rolling that could lead to hurt feelings and gunplay.

As Longarm hung his gunbelt over one bedpost and his hat over another he decided, "Too tame for this child. Better scout for a more serious tin-horn playing for more serious stakes. That old bird at the Silver Spur ain't about to bet the sort of money we need to qualify as bank robbers."

He sat down and started to shuck his boots. Then he wondered why he wanted to do a dumb thing like that with the night so young and Helena just waking up. So he rose to stride over to the corner washstand, explaining to his image in the shaving mirror as he ran a comb through his hair, "We got plenty of time. But not that *much* time to waste on trying to sleep. So what say we go scout up some chili con carne and black coffee before we explore some other establishments this evening?"

He was answered by a knock on the door across the room. He hadn't expected an answer from the mirror.

Figuring it had to be Sergeant Foster, since he didn't know anyone else in Helena at the moment, Longarm was unarmed when he opened the door to the darker hallway.

He could see right off this had been a mistake. The statuesque woman in maroon velvet, under auburn hair, with a sort of bird's nest perched atop it all, was holding a Dance

Brothers dragoon pistol on him as she demurely declared, "Permit me to introduce myself. I would be Pandora La Belle, the owner and manager of the Silver Spur. May I come in?"

Longarm was too polite to tell her that was a silly question. That Confederate antique was chambered for .45 caliber cap-and-ball rounds. So he said, "Please do," and asked her to what he owed the pleasure of her company as she kicked the door shut behind her without a waver of that unwinking gun muzzle trained on his gut at point-blank range.

He figured her for around forty, give or take some hard living, and she looked sober as she asked in a calm enough tone, "I'd like to know what you were up to at my Silver Spur, earlier, Mister . . . ?"

"Crawford. Buck Crawford." Longarm lied. Then he told her, truthfully enough, "I was bucking that roulette layout. It cleaned me out. If you were watching you know this to be true, Miss Pandora."

She said, "No I don't. I've been running joints like my Silver Spur longer than I care to admit and I guess I know when a man is bucking a game or nursing his chips while he cases the joint."

Longarm didn't answer.

She nodded and said, "You're a pro. I noticed the tailored grips on that double-action sixgun you were wearing. So tell me true and don't try to bullshit this child, Buck Crawford. Who were you figuring on holding up, later, our cashier who deals the chips or that mechanic in the corner? I couldn't be certain, thanks to that hat brim, but it did seem you were watching him more often than you glanced at our cashier's booth."

Longarm said, "You have my word I wasn't fixing to

rob your cashier, Miss Pandora. Might that fatherly old mechanic mean anything serious to you?"

She nodded grimly and said, "He certainly might. He's *my* father and now I'm *certain* I have to kill you!"

Chapter 5

"How in the hell did you ever do that and what in the hell did you just do?" asked Pandora La Belle from where she'd landed on her velvet-clad rump in a corner, looking mighty confused.

As Longarm loomed above her, removing the caps from her lethal antique, he calmly replied, "Practice. For what it's worth, never tell a man in advance you aim to kill him. As you likely just noticed, such talk can inspire desperate undeclared moves."

She started to cry.

Longarm snorted, "Aw, for Pete's sake, ain't it bad enough you came to kill me? Do you have to insult my intelligence as well? No offense, but ain't you a little . . . mature for maidenly vapors?"

She said God would get him for that but took the helping hand he offered and allowed him to haul her back to her feet as he soothed, "Seeing I got the drop on you, now, I hope you'll take my word as a gentleman of the Owlhoot

Trail I'd given up on taking your dear old dad before you came by to save him from me. As we both now know, he's too conservative a gambler to be worth my while. I was looking for higher stakes. Before you ask, I don't hold up gamblers. I beat 'em at their own game. When the game is worth the candle, I mean."

She asked, "What do you mean you have the drop on me? Isn't that your gun I see on yonder bedpost and didn't you just uncap the gun you're holding?"

Longarm held the now harmless weapon out to her, saying, "There you go insulting both our brains, Miss Pandora. Didn't I just dump you on your sweet shapely Fanny Adams with you aiming a loaded gun my way? Were you figuring on a rematch with that fool gun out of commission?"

She called him a big bully and moved around him towards the bed. He got to his pistol ahead of her, saying nothing about the Yellowboy in the closet as she said, "Oh for heaven's sake. I only want to sit down and pin my hat straight again. We've established that you're bigger than me. Run that part about high stakes past me some more."

As she sat on the bedding, Longarm removed the gunbelt from the bedpost to hang in the closet with that saddle gun, explaining, "I told you. I was looking to get into a serious game for serious money. Takes no more effort to win big than it takes to win modest, when you know what you're doing."

She said, "You'd never beat my father at poker, for any stakes you'd care to name. He's as good as they come. You're mistaking common sense for lack of skill. Getting shot in a card house, more than once, takes a lot of the flash out of a sporting gent."

Longarm shrugged and said, "If you say so, Miss Pandora. Since I won't be playing against your dear old dad, ain't this discussion academic?"

She said, "No. My father can beat anybody dumb enough to play poker with him. He's just not dumb enough to win big against the sort of men who play for high stakes. Are you with me so far?"

Longarm told her to go on.

She said, "We just established *you're* the sort of man my dad's afraid to gamble with and he'd best not mess with. I'll have to check with him, first. But what if the two of you got into a friendly little game with a certain high roller who owns a couple of mines and thinks he's too important to arrest and too dangerous to mess with?"

Longarm smiled thinly and suggested, "You mean what if your dear old dad threw the winning hands my way and let me catch any resulting hell from a sore loser?"

She beamed up at him adoringly and decided, "I'm glad you never let me kill you, Buck. We do seem made for one another, after all."

So, seeing she'd put it that way and there seemed to be no call to seek further amid the fleshpots of Helena, Longarm sat down beside her to gently remove her fragile summer hat and set it aside before he took her in his arms for a howdy-do.

She kissed back as friendly, French style, so the next thing they knew they were trying to undress one another without coming up for air, and then they were friends indeed, with her on top.

It helped a heap when folk dressed for high summer started out with no underwear. He didn't mind her high-button shoes and mesh stockings, gartered mid-thigh, once all the rest of her was bouncing stark naked up yonder, glowing from honest effort in the lamplight.

They naturally wound up on the rug, with him on top a spell before they stopped for a shared smoke and an attempt to catch their second winds back in bed.

As they shared a smoke with one of her mesh-sheathed limbs draped across his bare thigh, Pandora declared, "If my dad agrees, we're going to have to dress you more like a man of substance. The mark you'll be going up against doesn't play poker with strangers dressed like saddle tramps, and we're going to have to come up with a more impressive handle for you than Buck. I know what we'll call you. We'll introduce you to his copper majesty as Armstrong D. Weddington, the meatpacking king of Omaha. Our copper king, Vance Larson, hails from Saint Joe, so what might he know about a high roller from Omaha?"

Longarm blew a thoughtful smoke ring and asked when his copper majesty might show up at her Silver Spur.

Pandora said, "Never. High rollers such as Vance Larson don't gamble in card houses with the hoi polloi. My dad says he and other Montana moguls get together every week in a private hotel suite near Courthouse Square with the ante at ten dollars."

Longarm whistled and said, "Too rich for this child's blood. I don't have that money to play with."

She patted his naked thigh and said, "We do. Dad will stake you, introduce you, and see that you get the winning hands. Don't you see the beauty of it, Buck? Nobody could hope to excuse gunplay against a winner who couldn't have possibly dealt *himself* a royal flush!"

Longarm grimaced and said, "Sure they could, if he came in with the one who dealt him beans and ain't a royal flush pushing past common sense?"

She said, "My dad's going to have to deal him at least a straight flush if you expect him to hang tight as you keep raising. But you have a point about dad introducing you, you lucky devil. We're going to have to work on that angle. Tomorrow. Right now I've been wondering what it might be like, standing up against the wall, with a lover so tall."

So they tried and as it turned out, it hardly mattered how tall he was, once she had her own long legs wrapped around his waist like that.

Next morning Pandora took Longarm to a tailor she knew, and they had him gussied up like a rich dude from Omaha when she led him into the Silver Spur to introduce him to her dear old dad.

His name wasn't La Belle. He hadn't named his child Pandora, either. He explained she was just willful and after they got that worked out he said his real name was Thorne Townsend. So they were both inclined to dramatics.

Old Thorne, to hear him tell it, cottoned to the notion of cleaning out a copper king without getting killed his ownself, and said it would be easy to slip Armstrong D. Weddington, a sporting gent he'd never met before, into the game planned for that Friday, two days off. Copper kings with deep pockets who kept beating lesser lights and crowing about it caused a certain amount of resentment, and old Thorne knew a pissed-off mining man who'd no doubt be delighted to introduce a professional to his copper-mining pal as a rich bird ripe for the plucking.

Longarm and Pandora left the fatherly old fart to work things out. When Longarm allowed he meant to lay low at his hotel until they were ready to mine copper, Pandora wanted to tag along. But he pointed out it was early in broad-ass daylight and suggested she drop by his hotel after dark, when nobody at either end was likely to comment on old Thorne's daughter acting sneaky with a man who hadn't blown in from Omaha yet.

He was glad he'd talked her out of it when he found Crown Sergeant Foster waiting for him in the lobby.

Foster had a copy of the *Rocky Mountain News* he'd just picked up at the tobacco stand in his own lobby. The widely read Denver paper had run their payroll robbery over in Granite County in a banner headline on the front page. The story gave no names to go with fairly detailed descriptions of the both of them. But Marshal Billy Vail of the Denver District Court, Lord love him, had opined that those rascals who'd just pulled that robbery in Montana looked like the same ones who'd stopped that Overland stage near the Colorado-Wyoming line.

Foster waved the fool paper at Longarm, saying, "Your own lot have run the cover story we were waiting for. Why are we still here in Helena?"

Longarm led the Mountie in mufti to a more secluded corner of the lobby, saying, "Don't get your bowels in an uproar. Nobody's likely to suspect either of us as part of this desperate pair, as long as they never see us together."

Foster insisted, "You said once we were established as wanted outlaws we'd ride on to the gold camps along the westward slope and find a guide to Natova, damn it!"

Longarm said, "I did and I meant it. But we'll have less trouble finding us an outlaw guide if we show up with some outlaw *loot* and so that's what I'm working on now. If things work out the way I hope, we ought to be on our way west by this weekend."

Longarm explained how he and his new-found confederates planned to bilk the stinking rich Vance Larson, and Foster groaned, "That's all we need. Another loose cannon on deck as the sun pulls slowly from the shore and our ship sinks slowly in the west! What am I supposed to do if you manage to get yourself killed?"

Longarm shrugged and replied, "Won't be my problem. But neither of us figure to find the way to that hidden valley without help. Nobody but that one unlucky prospector ever has, aside from the original outlaws who set things up for all those others, I mean."

He let that sink in before he explained, "I figure the two

of us will show up somewheres closer, matching our descriptions in the newspapers as we flash some of the loot from that famous robbery and let it be known in low places we're sure worried about something. That's about the time some helpful soul ought to sell us on a swell mountian resort outside U.S. jurisdiction and offer to lead us there, for a price."

"How do you know that's the way it works?" asked Foster.

Longarm replied, "How else *could* it work: That not-too-bright Archie Croft you boys caught in Moose Jaw never found the place on his own and neither could others on Archie's list, hailing from all over. But why are we crossing that bridge before I can get us to it? Lay low until Saturday morning and if things work out I'll pick you up at youir own hotel on my way out of town."

Foster still didn't cotton to what he described as a cowboy crap-shoot. But seeing he had nothing slicker to suggest, they shook on it and parted friendly.

The next two nights were swell, whilst the next two days seemed to last two million years. And then it was Friday night and Longarm met with old Thorne Townsend and a chinless sore loser called Gordon who said he was a friend of His Copper Majesty, Vance Larson.

It would have been unkind to point out that a gent with the sort of friends Vance Larson had might have been better off playing poker with enemies. They needed Gordon to vouch his way into the private game.

Gordon did, with no trouble, at first. As the gussied-up Armstrong D. Weddington of Omaha, up Montana way to invest in a newly opened cattle range, shook with the nigh-as-tall and heavier-set Vance Larson, the copper king tried to impress him by shaking with a show-off nutcracker grip. Longarm suspected the somewhat older man had started at the bottom in hardrock mining, likely with a nine-pound hammer. But his massive paws were manicured and he had the outward manners of a man born to wealth.

As his gruffly gracious host introduced him around the hotel suite, Longarm saw it was staffed with liveried help, male and she-male, with a gal serving canny peas off the buff table in a French maid's outfit.

The balding gent serving drinks as often and as fast as anyone might want looked like a hardrock miner in an English butler's outfit.

He might have been one.

In another room nobody was using yet, a big round table stood stark beneath a hanging lamp, with eight places set up around it, indicating a serious game indeed if that minimum ante was ten dollars. As he waved at the scene with the back of a paw, the copper king explained he'd engaged a professional dealer for the night, called Thorne Townsend. When Armstrong D. of Omaha confessed he'd never heard of Townsend the copper king said, "He's more famous out this way. It's understood he's to deal all the hands to everyone but himself and place no bets in his own behalf. That way, we'll have no more discussion about just who might have dealt what to whom. For I just hate it when my guests get to calling one another cheating bastards."

Armstrong D. soberly allowed anyone could see there was nothing slow about his copper majesty and asked when the game might begin.

Larson said, "We're still waiting on a couple of guests and it ain't as if we ain't got all night. Or until the last player but one has had enough. We usually last well past three. With breaks for sandwiches and coffee, of course. Can't hardly play poker without plenty of coffee."

Armstrong D. allowed he just loved to see the sun come

up as he was packing it in for the night, and drifted away as Vance Larson headed back out front to greet a new arrival.

The fatherly Thorne Townsend came into the game room, not looking at his secret confederate as he produced a sealed deck of cards.

Others were drifting in, now, with or without highball glasses in their hands. Vance Larson was with a shorter bearded older man with a receding hairline. The stranger was smiling uncertainly as Larson led him over to where Longarm stood gussied up as Armstrong D. Larson said, "This would be my old pal, Abe Kramer, out of Omaha, the same as you, Weddington. You already know one another, of course?"

Kramer just looked confused. As Armstrong D., Longarm confessed he'd never had the pleasure, back in Omaha.

The copper king frowned thoughtfully and asked, "Do tell? I figured you had to know one another, seeing you're both in the same meat packing business back in Omaha."

Chapter 6

It was Kramer, Lord love him, who broke the long awkward silence with, "Omaha is a substantial city and we pack a lot of meat. But of course the name is familiar and didn't you officiate at our last state fair, Mr. Weddington? I'm good at faces and yours goes with that state fair."

Longarm modestly allowed he'd been to the fair but hadn't been in charge of anything and this was the simple truth when you studied on it. For he'd been there indeed after federal wanteds, planning to rob the ticket office, and it was a good thing Kramer's memory for faces wasn't quite as good as he fancied.

The last sucker, or guest, Larson had invited arrived, and after another round of drinks his copper majesty decreed the game should begin.

Armstrong D. chose a seat out of conversation range of Kramer's but not directly across, lest they wind up staring into one another's sort-of-familiar faces all evening.

Pandora's dear old dad commenced to deal eight hands as the permanent unwagering bank. On recent occasions, when he hadn't been screwing Townsend's daughter, Longarm had learned it had been just as well he'd never tried one of his own modest tricks on the slippery old cuss. For just as there was more than one way to skin a cat, there was more than one way to cheat at poker, and dear old dad knew them all.

He'd confided to Longarm, as they planned this very evening, how a man who kept skinning cats or dealing cards the same way was asking for a whole lot of trouble. So Longarm wasn't sure, this time, how the older man was doing it. But he was doing it, with Longarm and likely more than another experienced poker player watching him tight as he dealt everyone the cards he wanted them to have, just as he'd promised Longarm he could.

The old mechanic should have written plays. He had a swell sense for slowly building dramatics. As he'd advised Longarm and the weak-chinned Gordon in advance, he meant to narrow the field whilst allowing others to rake in suspicious pots. Nobody too smart to play three-card monte would buy consistanly big winners.

His copper majesty acted like he was used to winning every pot on those occasions Townsend dealt him the winning hand to keep him in a good mood. When he wasn't jeering about the bluff he'd called—Townsend had warned Larson always called—His Copper Majesty was bragging, on his copper holdings over in Silver Bow County. He seemed to think he was the first cuss on Earth who'd noticed you often had way bigger lodes of baser metals mixed in, and usually under a frosting of silver or gold. He'd bought into played-out silver mines in Silver Bow County, cheap, and developed them as paying copper mines. When he smugly asked anyone there to tell him why copper was likely to keep rising in price, Longarm, as Armstrong D., suggested, "Western Union?"

Larson chortled, "Along with the newer telephones and electric lightbulbs. They all run on copper wires and Lord knows where they'll get all the copper they'll need at the rate things have been going. You need miles of fine copper wire inside them new electric motors and the generators you can't have electricity without. You know that electrocuted social club the cattle barons of Cheyenne just outfitted with Edison lamps? I have it on good authority they used pounds of Edison bulbs and tons of wire for their generating plant alone!"

They all agreed his copper majesty was on to something, and he took it like a sport when the weak-chinned Gordon took him for the next pot.

Longarm had folded earlier. He'd been dealt a shitty hand, as planned. Old Townsend had instructed them to fold early with poor hands to show and only bet big when he dealt them at least a full house. That would be his signal the mark he'd set up for that deal would be holding a flush or straight. Either was likely to inspire a burst of optimistic raising, since there were only four other hands that beat a flush or five that beat a straight.

His Copper Majesty raised and called the butter-and-eggs man, who tried to bluff him when he'd been dealt a straight. So things were looking up. Old Townsend saw that his secret pals Gordon and Weddington won some and lost some, modestly, breaking about even as they hung in there. Two others had dropped out and they'd paused for sandwiches and coffee before Longarm figured how old Townsend had been doing it.

The older man fidgeted idly, or mayhaps nervously, with the cards he'd gathered in during the break. It seemed a harmless habit, like drumming one's fingers or scratching one's crotch, until you studied on it. But once you had, the answer was crude as a gob of tobacco spit on the table cloth. The old cuss was stacking the deck.

Not when he was fixing to deal, of course. Everyone was watching you when you were fixing to deal. But betwixt times, when it didn't seem important, the old pro idly shuffled and reshuffled as if anxious to avoid any suspicious luck. He shuffled and reshuffled the cards facedown so's anyone could see he had no way of reading their corners, unless one speculated on a shiny silver pinky ring old Townsend had chosen to wear that evening. Longarm could see it from where he sat. But he suspected that, like a Christmas tree ornament, the convex polished silver offered a distorted but magnified mirror image of anything passing above it.

One still had to marvel at the head for figures any professional card player had to possess if he ever wanted to amount to shit. It made Longarm's scalp tingle as he considered what it took to memorize fifty-two cards and a joker in their correct order, over and over for every deal. But he knew some could. The ones who beat blackjack layouts fair and square were called "counters" and ejected from the premises whenever they were spotted.

A stacked deck was simply a deck of cards the dealer had arranged in advance so that each player got the card the dealer wanted him to get as the dealer dealt, with not one sneaky motion. Unless he knew or suspected the deck had been stacked, there was no way in hell for the mark to detect it.

But as if he suspected something, or just aimed to show he knew it all, their gracious host called for a fresh sealed deck at midnight and instructed his hired dealer to discard that infernal joker.

It wasn't easy, but Armstrong D. managed not to grin like a shit-eating dog as he saw how much extra time it gave old Townsend to fiddle with the fresh cards, making sure they were shuffled right lest they'd come out of the pack stacked in order.

Refreshed with a new deck and black coffee, His Copper Majesty decreed it was time to buckle down to some serious poker. So another player dropped out, leaving five at the table as the game got serious indeed, with the table stakes getting ominous.

As Vance Larson knew, and banked on, all things being equal, the player with the deepest pockets tended to win at poker most every time. There was more than one notorious sporting cuss who used no more complexified methods. In a halfway honest game, everybody won some, everybody lost some, and as long as a man could cover his losses and hang in there, his luck was bound to change and so, as the game wore on, the player who nobody could clean out had to slowly but surely clean out everybody else. The only way you could beat a man with deeper pockets was by quitting while you were ahead, and high rollers with deep pockets found this mighty rude. A true sportsman wasn't supposed to count his winnings at the table or leave the table until there was nobody there to play against.

Knowing this, His Copper Majesty didn't look worried when he was in the hole. He wasn't figuring on staying there.

Pandora and her dear old dad had staked their meat-packing associate from Omaha. But the others were *real* high rollers, and the stakes rolled high indeed as they threatened to climb past Longarm's grubstake.

Then a cattle baron called Dixon, bless him, allowed he was low on pocket jingle and asked if the bank would take his marker. Old Townsend shot a glance at his copper majesty, who nodded and said, "My own marker has ever been good and I don't play cards with four flushers." He fished out an alligator-hide wallet to cover the cattle baron's marker with cash silver certificates as he expansively added, "Friend Dixon can settle up later, after I win this loan back. So let's deal the damn cards and play some damn poker!"

That gave old Townsend time to fiddle with the deck to make certain it was properly shuffled, and stacked, before he dealt another round.

He never made eye contact with his confederates at the table. They'd been told in advance how to bet the hands he meant to deal them.

Gordon won the next pot because not even a copper king was fixing to bluff with the rotten hand the old mechanic had shoved *his* way. But as Gordon raked in the substantial pot and proceeded to pocket his winnings Larson scowled and demanded, "Where do you think you're going with all that money, friend?"

Gordon rose easily and replied with what seemed a clear conscience, "Home. Like I promised the wife I would before midnight, Vance. Weren't you listening when I said I had to leave early? I was, and I'm a man of my word. So Merry Christmas to all and to all a good night!"

His copper majesty considered, shrugged and conceded, "Kiss her once for me, then, spoilsport!"

As Gordon left with his share, Vance Larson growled, "Deal, Professor!" and when he saw what old Townsend had dealt him, his face went cigar-store Indian and he quietly declared, "I see and raise a hundred."

As His Copper Majesty added five golden eagles to the pot, Longarm saw he'd been dealt a royal flush. So he knew what Larson was feeling so good about. Pandora's dear old dad had told him he meant to deal Larson four of a kind when it came time to strike. They knew Larson would know only one hand beat four of a kind and the odds on drawing a royal flush were 0.0002 percent.

So Longarm hung in as others raised or folded until only he and Larson were left, with better than ten grand in the pot.

When the overconfident copper king not only covered that but raised another thousand, Armstrong D. Weddington from Omaha allowed he was low on pocket jingle and asked for paper, a pen and some ink so's he could see Larson and raise him a million-dollar marker.

His copper majesty looked startled and asked, "Are you saying you got money in a bank to cover such a marker, Omaha?"

To which Longarm sweetly replied, "Did I just hear somebody intimating I might be a liar?"

As he rose to allow the grips of his .44-40 to peek coyly from under the tail of his fancy frock coat, His Copper Majesty decided his invited guest was either rich as hell or not long for this world.

He folded his hand and said, "You win. Nobody bluffs a million. What will it cost me to see what you were holding?"

Longarm turned his royal flush face up with a smile to gracefully reply, "Read 'em and weep, seeing this was a friendly game."

Larson nodded soberly and conceded, "I knew you couldn't be bluffing. But how might you have managed that hand, Omaha?"

Longarm's smile grew wolfish as he suggested, "You tell me. I never dealt myself shit. Are you saying this tinhorn you hired for the night dealt you four of a kind and me a royal flush because you *told* him to?"

Larson sighed and said, "Aw, set yourself down and let the game proceed so's I can see you do that again!"

But the tall dark winner remained on his feet, stuffing his pockets as he replied in a deliberately injured tone, "I don't play cards with sore losers, Mr. Larson. I'd tell you what happened to the last man who implied I might be cheating. But you'd only think I was bragging."

"Come on, you can't leave now!" gasped out His Copper Majesty.

But Longarm sweetly asked if anyone there meant to stop him, and when nobody did, he was out of there and moving *up* the stairwell on the balls of his feet instead of down the same, lest his copper majesty prove a sore loser indeed.

Anybody moving *down* the stairs after him moved to cat pawed to hear. Longarm still circled some to make sure he was alone on the dark streets of Helena before he headed home to Pandora with their winnings.

She insisted they count it and divvy up, as agreed, before she got in bed with him. When their net profit totaled over fifteen grand after Longarm returned the five he'd been staked, he was big about loose change.

It was easy to see why she'd given herself a fake French name, and a man had to admire a gal who took so much pride in getting down and dirty. Longarm liked women too much to risk hurting one and knowing how few really enjoyed it, save as a down and dirty diversion, he was never the one to ask for an invite around to the back entrance. But when Pandora asked if they could make it a Holy Trinity in celebration of a night she never wanted to forget, Longarm allowed he was game for anything that didn't hurt, and she said it didn't hurt at all when he came in her all three ways.

When the time for parting came she was less sneaky

about it than Maria had been and Longarm had to remind her big girls didn't cry when they headed home with all that money.

Crown Segeant Foster took things more cheerful the next morning at his own hotel. They divvied up Longarm's five grand share in front of a set-down breakfast of scrambled eggs, sausages and home fries before they split up to redeem their ponies and meet saddled up and ready to ride on the outskirts of town.

As they did so with the morning sun clapping both of them on their backs warm and friendly, Foster asked if Longarm thought it wise to return to the scene of their fictitious crime.

Longarm said, "Aw, we ain't headed for West Valley where he robbed this payroll, pard. Don't you remember how after all that zigging and zagging along the Anaconda Range we wound up with them trashy sisters on the far slope of the Beaverheads?"

When the Canadian lawman dryly allowed it was all coming back to him, Longarm continued, "It's a shame we got suspicious of them gals and cut out on 'em. But seeing we felt we'd better, and seeing we don't know the country all that well, we did, and here we are, once we get there, up in let's say Powell County, not more than, say, sixty miles from the scene of our payroll robbery and clearly needing guidance as we scout for a place to fort up."

Back in the town they'd just left, a lean and hungry sort in a more expensive riding outfit found his copper majesty enjoying breakfast in bed as he reported in. He said, "That meatpacker you're concerned about just left town, dressed like a trail driver, with another rider of the same description. I have McCord tailing them. He's to wire me once he sees where they wind up."

"Why?" asked Vance Larson, spearing some french

toast with a sterling silver fork as he added, "I don't give a fuck where he thinks he's going with my money. I want him dead with my money back, God damn his eyes!"

"I'll wire McCord to that effect as soon as I can find out where all of them wound up for the day," replied the copper king's boss trouble shooter.

Chapter 7

The two lawmen pretending to be outlaws had two conflicting impressions to worry about, or, in point of fact, one impression to avoid leaving in their wake. Outlaws who'd ridden as light, fast and far would hardly be in need of a hideout. Frank and Jesse had gotten away clean after the disasterous Northfield Raid by riding fast and far in an unexpected direction as other gang members had been rounded up nearby. Everybody along the Owlhoot Trail knew this. It was important that once they did break cover a few days' ride from that mythical robbery they'd pulled, nobody would recall them having been farther away.

After that there was more than one way to skin a cat, cheat at poker or cover ground on horseback. All of them involved some understanding of horseflesh. Neither cowboys, Indians nor the U.S. Cav treated a horse like a pet or an unfeeling machine. There were good and bad riders of all complexions. The good ones understood a horse was made of flesh and blood and feelings, with no self-sacrificing desire to die or even feel uncomfortable for a master it was devoted to. The old saw about leading a horse to water without being able to make him drink was only the half of it. Horses varied, just as riders did. But a good rider worked a horse within limits set by generations of good horsemen.

You could ride a horse all day if you rode it slow and gentle at a three-mile-an-hour walk, with plenty of trail breaks for water and some grazing, with square meals of grain at least once a day. That was how the U.S. Cav covered ground in the field betwixt skirmishes, averaging thirty miles an etape, or twelve hour ride.

Cows walked even slower. But cowboys driving trail herds were set up with five to seven horse *remudas* so's they could work with a fresh mount every day. A trail drive was mostly poking along, with sudden bursts of zigzagging speed that could leave a cow pony in need of a good, long rest. Muscles of men or other critters that had been overtaxed tended to stiffen most by the third day after and recover within a week.

Stories about cowboys having personal mounts smarter than any sheepdog were so much sheep dip. Horses were harder to teach new tricks to than dogs, but better than most critters at *remembering*. So you got a horse to do what you wanted it to by giving it pleasant and unpleasant memories about the likely puzzling midgets who kept after it to make mysterious moves that couldn't mean much to a natural critter more interested in eating, drinking, lazing about or, in season, rutting.

Once a horse had been taught to accept a saddle or harness and understood what the bit in its mouth seemed to want from it, you could ride it at a lope for twenty minutes or ride it at a dead run for say, five, if you were trying to hurt it, with at least a half hour of resting or slow walking before you tried it again. Riders in a hurry could and did push a horse harder. Riders in a hurry wound up with jaded mounts that would barely take another step, or a foundered mount that fell down and just lay there no matter what.

So the short-lived but famous Pony Express had carried the mail eighty miles or more a day as a sort of relay race, with young, skinny riders switching butts and the mail to fresh mounts every dozen or so miles. Stagecoaches averaged nine miles an hour, trotting about the same distance betwixt team changes.

Such were the rules set by Mother Nature and her limitations as to horsepower. So Longarm and Foster rode hard as far as the mountain town of Marysville, swapped their jaded mounts and five dollars for fresh ones and walked 'em more sedately over the continental divide by way of low-slung Mullar Pass, from whence it was all downhill to Clarkside, where they meant to spend the night.

They had no way of knowing the hardcase Clay McCord was tailing them. McCord knew his oats. Following them through open high country at spyglass range, McCord had ghosted the bay rumps of the mounts they'd changed to in Marysville aboard the fresh mount he'd picked up a few minutes later at the same livery.

The hired gun who'd moved in closer as trees grew closer together at lower altitude paused in the shade of some trailside aspen, as he saw the riders he'd been following rein in at a trailside stage-line stop. Likely the last one before Clarkside.

As that meatpacker from Omaha and his mysterious sidekick entered the station, McCord assumed they'd stopped to grub up.

Stage stops offered set-down meals and often served as local restaurants, whether you rode their fool coaches or not.

Money was money, and that was what the line was set up to take in. So, seeing it had constant upkeep of its live as well as rolling stock to see to, its smithee and remount corral attached next door catered to passing riders and their mounts too.

After that there came a cluster of family quarters and, seeing there was a Western Union branch line to the mining towns to the west, both following the same trace, there was a telegraph shed on the far side of the tiny town, open on demand, like a railroad flag stop.

So Clay McCord rode on past the stage stop, where the two ponies he'd been admiring from a distance stood tethered side by side. He'd been told to try and keep in touch by wire, and telegraph sheds were a sometimes thing as you got ever farther from the hub of Helena. So McCord reined in out front to read the sign posted on the padlocked door without dismounting.

The sign said anyone wanting to send a telegram should scout up the part-time Western Union clerk at his full-time chicken farm across the way. McCord glanced back the way he'd come to see that those ponies hadn't done anything exciting. So, knowing he only had to keep their route west in sight, he rode on across the trace they'd have to travel to dismount in front of the log cabin, this side of a long wire-mesh chicken run.

Before he could knock, a motherly old gal came to the door to tell him, "My man's around the back chopping firewood, if you want to send a telly-gram, good sir."

The hired gun thanked her with a tip of his hat brim and circled the cabin, making sure he could see the wagon trace to his north all the way 'round. He could still keep an eye on it, he saw, as he strode over to an older man splitting cord-wood betwixt the cabin's back door and its outhouse.

The chicken-growing telegraph clerk sank his axe-head

into a nearby chopping block and let go of the handle to straighten up with a smile, asking if McCord wanted to send a wire.

The hired gun glanced at the stretch of wagon trace he could still see, as he nodded and replied, "If it ain't too much trouble. We're talking a nickel a word, right?"

The older man nodded but conceded, "I can send your message cheaper at night rates, old son. They'll get it tomorrow morning if a nickel a word strikes you as dear."

McCord smiled thinly and said, "What I have to say won't cost me but four bits. My message will be terse."

He didn't add that it would be in code.

The telegraph-clerk-cum-chicken-farmer wiped his sweaty hands on his bib overalls and allowed they'd best get cracking, then.

McCord left his own pony tethered by the cabin as he and the older man crossed the trace on foot. A single glance assured McCord that those two ponies still stood out front of the stage stop. The rascals he'd been trailing were likely dawdling over dessert, the sons of bitches. McCord was getting hungry as the long day wore on, and it hardly seemed fair.

As the older man unlocked his telegraph shed, McCord saw at a glance that you could stand at the counter inside and still watch out a side window overlooking the trace. The older man went in ahead to open a drop-leaf at one end of the counter, swing around, and shove a pad of yellow forms and a stub of pencil McCord's way, saying, "Be our guest, old son."

With another glance out the side window, the hired gunhand blocked his short message to the effect that he expected to join Cousin Fred down the way in Clarkside, and that he'd wire again when he was sure Cousin Fred was home."

He paid for the simple telegram at day rates and the older man said he'd put her on the wire directly, adding with a chuckle, "Beats chopping kindling at this hour. I doubt we'll need much firewood tonight in any case, seeing we're going on the ides of June."

McCord didn't have any call to argue. He knew how fickle the weather was in the Rockies. As he stepped out into the dazzle of a now lower but still hot sun to head back across the trace, he glanced to his left, and then he stopped to swing around and stare harder.

There were no ponies tethered out front of the stage stop now. That meatpacker from Omaha and his mysterious sidekick had ridden on!

McCord started to run for the stage stop, thought better of it, and ran to untether and mount his own pony so's he'd be free to gallop any way the bastards might have gone.

He ran his own mount the short way, slid it to a stop with a vicious yank on the reins, and dashed inside, trusting the grounded reins to hold an already well-ridden mount.

Drawing his six-gun, McCord threw down on everybody there, only to find the trestle table in the middle of the main room empty. When the young gal clearing the table saw the gun in McCord's hand, she let go enough cups and saucers to punctuate the hell out of her high-pitched scream.

A fat man in a grease-stained apron appeared in the doorway behind her to freeze, throw up his hands, and plead, "Hold your fire! Everything we have is yours! But that ain't saying much! Will you let us live for the seven dollars and change in the till?"

McCord snapped, "This ain't a holdup. I'm looking for them two riders who tethered them two ponies out front! Where are they?"

The cook looked at the waitress and asked, "Tillie?"

She gasped, "Next door. They asked me about them ponies and I told 'em to take it up with old Ed!"

McCord didn't ask who old Ed might be. He dashed back outside and ran the short distance to the neighboring smithee, holstering his six-gun as it came to him how some might take it, and seeing he didn't seem to need it in hand at the moment.

Dashing in through the open front of the smithee, he saw at a glance that the forge was banked and nobody was working there. He ran on through and out the open back door to see a trio in overalls rubbing down the very pony that meatpacker had been riding. The bay his pal had just been aboard was tethered to a corral rail on the far side. Neither mount wore a saddle or its original bridle.

When McCord asked in a more reasonable tone where his pals from Omaha had gone, the gray-haired hostler who seemed in charge looked puzzled and answered, "Omaha? Ain't nobody from Omaha been around here today, pilgrim. Only trade we've had since the morning stage came through was a couple of laid-off cowhands from Wymoming. Looking to sign on as hardrock helpers over in the gold fields."

"Might they have been the ones who rid in on them two ponies?" the hired gun demanded.

The older man nodded and replied, "Fine enough ponies, as you can see, but jaded some. Being in a hurry, they offered us a swap with four dollars throwed in. They must have been in a hurry indeeed. Are you the law?"

"Just a pal," McCord replied, adding, "How much of a lead might they have on me?"

The three of them compared notes. The older one allowed, "Fifteen, mayhaps twenty minutes since they rid out of here on fresh mounts. Brown-and-white paint with four white stockings, along with a blue roan, if that helps."

McCord dashed off without thanking them. By the time the stranger had ridden off on his own sorrel barb, Tillie from the kitchen had joined them out back, flush-faced and out of breath, as she gasped, "Oh, praise the Lord he never shot you boys!"

The fatherly cuss she knew as old Ed smiled uncertainly and asked the flustered gal what she was jawing about. Once she told him, old Ed turned to one of his helpers and said, "Tommy, you'd best run up to the Western Union shed and have Chuck Lawford wire the sheriff up in Deer Lodge. Something funny's going on and that's his department!"

The stable hand asked, "What should I tell the sheriff might be going on, Ed?"

Old Ed said, "I just now told you it wasn't my department, Tommy! You were standing right here with your bare face hanging out! Wire the sheriff everything you remember about all three of them strangers and let *him* sort it out!"

So Tommy ran for it as, out on the trace, McCord and his trail-weary sorrel were already out of sight, backtracking towards Helena.

McCord had no idea why anyone would ride west this far, change to fresh ponies, and ride back the way they'd come. It made no sense. But he was certain they hadn't ridden past him to the west, and Keystone had said the boss was pissed about that meatpacker pulling a royal flush out of thin air. Meaning he had sneakier habits than your average meatpacker and why would he tell anyone he was a laid-off cowhand?

McCord had loped his well-ridden sorrel half a mile before it broke stride and refused to move faster than a slow trot, no matter how he spurred and lashed with the rein ends.

McCord cursed and muttered, "Shit! I should have thought to offer a swap back there! I'll never catch up with two fresh mounts aboard this one!"

He reined in, started to wheel his jaded pony around and then declared, "Fuck it!" take me the better part of another hour before I'll ever get to chase 'em with a fresh mount and by that time they'll be too far ahead, in any case."

He spurred his sorrel foreward as he half sobbed, "Well, shit, we got to go back and face the music in Helena if we've lost 'em. So let's hope Keystone spotted 'em cutting back and knows where they're at!"

Far behind them, in the shade of the tree line far up the grassy slope south of the wagon trace, Crown Sergeant Foster rose from where he'd been seated on a log near his tethered roan to say, "I don't know about you. But in my opinion we've lost that bird on the sorrel, if he's trailing us as you suspect."

Longarm got to his own feet and stretched, saying, "Oh, he had to be following us. Why else would anybody ride west to a stage stop, send him a wire, tear ass into the stage stop with a drawn gun, and light out for the east?"

Foster shrugged and said, "You'll get no argument from me, Longarm. But how did you ever spot him? I was watching our back trail and I never saw anything."

Longarm said, "He didn't want you to. I'd say he was an old pro. I never spotted him following us. I wasn't dead certain anybody was. But having rid through Indian country in my time, I figured we'd best make sure before we rode on. So now we're sure and let's ride on."

Chapter 8

Clarkside stood beside the River Clark. It was modest in population, and it was always best to ride into a small town around suppertime, when folk were usually more intent on where *they* were going or coming from than they were about where *you* might have come from.

Also, strangers riding in as if they belonged there were inclined to attract less attention if they didn't have to ask directions as if they didn't belong there.

Having had an eye on time and distance as they rode that afternoon, Longarm called a halt an hour short of quitting time in the town ahead to see if they might wrangle an early supper at a homestead a handy haul east of the county seat. He was not at all surprised when a rangy homesteader and his raggedly dressed old woman allowed they surely could.

That Homestead Act Honest Abe Lincoln had come up with worked better where it rained more, west of say longitude 100°. But that song about starving to death on one's government claim was less accurate in high country where the grass stayed green when it wasn't snowing.

Western Montana Territory was too far from any mass markets to go for one all-out cash crop, even if farmers had been able to grow wheat or corn at that altitude. But mining men and all the supporting service workers who went with the ever-growing mining of Montana were well paid and had to eat. So you found folk raising pigs and chickens along with dairy stock and barley for the local breweries 'round any mining town of any size.

The homesteaders Longarm and Foster had dropped in on, as if in answer to their prayers, were new out that way, Longarm could see at a glance.

They naturally had a chicken run and a messy pen of hogs to slop. But if Longarm was any judge of weeds, they'd drilled in close to forty acres of puny cornstalks on a twenty degree slope. The team of mules he'd used in such an exercise of futility were grazing the sort of vegetation that belonged up that way in a paddock fenced in with lodgepole rails.

The thin, dry, overheated air all around would cool fast after dark. But it wasn't fixing to get dark yet. So whilst the lady of the house ducked inside to rustle up some grub, the homesteader led his welcome guests around to where planks on sawhorses and backless stools were shaded by some aspen he'd been smart enough to leave alone.

A lot of greenhorns didn't. Aspenwood didn't burn worth shit, whilst the fluttering leaves offered shade through the few hot spells at that altitude.

As he seated them, the homesteader explained that they'd have to settle for biscuits and gravy with coffee, if his old woman could manage it with the little they had left.

Neither Longarm nor Foster were rude enough to comment. But the homesteader felt obliged to explain, "We're scraping the bottom of our credit and our corn don't seem to be ready to pick."

Longarm nodded soberly and said, "It's none of my never-mind but it's my understanding barley is about the only grain that thrives up this way. Corn and wheat need a longer growing season than you get where the ground don't thaw in time for April Fools' day."

The lean and hungry-looking homesteader sighed and said, "Tell me a tale I ain't heard from the neighbors. But what can I do at this late date? Ain't got time to start all over, even if I had the seed money. So I reckon we'll just have to pray for late first-frost."

He looked away and muttered half to himself, "It ain't like we got any choice."

Foster sat down at the bare table. Longarm remained on his feet with their rangy host, fishing out a couple of cheroots as he said, "Might have a deal for you, seeing you're short of pocket jingle and we've rid a fair piece today with miles to go before we sleep."

The homesteader cautiously asked what Longarm had in mind.

Longarm got their smokes going with a waterproof Mex match as he told the rangy greenhorn, "Swap you those two ponies around the front with five dollars thrown in for those frisky looking mules out back."

"Are you serious?" asked the homesteader. "Neither of them mules are worth the opening price of either of those ponies."

Foster looked up to say, "Listen to the man. He's right."

Longarm said, "That well may be. But mules last longer on mountain trails if you ain't worried about speed, and, I don't know. Let's just say I'm tired of staring at the rump of your roan. Mayhaps because I ain't used to it. Blue roans ain't all that common out our way, you know."

Foster brightened and said, "I follow your drift, as they say out our way. The paint you rode in reminds me of a pony I fell off when I was little. I vote we swap 'em both for those fine nondescript mules."

So that was how they rode on, after a piss-poor supper of biscuits and some brown slime the lady of the house had described as gravy.

As the hitherto desperate homesteaders watched them ride off on the matching Corovan brown mules, the woman who'd sort of fed them asked her husband, "You know who those stangers must have been, don't you, Old Man?"

To which he replied, jingling the silver dollars in his worn jeans, "Of course I know who they must have been. Do you think you married a moon calf, Old Woman?"

She said, "They was them! The outlaws who robbed that payroll down to the Anacondas! The papers say they was both tall and well built, with the lighter complected one smooth-shaven and the darker one sporting a heavy mustache!"

Her husband snorted, "That's what I just said. I'd have thought they'd have rid farther by this time. They must have circled some, with all them lawmen on their trail. Lord only knows how many times they've swapped mounts by this time. Them handsome ponies we got for our mules are likely safe to put on the market and we're already way out ahead in grocery money!"

He laughed and added, "Damn my soul if I don't mean to buy you a new dress, Old Woman! Saw a handsome summer frock in Peterson's window the last time I was in town. Going for a dollar fifty on sale!"

She half sobbed, "Never mind that fool dress, Old Man.

Don't you mean to blue-streak in to tell the law as soon as it's safe?"

He shook his head and said, "Not hardly. To begin with, it won't never be safe as long as them two boys are running loose with them six-guns they wore like man accustomed to the heft. For another thing, it wouldn't be Christian to turn in men who just rid in like angels in answer to our prayers."

When she declared, "Reckon so," he wrapped an arm around her scrawny waist to add, "Even if they wasn't angels in disguise, no man who'd rob them stuck-up mining moguls could be all bad, and I'll be whupped with snakes if all these pleasant surprises ain't got me feeling frisky! What say we duck inside for some slap and tickle, Old Woman?"

She protested with a broad smile, "For land's sake, Old Man, it's still broad daylight!"

To which he replied with a leer, "All the better, Old Woman, for I mean to show it to you hard and I wouldn't want you to mistake it for my clenched fist in the dark!"

But as they raced one another inside neither Longarm nor Foster knew or cared what they might be up to. By then the sun was already taking its last few breaths before diving behind the lofty Bitterroots off to the west. Foster demanded when, if ever, they'd be heading, damn it, to the north.

He pointed out, again, "Thanks to all this riding round Robin Hood's barn we're over a hundred and eighty miles south of the border, and they say Natova is somewhat *north* of the border!"

Longarm said, "It was your grand notion to meet me in Great Falls. The towns to our west may be our last chance to get at a telegraph office for a spell. Once I bring my home office up-to-date, I vote we ride west to Sliderock and if nothing happens in Sliderock, just keep trending west as far as mining camps hold out. We don't want to wander north to where we're off the map, like that hidden valley and its one entrance opening on trackless U.S. wilderness."

"Then how in the devil do you propose we find it without looking for it on your side of the border?"

Longarm said, "I keep telling you. We let it look for us. If any other stangers have ever rid this way looking more like outlaws on the dodge the poor bastards have been caught. We know Archie Croft, a not-too-bright outlaw from clean out of the country, made his way, or got invited, to stay in Natova as long as his money held out. I doubt he was looking for any hideout in particular when someone noticed he was in the market for a hideout and had the jingle to pay his way in."

Foster asked, "Why do you suppose they let him pay his way in? He was a long way from home with that jingle you mentioned. What was to stop a gang who'd recognized Croft for what he was from simply robbing him? Who was he going to complain to?"

Longarm said, "Other crooks. Even if all he did to bitch was vanish from the ken of other riders of the Owlhoot Trail. You can't run a hotel by charging guests for a room and planting them in the cellar. Not very long, least ways. A wary cuss on the prod has to feel safe about any door he knocks on. Would you go down a dark alley with a gal you'd met through a pal if said pal was missing?"

"I see your point. What if we're picked up by the law before our . . . outlaw associates take notice of us?"

"Our mission will be all fucked up," Longarm conceded easily, adding, "Wouldn't need to worry about such things if you didn't ride for such a fucked-up government."

Foster blustered, "Now just one minute, Yank! I'll admit

Sir John is a bit of a blockhead if you'll admit you blighters have always had it in for Canada!"

Longarm snorted, "Most of us blighters don't have any feelings one way or another about that pink space north of our yellow space in the school-house globe we used to spin when the teacher was out of the room. Some few of us have heard talk about birch bark and maple syrup and of course you Mounties do look pretty on parade to American visitors to Niagara Falls. But it comes as a total shock to most Americans to hear, if they ever hear, that Canada is braced for Sherman to march for the north pole any day, now."

"You did invade us in 1812, didn't you?" Foster demanded.

Longarm said, "I wasn't there. But I understand we fought each other to a draw and agreed to let her go at that. The few of us blighters I know who've ever spent fifteen minutes *thinking* about Canada seem to *like* Canadians next to *most* furriners. Of course, at the rate your Sir John is going, his prophecy will be self-fulfilling and you'll wind up with neighbors who don't cotton to *you*, neither."

Foster tried to change the awkward subject by asking what the game was if they were challenged by other lawmen as they tried to pass for outlaws.

Longarm said, "We go along with the game as far as we can without it starting to hurt. You'd be surprised what you can pick up spending time in a holding tank before you explain things in the morning to the judge."

"If you're lucky." Foster declared in a superior tone as he pointed out, "You wild western blighters have this awkward custom of mobbing a jail and lynching the contents. How many times would you say one of your vigilance committees has hung the wrong man?"

Longarm shrugged and allowed, "It happens, albeit not

as often as the sob sisters will go on about. A good part of the time, the old boy the vigilantes strung up had it coming."

"Then why did they lynch him? Why not let the law take its course?" asked the visitor from the north.

To which Longarm could only reply, "Like you said, it's a wilder west. More populated and not as well policed, least ways."

They fussed at one another in the same circles as they rode on into the county seat through the tricky light of sundown. Lampposts stood at regular intervals along either side of the unpaved main street. There was nothing slow about Clarkside, once you found it on a map. But none of the street lights had been lit yet and betwixt the tricky twilight and the dust kicked up by all the coming and going, Longarm suspected they could have ridden a circus bandwagon in without anybody giving a damn.

Anybody watching out for suspicious characters would have an eye on the telegraph office. Nobody had enough eyes to watch all the crowded saloons at that hour. So they tethered their new mules with the horses along the hitch rail of a through-the-block establishment advertising itself as the Last Chance.

There were Last Chance saloons in every town in Montana Territory, named in honor of the first big gold strike back in '64 in Last Chance Gulch near Helena.

This particular Last Chance offered German potato salad, deviled eggs, pickled pigs feet and assorted cold cuts at the bar, farthest from the front door, to customers serious enough to order at least a needled beer.

So Longarm and Foster ordered boilermakers, lest anybody comment on their appetites as they made up for that miserly supper they'd had off to the east. The plan was to settle in, get the feel of the town, and let the town get used to them before they sent any wires up the street.

With the two mules left right where they were.

But as that Scotch poet had warned, poetic, the best-laid plans of mice and men had a habit of going to hell in a hack.

They'd just about rinsed a few swallows of free lunch down with the beer chasers of their boiler makers when they were joined at the bar by an older and stubbier gent wearing a gray walrus mustache and a gold-plated star above an impressive brace of Colt '74s.

Getting right to the point, he declared, "I'd be under-sheriff Howard Ebsen of Powell County and we just received a mighty interesting wire from our county seat at Deer Lodge."

As Longarm set the makings on the zin-topped bar, the county lawman said, "Understand the two of you rode in on them Cordovan mules out front. Ain't horses good enough for you?"

Foster just stood there as Longarm answered, "If we could afford 'em they might be. Mules are good enough in mountain country and we were just handed the shovel down Wyoming way. Outfit called the Lazy B. New outfit. Signed us on long enough to help them move their herd up from Cheyenne and then . . ."

"Spare me the sad song I've heard so many times before," Ebsen cut in, to explain, "We got a wire earlier this evening, about two tall galoots. One smooth-shaven and one with a mustache. Swapping jaded mounts at a stage stop as if they was in a hurry to get somewheres, or away from somewheres. They was last seen aboard a brown-and-white paint and a blue roan. I don't suppose you could tell us anything about that, right?"

Longarm started to shake his head, then he brightened and said, "Oh, *them* two? Now that you mention it, we did think something funny might be going on."

"How so, funny?" asked the older lawman.

Longarm said, "They acted innocent enough as we met on the trace. It must have been east of that last stage stop out of here. We passed it later. Didn't see anything funny *there*."

He turned to Foster to say, "You remember me saying that other rascal on that lathered sorrel looked sneaky when he asked us if we'd seen his pals, riding a paint and a blue roan. Don't you. Dusty?"

Longarm had thought the Mountie had the makings of a good poker player. Foster proved it by shrugging and observing, "He looked more worried than sneaky to me. You're always saying somebody who hasn't done anything to you is up to something."

Old Ebsen shifted back and forth in his boots like a schoolboy who had to pee as he cut in, "Never mind all that bullshit. You say this jasper on the sorrel was chasing after the other two, headed east for Helena?"

Longarm replied, "None of 'em said where they was headed. But all of them seemed anxious to get there."

A younger, taller cuss wearing one six-gun and a deputy sheriff's badge joined them as others along the bar fell silent. Ebsen nodded at the deputy and dropped a casual hand to the grips of his right-hand Peacemaker as he calmly asked, "Well?"

The deputy stared at Longarm and Foster as he answered, "Can't say which saddle gun rode in with which. But one of 'em's a seven-shot Spencer and the other's a '63 Henry."

Undersheriff Ebsen smiled for the first time and said, "These boys were just telling me the rascal riding a paint with a Yellowboy and his pal packing a newer Winchester '73 were chased east along the Helena trace by that *other* suspicious jasper the stage stop crew wired us about."

The deputy asked, "The one who scared the liver and lights out of poor little Tillie, with a drawn gun?"

Ebsen said, "The same. So now we know for certain all three rode east. Tommy at the stage stop wired they were only certain about one tearing east on that sorrel."

The deputy asked, "You want me to posse up some of the boys?"

Ebsen shook his older and wiser head to say, "Not hardly. They got too good a lead on us even if it wasn't already dark out. Time we ever cut their sign in the morning they'd have made it back to the more settled parts east of the divide and gone to ground. Our best bet would be to wire Lewis and Clark County or, hell, Helena so they can worry about the mysterious rascals."

He nodded at Longarm and the ramrod-straight Foster to say, "Enjoy your visit to Powell County and we're much obliged. You've been a great help."

Then he and his deputy were heading out the front way. Longarm grabbed Foster by the elbow and muttered, "Stay put and let me buy you another, pard."

"I want to see about those . . . mules!" Foster insisted.

Not knowing how many others might be listening, Longarm soothed in a desperately casual tone, "That lawmen just told us our saddles and saddle guns were as we left 'em. Like I told you riding in, nervous nellies entering saloons in a strange town with rifles can occasion more trouble than the risk of pilferage is worth, and, as you just heard, ain't nobody swapped out saddle guns for antiques. So, you ready for another boilermaker?"

The Mountie allowed he could use a stiff one, with a muttered aside under his breath about thieving Yanks. So Longarm ordered and the barmaid refilled their beer schooners and poured two shots of fairly good spirits. It was likely corn squeezings colored with tea but it was *good* corn squeezings and they'd already noticed the better-than-usual cold cuts and fairly fresh rye bread. This particular Last Chance gave you a sporting chance at an enjoyable evening without needing a stomach pump in the morning.

The four barmaids working the long bar, instead of the usual he-men, cheered the atmosphere even more. You had to watch close to see the he-men lounging near the front and back entrances. The one guarding the stairs up to the mezzanine surrounding the main floor was less subtle with that baseball bat cradled in his burly arms. But he smiled a lot.

From time to time a sober enough customer would go up or down the stairs. The bouncer smiled at the one liquored up rustic he turned away. The gals working the cribs up yonder never showed themselves, as they did in some such establishments. In sum, the Last Chance in Clarkside was a well-run joint.

There was no stage and the piano so common to the species wasn't there to slow the flow of orders across the bar. There was no faro layout or wheel of fortune. But from the way the door to the back room kept opening and closing there was heavy wagering going on behind it.

Any strongarm man guarding the boys in the back room was posted on the far side, likely with a gun. Nobody who hadn't been invited tried to bull his way into a back room unless he was serious.

Now and again you'd see a gal in Rainy Suzy skirts and more makeup than Queen Victoria approved threading through the crowd with a tray, or just smiling a lot. So Longarm wasn't startled when a pretty little thing with a black velvet band around her bare throat, as if to make up for how much of her chest was exposed joined them at the bar to smile up at them and ask if they'd care to go upstairs with her.

She was more tempting than most with her henna-rinsed hair smelling of shampoo and her duds freshly laundered. But without having to consult with Foster and without sounding lofty, Longarm politely declined by allowing they were expected in other parts that evening and just fixing to leave.

The tarted-up play pretty coyly asked, "Without your guns?"

The two undercover lawmen exchanged glances. Each knew what the other was thinking. It was a close call. Sending a coyote bitch-in-heat to lure a yard dog out on the lone prairie was as old a ruse as there was. You could read of such doings in the Good Book.

On the other hand, curiosity had killed the cat with good reason. The human race would still be dwelling in caves if, every now and again, somebody hadn't risked looking for some answers.

So Longarm said, "Why don't you stay down here and wait on me whilst I go see what this is all about, Dusty?"

It didn't seem to fluster the tart when the Mountie allowed he'd be sitting at a table near the front door. So Longarm followed as the pretty little thing led him through the crowd to the stairs and up the same.

The doors to the cribs they passed were all shut and nothing louder than a girlish giggle or two broke the more sedate atmosphere of the second floor. She led him 'round to chambers that likely overlooked the street out front and opened the door, murmuring, "The Madam is expecting you."

She never followed as Longarm went on in. Things were darker and smelled of sandalwood incense as he moved on towards the lamplight on the far side of a beaded curtain across another doorway. When he parted the curtains he saw that the junoesque gal reclining like Goya's *Naked Maja* on a blue-velvet lounge was cheating with a flesh-colored chemise and black silk stockings gartered at mid-thigh with black lace. The outfit made her look more naked than Goya had managed in that nude painting.

After that, her hair matched her black silk garters, save for being combed more smoothly before she'd pinned it up. She wore no makeup. She had no need for makeup with those long lashes and big brown eyes. He figured her for around thirty-five, shooting for sweet sixteen and almost making it.

Doffing his Stetson with a flourish, Longarm allowed he was her servant. She said, "I know. That's why I sent for you."

Longarm just stood there, waiting for the other shoe to drop. She said she was going by the handle of Last Chance Charlene these days. She disremembered what they used to call her when the world was young and green. She allowed Buck was a good enough name for him and went on to explain, "We have connections with the local courthouse gang. When that wire about you boys came in this afternoon, I was advised you might be heading this way and warned I'd best keep an eye peeled for you. So I did. One of my boys reported you were in town before you made up your mind to tether your mules out front."

She let that sink in before she patted the blue velvet she reclined on and said, "Set yourself down and take a load off your boots. Where might you have swapped that paint and that roan for those mules?"

Longarm perched his rump gingerly on the space she'd made for him by shifting her own rump back as he answered, innocently, "Who said we ever swapped any riding stock, Miss Charlene?"

Last Chance Charlene demurely replied, "The wire from the stage stop warned the two of you looked armed and dangerous, with a Yellowboy and a newer Winchester keeping company with your centerfire saddles. Most roping men up this way favor double rig and Yellowboys are getting rare as a Mexican song without the word *corazón* in it. We have them on tap for you when you're ready to leave, unless you want to ride off smart with *two* Winchester 74s. I had my boys switch more innocent hardware in your saddle boots. Do we have to drone on with this bullshit or are you ready to deal?"

Longarm allowed he was listening.

The softly curved but firm-jawed brunette said, "First hear my offer. You and your friend downstairs stay here, with free . . . room service, as long as the job may take. When you're ready to leave you'll ride on with five hundred dollars apiece, along with fine fresh horses, new saddle guns with local bills of sale, and no wads worth mention left in your balls. Do I have to tell you what the alternative is?"

Longarm soberly replied, "We were just talking to the alternative down at your bar. What's the job?"

She said, "I'm being muscled. I'm a live-and-let-live sporting girl, as any man here can see. So I stand ready to compete fair and square if you want to open another joint across the way."

Longarm said, "I ain't been planning to, ma'am. I take it somebody else might of?"

She said, "He calls himself Honest John Jenkins. His beer is watered. His games are fixed, and those few of his girls who aren't clapped up are ugly!"

Longarm nodded and said, "Old Dusty and me gave the place across the way a glance before we were attracted to your brighter paint and cleaner smells. So what's your problem? Seems to me you already have the cuss whupped fair and square."

She said, "Honest John doesn't play fair and square. He's demanded a sixty-forty split on my profits, with guess who's getting the lion's share!"

Longarm grimaced and said, "You're right. He don't sound fair or even reasonable. What's he offering for you cutting him in for anything at all?"

She answered, simply, "My staying in business at all. He's already burned out a couple of others who refused him. As of now he's raking off sixty percent from Lord knows how many others in town. Such deals are not deals one brags about. He's given me to Midsummer's Eve to make up my mind, intimating big bonfires on Midsummer's Eve were the custom in Viking times, with Midsummer's Eve a little less than a week away."

Longarm smiled thinly and said, "He sounds more like a plain and simple extortionist than a Viking to me, Miss Charlene. But, no offense, you already seem to have some tough-looking boys on your payroll."

She grimaced and said, "They're bouncers, not gunslicks, like you and your friend downstairs."

Longarm let that pass and asked, "I take it this Honest John has a gunslick or more on his own payroll?"

She said, "A whole crew. We're not certain how many. We do know they take orders from one Edwin Chambers, who tells you to call him Empty Chambers as he stands there sneering down at you."

"Big gent, you say?" asked Longarm.

She said, "As tall or taller than you, built heavier, packing two double-action six-guns instead of the one you seem to be wearing."

Longarm never told anyone about his double derringer unless he had to whip it out on the end of his watch chain. He said, "I wouldn't want a pretty lady to take me for a sissy, Miss Charlene, but the dust is still settling from a similar situation down New Mexico way. They called her the Lincoln County War. Folk are still arguing about who was most at fault. Neither side were angels and neither side showed much common sense."

She said, "I know all about the Lincoln County War. I read the papers and we get customers from all over. I find myself in the position of the Chisum, Tunstall and McSween faction, bullied by the Murphy, Dolan, Brady gang!"

He said, "Never leave out Ryan. It was Rancher Ryan's beef Major Murphy and Jim Dolan were selling to the army and the nearby Mescalero agency. They were there first. If anybody was crowding anybody it was Uncle John Chisum and his younger business partners, out to sell beef Uncle John had bought on credit in Texas to Major Murphy's established customers."

She said, "Oh, piffle. Don't split hairs. You know what I mean. No matter who was offering what at any price didn't the Murphy, Dolan, Brady gang murder poor young Tunstall in cold blood?"

Longarm nodded and said, "Then Tunstall's foreman, Dick Brewer, got a gang of his own together and commenced to murder the other side. They got Sheriff Brady on April Fools' day and Dick Brewer lay dead eight days later with the top blown off his head."

He sighed and said, "After that things started to get rough, with both sides ruined in the end. Such wars are expensive two ways, Miss—guns draw top dollar, and you don't do much business with bullets in the air instead of flies. Had either side down Lincoln County way folded their hands and got up from the table when they saw how steep the stakes were rising . . ."

She said, "I told you I know all about that poorly thought-out feud!" Then she added, "The mistake Tunstall's partners made after the other side murdered him was in going after the other side from the bottom up. It was Murphy's top gun, Jim Dolan, holding their faction together. If Dick Brewer had killed him first, Murphy and the others would have run for it."

She let that sink in and said, "Empty Chambers is the linch pin holding everything across the way together. Neither Honest John nor any of his own boys in the back room add up to half as much."

Longarm asked what she expected him to do about Empty Chambers.

She said, "Kill the son of a bitch, of course."

To which Longarm could only reply, "Oh, I was afraid you were going to ask me to move some furniture."

Chapter 9

When Longarm rejoined Foster downstairs, the Mountie marveled, "What's your secret? Do whorehouse madams fall for you everywhere you go?"

Longarm said, "Aw, neither the Silver Spur in Helena nor this place are exactly whorehouses. They're more like saloons with extra trimmings, and neither gal could be described as falling for me. They both wanted favors. Most sensible women do. Professor Darwin explains all that in his theory of revolution. Most all our maternal ancestors back to Mother Eve hooked up with some hombre willing to favor a gal with food, shelter and protection. Gals dumb enough to put out without expecting nothing never got to *be* ancestors. So the ones who did revolved expecting to be treated right."

Foster said, "Good Lord, you make it sound as if all women are cheap whores!"

Longarm shook his head and said, "Only the ones we call whores come cheap. Would you say a vaporous young thing who demands a ring and a contractual obligation to support her for the rest of her life before you get to feel her tits is offering you a *bargain*?"

Foster protested, "Oh, come now, a good wife offers a man more than bedroom priviliges. She cooks and sews and keeps house for man and their nippers, you know."

Longarm shrugged and conceded, "Average housewife must work half as hard as one of them gals putting in twelve-hour days in a factory for two bits a day. But none of this is here nor there. We're set here for as long as I can stall Madame Charlene. Like I said, all she's expecting in return is that we take out this Empty Chambers bozo."

The Mountie in mufti demanded, "How? We're only allowed to bend the rules within limits while we're working undercover, and assassination would be bending the rules indeed!"

Longarm shrugged and said, "I know that, and you know that, but what does *she* know, and the deadline Honest John set is way off in the future, a good six days away."

Foster shook his head and insisted, "Ridiculous! I was hoping we'd be far as Sliderock by this time tomorrow!"

Longarm demanded, "On jaded mules, with antique saddle guns and the county law snapping at our heels? She'll have the law on us if we light out on her. She's offering fresh mounts, new rifles and a thousand bucks betwixt us if we save this saloon for her. So we'd best stick around a spell."

Foster insisted, "To what end? Sooner or later she'll see we don't mean to kill anybody for her and won't that brown her off even more? Even if there was some way to solve her problems without becoming outlaws sincerely indeed, we can't afford to waste that much time!"

Longarm mused, "Ain't certain we'll be wasting it. Somebody's kept our gracious hostess up on recent gunplay as far south as New Mexico Territory and the more shady characters we sell on our being Owlhoot riders on the dodge, the more likely we are to fall in with some Montana riders who know the way to Natova. Up to now, we've only managed to *resemble* outlaws wanted for a robbery that never took place. Letting it be known in whispers that we're hired guns working for a more famous shady lady . . ."

"It won't work!" the Mountie cut in, insisting, "Even if we were mad enough to stay down this way late as the twenty-first of June, we'd have to kill somebody or cut and run by then, with your Last Chance Charlene just as enraged, if not more so, than if we were to simply be on our way before anyone knows we've left."

Before Longarm could answer, Foster went on, "We've money to buy new rifles, new ponies, even new saddles in the morning without anyone here the wiser, see?"

Longarm shrugged and said, "Might get halfway to Sliderock before they posse up. Meanwhile, the night's not getting any younger and her nibs is expecting me to bring you upstairs like I said I would. So why don't we sleep on it? I can't go wiring my home office this late at night, in any case. Nobody will deliver a telegram late on a Sabbath night to begin with and I want to drop by when things are busy."

Foster asked if he thought it wise to file progress reports in any case, explaining, "My supervisor gave me some time off and told me I was on my own until I had something really worth reporting. I somehow doubt anyone at Fort MacLeod is concerned about where I'll be spending the night nearly two hundred miles south of the perishing border!"

Longarm said things were tough all over and led Foster upstairs to meet the gals. The gals waiting on them were plural, now, because Last Chance Charlene had told two of her best-looking gals to see to the needs of the two distinguished gents who'd be boarding there a spell.

She'd already ordered some of her male help to lead those mules out back to her private stable and store their gear in her tack room. Having introduced her new gunhands to Mabel and Jo, Last Chance Charlene retired to her own quarters before Longarm could stop her.

He hadn't been anxious to stop her because there was anything wrong with the younger Mabel and Jo. He doubted either could have been to bed with as many other men before him and you had to hand it to a boss too smart to sleep with the hired help. But he still had scores of questions to ask her, starting with whether she'd ever heard tell of an outlaw mountain resort in them there hills.

The brown-haired Mabel seemed to be with Foster and it wouldn't have been reasonable to say he was *stuck* with Jo. For as things turned out in her perfumed lamplit crib, she was blond all over and as the old trail song best described her, "Young and pretty, too, and had what they call a ring-dang-doo!"

After that, like the madam herself, the choice stock only served the more clean and prosperous customers, and once Longarm adjusted to not having much choice if he meant to pass for a knockaround hairpin, he discovered the not too bright but mighty friendly little thing seemed naturally warm-natured as well as anxious to please, and he was able to rise to the occasion.

Jo seemed impressed and allowed she couldn't wait to tell the other gals she'd taken that much manhood to the roots, from on top. He knew better than to ask her not to. The cynic who'd described the three fastest means of communication as the telegraph, the telephone and the tell-a-woman had likely asked a gal or more to keep a secret.

He knew that whether her girls gossiped or not, Last Chance Charlene was sure to let Honest John and Empty Chambers know they'd be crowding her further at their own peril. There was no sense buying a bulldog unless you posted BEWARE THE DOG signs. The ancient Romans had known that, even though the sign dug out of those Roman ruins had read CAVE CANUM.

Such signs only worked when the other side was afraid of dogs, or didn't have a bulldog of its own.

He didn't have long to wait before he was certain he'd been on the money about she-male gossip and how impressed the other side might be by the same.

After joining Last Chance Charlene in her quarters for a demitasse after she'd broken fast alone, Longarm allowed he meant to mosey about and get the feel of her neck of the woods. She said he'd find there wasn't all that much of it and she'd been there, damn it, *first*. When she asked if he could use a sawed-off ten-gauge Greener she kept for rough trade when he dropped in on Honest John across the way, Longarm told her he wasn't planning to, adding, "That would amount to an outright declaration of war, Miss Charlene, and I just got here. Ain't ready for a showdown before I scout the fields of fire."

She said, "They know you and Dusty are working for me. Won't they think you're afraid of them if you sniff around like a dog scouting a gate post?"

He soothed, "Won't matter what they think of us, earlier, if we win in the sweet by and by. Napoleon likely thought the Duke of Wellington was scared of him at Waterloo. Then he sent massed cavalry to charge the British squares from the flank and, guess what, the French had scouted the terrain ahead sloppy, and all those men and horses piled up in one bloody windrow when they hit a sunken road they hadn't known was there."

The voluptuous brunette shrugged her creamy, bare shoulders and sipped her demitasse without answering.

Longarm downed the rest of his—there wasn't but a few sips in such a sissy cup—and rose to his considerable height, saying, "I mean to circle every block for blocks around and cut through as many alleyways as ain't posted. If push comes to shove, I want to know what's where. I understand when that Lincoln County War came to a head in the summer of '78, with both sides forted up right across the street from one another, Murphy-Dolan gun-hands had the higher vantage point as they fired down into the McSween complex from Major Murphy's big store."

He put his hat on as he added, "That was before Murphy's army pals from Fort Stanton showed up to make things hopeless. Have you looked into which way the local courthouse gang is likely to throw its weight if and when Honest John makes good on his threats?"

She looked away and said, "They've told me it's between the Jenkins-Chambers faction and us. They say the taxpayers can't be expected to pay for business rivalry. That's what they call it when those thugs burn saloons down, 'business rivalry.' "

What they'd meant, of course, was that the Women's Christian Temperance Union wasn't about to approve of officials taking sides in a saloon fight in an election year. Things could have been worse. Tunstall and McSween had gone up against gents backed by the Lincoln County courthouse gang, with Uncle John Chisum offering to hold their coats.

Down by the bar, Longarm found Crown Sergeant Foster drinking alone, with a sober expression. He didn't ask whether the stiff-backed Mountie had managed to get through the night by shutting his eyes, gritting his teeth and thinking of Queen and Empire. He told Foster he meant to scout around and get that wire off to Denver if nobody followed him to the telegraph office.

Foster offered to tag along and back his play. Longarm shook his head and said, "Best if the two of us are never in sight at the same time. You know how hunters worry about a mountain lion's mate when they ain't certain the time to fire has come. I'll hole up with old Jo while you mosey around out yonder, later on, if you like."

Foster looked disgusted and asked, "How long do you mean to whore and swill free liquor, here, before we continue our search for that hidden valley to the north?"

Longarm said, "We're searching for it swell. Last night Jo told me she'd heard gents saying those outlaws who robbed that payroll, namely us, had likely made it to that robbers' roost in the high country by this time. After that she couldn't recall any directions to Natova.

Somebody had surely been posted at a window across the way, for as Longarm parted the bat-wing doors of the Last Chance to step out into the late morning light, a tall, broad-shouldered figure in a tailored *charro* outfit of dark oxblood leather trimmed in German silver seemed to be headed catty-corner, as if to meet up with him.

Longarm kept moving the way he'd intended up the shady side of the street as he took in the black Spanish hat and twin Schofields riding in a silver-trimmed Buscadero rig, side drawn and tied down, or, in sum, the way a killer who meant to do most of his fighting on foot in town wore his guns.

Longarm naturally carried his .44-40 cross-draw, higher on his left hip, where a man could get at it afoot or astride, seated at a table or standing by the bar. Cross-draw was a sort of Jack-of-all-trades-and-master-of-None for a man who just never knew when he'd need to fill his fist in a hurry. The stranger heading him off would have the edge if they went at it mano a mano on their feet.

Longarm locked eyes with the Fancy Dan who'd cut across the dusty street, nigh empty at that hour, to plant a boot on the boardwalk ahead as he demanded, "Might you be one of them birds who just signed on with Last Chance Charlene?"

Longarm stopped, a most within fist-fighting range, to nod agreeably and reply, "You can call me Buck Crawford."

The other man said, "They call me Empty Chambers and I'll call you anything I feel like, once I take your measure."

Longarm went on smiling as he said, "Measure away, Empty. No offense but the name sure seems to fit you, far as I can see."

The top gun for the other side smiled wolfishly and shot back, "Well what have we here, a big brave pimp playing big bad wolf?"

Longarm calmly replied, "Watch who you call a pimp. That ain't the position I applied for."

Empty Chambers sneered, "Oh, no? Suppose you tell this child what sort of a position you applied for."

Longarm wasn't smiling when he said, "Fly swatter. Pesky flies get to buzzing in my ears and I'm likely to swat 'em."

There came a long moment of silence. Then Empty Chambers grinned a bully's grin and replied in a lighter tone, "You sure must have got out of the wrong side of bed this morning, dear. If I didn't know better, I'd think you were trying to provoke a gunfight, right here on Main Street in broad-ass daylight!"

Longarm calmly asked, "When do you *usually* draw on a man, on a *dark* street when his back is turned to you?"

The bully who'd bluff had been called said, "See here, I ain't used to being spoke to that way, ah, Buck."

Longarm said, "Don't crowd me and I won't talk to you at all. If that ain't good enough for you, feel free to fill your fist any time you fancy. You know where to find me."

"I'd best talk to the boss about this," Empty Chambers growled, trying to sound more ominous than he likely felt. Then he turned to head back where he'd come from as Longarm strode on.

As he drifted on towards the telegraph office up the way, making mental notes of vantage points overlooking the street from all sides, Longarm was trying to picture where he'd seen Empty Chambers before, if he ever had. It was his business to remember names and faces, and Empty Chambers rang no bells. If he'd seen that know-it-all sneer and cocked eyebrow before, it didn't go with a fancy *charro* outfit or . . . fancy duds at all. In the army, back in that war they'd held in his honor? In some line-up or mayhaps some holding cell?

Longarm strode past the Western Union office to circle the block and make certain nobody was following him. He wasn't ready to file a coded progress report from Clarkside as yet. He hadn't been there long enough to know what he was doing there, and what the hell could his pals back in Denver do for him in any case?

Chapter 10

When Longarm got back from Western Union he found the vapidly pretty Jo tending bar. As she served him a boilermaker it made him feel better about the way she'd saved him the night before.

Before they could talk about it much they were joined by a young squirt wearing a seersucker summer suit and horn-rimmed glasses, thick as the bottom of Longarm's shot glass. He introduced himself as the society editor for the *Powell County Advertiser* and said he wanted to be sure he'd have the spelling right when he typed up the obituaries of Buck Crawford and Dusty Rhodes.

Longarm asked Jo to set one up for the cheerful cuss and allowed it seemed a tad early to be jawing about obituaries for anybody.

The newspaper squirt said, "I wouldn't be so sure. They say Empty Chambers has already told you not to be in town on Midsummer's Eve and that's only six days off."

Longarm didn't ask who "they" were. Someone was always watching everything along the main street of a small town. So as Jo poured the squirt a shot with a beer chaser, Longarm said, "Me and old Empty have only met on one occasion. I don't recall him telling me to get out of town."

The society editor knocked back the hard liquor, gasped, and gulped some suds before he wheezed, "I've been given to understand Chambers isn't one for protracted negotiations. Partners who owed the Hardrock Saloon hired a couple of mysterious strangers to stand up to Honest John on May Day. Honest John seems to favor easy dates to remember for his deadlines."

Longarm didn't ask what might have happened to those other hired guns. He knew the newspaper squirt was fixing to tell him.

The newspaper squirt said, "The coroner's jury declared it a clear case of self-defense when one of them strode down the street from the Hardrock like he owned it. The street, that is. Empty Chambers allowed he was minding his own business in front of the pool hall when he saw this notorious gunman bearing down on him and only did what he had to do."

It was Jo, Lord love her, who asked what had happened to that *other* gun the Hardrock Saloon had sent away for.

The newspaper squirt said, "Nobody knows. He never left town by stagecoach. Must have left town on the sneak. Nobody ever saw him again. The one they buried had papers on him indicating he might have been named Roy Wojensky. A security man from one of the local mines said he'd heard of a hardcase private detective called Bohunk Wojensky. If that was him, old Empty Chambers defended himself pretty good against a cuss who'd won big, more than once, in other parts."

Longarm sipped more suds and said, "He intimated when we spoke a spell back he thought he was the bee's knees. I take it Honest John now owns a piece of this Hardrock Saloon?"

The newspaper squirt shook his head and said, "He owns it all. Said he had no use for partners who'd sic hired guns on an honest businessmen. So they left. By stage. Honest John pays their fare as a gesture of goodwill."

Longarm drained the last of his beer schooner and set it back on the bar expectantly. So, seeing it was his turn to buy a round if he meant to stay, he left. As he parted the bat-wings of the front entrance, Crown Sergeant Foster rose from where he'd been nursing his own suds at a nearby table with his back to them and joined Longarm at the bar.

Foster said, "I hope you read that conversation the way I did?" Longarm said, "Sure. Honest John must advertise in the *Powell County Advertiser*. Things are looking up if they've commenced a war of nerves. Our Honest John's a smarter businessman than the late Major Murphy of Lincoln County fame. Or maybe the courthouse gang up this way is really neutral as Last Chance Charlene says. In any case, they've given us six days' grace to study on it and a lot can happen in six days."

"We could ride north to the perishing Canadian border in less than ten days, and have you forgotten where we're supposed to be, right now?"

Longarm shot him a warning glance without looking at Jo as he asked her to fix the two of them up.

As Jo poured, Longarm said, "We've been over that, Dusty. Ain't hardly anybody to talk to up in the glacier country near the border, and look at all the friends we've been making down here in the mining district."

Foster looked disgusted as he muttered, "With friends like you make, who needs enemies? Don't you see how Empty Chambers sets things up?"

Longarm nodded and replied, "That newspaper squirt just told us. As a local boy with a steady job in town, old Empty lets it be known far and wide he's had words with a stranger before he shoots said stranger in self-defense. It ain't too subtle and it ain't at all new. But it works when the boys on the coroner's jury include just a few boys from your back room. They say that after the Murphy-Dolan guns finished off her man, the Widow McSween hired a lawyer, an unwarmed one armed lawyer from Las Vegas by the name of Hustin Chapman to help her settle up her dead husband's estate." Foster reached for his fresh shot glass as he allowed widows usually did retain a lawyer at such times.

Longarm said, "Jim Dolan, party to the killing of Sandy McSween, shot the unarmed crippled Chapman down like a dog on the streets of Lincoln Plaza and pled self defense."

The Canadian said, "You can't be serious!"

Longarm downed his own whiskey, chased it with some suds and sounded just as disgusted when he said, "Nobody laughed. He won an acquittal. He and some of his gun waddies were still standing. Tunstall and McSween were dead. Uncle John Chisum was holed up at South Springs, miles away, and the few young guns of Dick Brewer's avengers were scattered to hell and breakfast. Seeing things Dolan's way saved the county a trial that might have still been going on to this day, what with witnesses leaving town unexpected and so on."

Foster declared, "In sum, if you step out that front entrance in the tricky light of Midsummer's Eve, someone from across the way is liable to take an awful fright and shoot you in self-defense, from cover?"

"Empty Chambers may try to make it look less blatant," said Longarm.

He pointed out, "As I read the sad end of Bohunk Wojensky, Chambers stepped out of a pool hall, unexpected, as Wojensky was starting down the street ahead. Chambers wears his six-guns slung low and tied down. Popping out at another man liked an armed and dangerous cuckoo clock bird with its mind already made up gives our boy the edge he feels he needs. I gave him a shot at a fair fight this morning. He never took it."

"My God! You didn't!" gasped the Canadian lawman, pointing at his empty shot glass for Jo's edification as he warned Longarm, "I've chided you in the past about your notions of rough justice, ah, Buck. If you think you can shoot it out with a man in his own town and get off without, ah, explaining in detail to the powers that be, you must have been lying in mind as well!"

"A man does what he has to." Longarm shrugged.

The Mountie stiffly replied, "I agree. When I've sworn to tell the truth, the whole truth and nothing but the truth, I feel I have to tell the truth!"

Longarm was saved from having to answer when they were joined by Under-sheriff Ebsen.

The older and stubbier local lawman declined Longarm's offer of a drink and said, "I'm here on county beeswax. I just come for a meeting with the our mayor and city council, over to the town hall. What's all this they say about you backing Empty Chambers down this morning?" Longarm allowed "they" sure had a lot to say behind men's backs and soothed, "Wasn't that dramatic. Old Empty just wanted to know how long me and Dusty, here, meant to stick around."

Ebsen nodded at the Mountie next to Longarm as he told them both in a morose tone, "Wire came in this morning from Marysville. Seems somebody helped hisself to a stabled pony, leaving a lathered sorrel in its stead. So like I just now told them over to the town hall, you gents just won't work as the strangers we was hoping you might be."

Longarm smiled down at the older lawman innocently to allow he was glad to hear that.

Ebsen snapped, "So who are you? What are you? Don't give me any more of that shit about honest young cowboys, looking for honest work. Last Chance Charlene don't have no cows and if she did have they say you was smiling like a wolverine in a henhouse when you backed Empty Chambers down out front. Do you take me for a moon calf? Do you think I can't read tailored grips on a double-action six-gun as the tools of the gun-fighting trade?"

Longarm said, "Have her your own way, then. Let's say me and old Dusty, here, have smelled some gunsmoke in other parts, if that suits your fancy. What's the charge, if you have any charge to prefer this afternoon?"

Ebsen's voice was pleading as he answered, "Aw, shoot, be reasonable, Buck. This is an election year and we just can't let Empty Chambers off on shooting out-of-town guns! I mean, it don't look civilized!"

Longarm was too polite to ask why they hadn't arrested the murderous son of a bitch already. He figured if he asked a silly question, he'd get a silly answer.

He said, "If it's any comfort, you can tell the courthouse gang we don't aim no walkdown such as Ned Buntline descibes in those western fairy tales he publishes. Come Midsummer's Eve, we mean to celebrate her like everybody else with a late supper and a jug of hard cider to pass around."

Ebsen said, "I've got a grander suggestion for you boys, with Powell County paying your stage fare to the nearest railhead of your choice. That way you could celebrate Midsummer's Eve right, out by the Frisco Bay or under the bright lights along Chicago's State Street. In six days you could be most anywhere in the U.S. of A., thanks to the wonders of modern transportation, and why go down with a sinking ship, out here in Clarkside?"

Longarm figured he'd had enough to drink for the time being and went for a cheroot in his shirt pocket as he calmly replied, "We'll see whose ship goes down, come Midsummer's Eve."

The charter member of the local courthouse gang snorted, "Aw, come on, Buck. Last Chance Charlene's a good old gal, but she's a woman alone, up against ruthless, powerful men!"

Longarm said, "No she ain't. Not since me and Dusty, here, signed on with her. You tell Honest John for all of us that he'd best not grab for the lady's property unless he'd like to draw back a stump."

"Who said I'm carrying messages back and forth betwixt two camps?" asked Undersheriff Ebsen in a defensive tone.

Longarm smiled like a wolverine indeed as he replied, "Ain't you? I stand corrected, then. Guess we'll just have to let Honest John learn the error of his business methods the hard way."

As the undersheriff grumped out, Crown Sergeant Foster of the Northwest Mounted Police quietly said, "Count me in. That remark about a woman alone was uncalled for, and I've never cared for bullies since I was thrown out of a fine public school in Ottawa."

"You licked the class bully?" asked Longarm, knowingly.

The Mountie who wore stripes in spite of acting like an upper-class twit said, "Actually, it was the headmaster. Had this unfortunate habit of beating little boys with a hickory cane. I fear I upset my poor social-climbing mother quite a bit. But my dad said he was proud of me."

Without describing the injuries a Canadian stripling had inflicted upon a sadistic headmaster, Foster asked, "But how are we going to satisfy the coroner's jury without lying under oath?"

Longarm shot him another look and said, "We got this old church song down this way, as assures us that farther along we'll know more about it. Six days is a long time."

"The hell you say!" the Canadian lawman replied, adding, "We just got here. The other side knows every back alley and shortcut in Clarkside and what if Empty Chambers posts snipers covering every field of fire we have to work with?"

Longarm said, "I mean to know the town better by the time I need to know it that well. I've already done some scouting. There ain't that much to scout. What there is began as just another gold camp and got sort of big for its britches when they chose it for a stage junction because it was located more central than some. Most of the gents you see in town with free time and money to spend work the mines all about, 'round the clock in twelve-hour shifts. You see more bellied up to the bars after dark when farm and ranch hands ride on after work. Streets figure to be more crowded than usual on Midsummer's Eve. Won't be open space for one of those Ned Buntline walkdowns if we were dumb enough act like that. I figure Empty Chambers will make more war talk betwixt now and then, so's everybody will know he has just cause to fear for his life when we meet unexpected. I'm still working on where he expects that to be. He's already used up that pool hall."

Another gal came down the stairs to declare supper was

being served and that ended their discussion for the time being.

It was after supper, with the shadows lengthening outside, when Last Chance Charlene sent word "Buck" was invited for another demitasse and maybe more dessert in her private quarters up front.

When he joined the sultry brunette she was wearing more perfume and looking more sultry than before as she patted the blue velvet beside her and said, "Jo just told me what she overheard downstairs this afternoon. That isn't all she told me. There seems to be more to you than meets the eye and there's a lot of you that meets the eye, you big moose."

He modestly allowed his poor but honest parents had managed to feed a growing boy tolerable back in West-By-God-Virginia. Then he asked where those bitty cups of coffee might be.

She purred, "Maybe later. Right now I don't need anything to wake me and I doubt you do, either. I was touched by what you said, downstairs, about my no longer being a woman alone."

Her sloe eyes were filled with tears as she sobbed, "Oh, Buck, you've no idea how alone I was feeling when you and that other Owlhoot rider reined in out front, one jump ahead of the law! But you did and now you *are* with me and I'm *not* alone anymore, right?"

Hoping he was reading the smoke signals she was sending with her big brown eyes correctly, Longarm took her in his arms to assure he was with her. She kissed back passionately and as his questing free hand soon determined, she had nothing on under that flesh-colored chemise.

So as he proceeded to rock the little man in the boat for her she got to work on the buttons of his jeans with neither saying a word as they went on swapping spit.

Then Last Chance Charlene got a firmer grasp on what she was letting herself in for and twisted her lips away to gasp, "My God, Jo might have warned me! But she only said you were great in bed and I don't know, Buck. It's been a while and never with anyone this . . . tall."

But as things turned out, once they managed to get it in her, Last Chance Charlene just couldn't seem to get enough of all he had to offer.

Chapter 11

Last Chance Charlene said, and Longarm had no call to doubt, that she was not inclined to put out to customers or hired help as a rule. But rules were made to be broken and despite her business sense the soft and curvacious little thing was mighty warm-natured inside her imperious shell—as she proved by leaving the two of them nursing rug-burns over the days and nights that followed.

Longarm tried to tell her he'd read the fool book and that half the positions in the forbidden *Kama Sutra*, sold from under the counter in a plain brown cover, were impratical if not downright painful. But like most every other gal who'd ever blinked at the illustrations, including a good many late Victorian brides, the usually more dignified brunette just had to see for herself which positions worked and which might not. She was a good sport when a joint popped or they fell out of bed again. And on those occasions she was content with the missionary position, she came close to bucking him off.

If Jo or any of her other gals were jealous, or even knew just what was going on, they never said anything. So the nights that followed were warm and friendly while each day got more growly and tense.

Neither Honest John nor Empty Chambers proved dumb enough to set foot on the opposing faction's side of Main Street as they dispatched ever more ominous veiled threats along the grapevine. Their position was a flat contradiction in terms. Honest John Jenkins wanted it known he'd made an honest offer for a mutually profitable business merger and been met by threats against his very life. Last Chance Charlene had up and hired known gunslingers, whover they were, and Honest John's associate, the live-and-let-live Empty Chambers, had merely *advised* Buck Crawford and Dusty Rhodes to get out of town by Midsummer's Eve. Longarm had no idea what might happen if they didn't. But anyone could see the town just wasn't big enough for so many gunslicks with uncertain dispositions.

A day or so after he'd changed bed partners at the Last Chance and was walking sort of stiff, Longarm met with another businesswoman who had a rooming house with a mansard roof near the stagecoach terminal down Main Street. She allowed that as he'd expected, the dormer rooms under sloping, sunbaked shingles were tough to rent with high summer coming on. When she showed "Buck Crawford" around up yonder he saw one dormer did offer the view he'd hoped for, down Main Street and covering the lower rooftops on either side.

When he said he'd take her whole top floor she offered him a fair price and asked when he'd be moving in. He said, "Ain't certain. Why don't you just give me my keys to the one door at the head of them stairs and your alley door, downstairs, and let me worry about it?"

His new landlady, a wordly middle-aged Irish type, put a finger to her nose, handed over the keys and allowed she'd heard his love life at the saloon sounded complexified.

He didn't argue. Gossip was about the only cultural entertainment in a town that had no opera house, and it might have been worse. She might have considered how his hiring the best bird's-eye view of the pending field of battle precluded it to anyone else.

Having covered all the bets he could think of in advance of Midsummer's Eve in broad daylight, Longarm had to ask Last Chance Charlene to hold the thought until he got back, as he did some late-night pussyfooting over by the dormer rooms he'd rented near the stage terminal.

He found that, as he'd hoped, he could let himself in that side door from the dark alley and ease up the back stairs without disturbing any of the others rooming in the big frame pile. They'd told him over in the stage terminal, when he'd dropped by to gossip, that the way-taller rooming house had been built as the town house of a mining mogul, back in the boom of the sixties, and sold as a white elephant when his fancy young wife refused to dwell downwind of the stage terminal and municipal corrals.

Peering down from that dormer window like an owl bird with no lamplight to outline his head from behind, Longarm could make out everybody moving along Main Street through the circles lit up by the streetlights to either side. Some distant figures seemed to wink in and out of sight as they moved through the darker stretches between. But he figured at street level you could make out anyone outlined by the lighting behind them if they were within pistol range, and you hardly had to worry about anyone farther away, who'd doubtless have as much trouble drawing beads on *you*, so what the hell.

Taking nothing for granted in such an uncertain world,

Longarm came by late at night more than once. He was never challenged when he moved in sneaky, moving from a side door of the Western Union through the waiting room of the stage terminal and into the alley on the far side, offering dark shadows all the way to that side door and from there up the stairs to those empty rooms he'd hired.

Except for the third time he tried it.

It was going on ten, and Last Chance Charlene had said she'd start without him if he didn't get back by midnight. So he only meant to test the approaches to his owl's nest that time. But the plain and dumpy Irish gal who owned the place caught him on the back steps.

She gleeped, "Oh, me eyebrow, I was after taking out these table scraps to put in the can and how was I to know I'd meet a soul in me birthday suit?"

Longarm tipped his hat brim to the naked lady and assured her he could barely see anything in that light.

She laughed and replied, "Sure it's a good thing we're both drunk, then. Go on up the stairs while I get rid of this garbage and I'll say I didn't see you, either!"

He went up the stairs. He had to. Lest she wonder what he was really up to. The way you kept folk from figuring what you were up to was by not getting them to wonder what you were up to.

The rooms he'd hired were furnished, albeit there was no bedding on the bare mattress of either bed. He later realized she'd known that. Seeing they were her beds. He smoked a cheroot to give the house below him time to settle down. Then he rose, locked up, and eased down the stairs to get on back to Last Chance Charlene.

But he met the lady of this house on the stairs, heading up them in a kimono with bedding over one arm and a covered lunch pail in the other.

"And where might you be going at this hour after compromising a lady and getting her all hot and bothered?" she demanded.

He said it was still stuffy upstairs after such a late sunset as one got late in June.

She said, "Let's duck into me quarters then, and whist, before anyone sees us and draws the wrong conclusions!"

Longarm had to wonder what other conclusions anyone might draw as she hauled him into her own rooms off the stairs and shucked that kimono to welcome him indeed. Atop that bedding. Spread across the rug.

Such light as they had to work with came from the street through the lace curtains of a distant window. But Longarm figured it was just as well, seeing what she was built like, next to Last Chance Charlene.

But after that there was much to commend a change in pace that had in truth began to feel a tad like *work*. Longarm was prone to tell gals who asked that he was single because he'd attended too many funerals of men who wore badges, and this was partly true. But the few times he'd spent enough time with a really great gal to feel tempted, he'd noticed how, after you've been having steak for a while, you get to hankering for beans.

She said her name was Maureen and she'd been married once and found it confining. After that she was plain of face and more than pleasantly plump, with a thirsty wet ring-dang-doo that grabbed a man's old organ grinder like the greased-up fist of a mighty experienced milk maid and never let go, as she moved her generous hips with no need for a pillow under them.

So it was after midnight when he finally got back to the Last Chance and, finding the way prettier brunette asleep, slipped in beside her for a cuddle and damned if he didn't feel himself rising to the occasion.

But Last Chance Charlene muttered, "Leemealone!" in

her sleep, as gals are prone to once it gets to the chore stage, and he was able to catch a few winks and treat her right, after all, as they tore off a sunrise quickie.

So a good if somewhat complicated time was had by all as Midsummer's Eve bore down on them, with Empty Chambers sounding ever more like a homicidal maniac, or a man with a worried mind, as he let it be known he'd been praticing out back by placing a silver dollar on the back of his gun hand to draw, cock and fire before said silver dollar could hit the ground.

Longarm had no choice but to confide to some extent in old Maureen as he managed a game of musical beds that helped him pass the time as the whole town waited with bated breath for the coming showdown.

He was forced to trust her at least part way, just as he couldn't go pussyfooting from the Western Union, through the stage terminal and up those stairs without taking Western Union and the terminal manager into his confidence, telling them no more than they had to know unless he wanted to risk their idle gossip as to what he might or might not be up to.

Thus, old Maureen knew about "Buck" having to keep his boss lady satisfied and thought it made for some spice in their own slap and tickle when they had the chance for some. She seemed to be one of those natural conspirators who lusted more after the men of other women than poor hard-up johns who had no gals and really needed it.

Longarm felt no call to tell Last Chance Charlene where he was headed or what he might be up to after dark, of course. He made sure neither she nor any of the other gals who worked for her mentioned his prowling back alleyways after dark and after dark kept getting shorter as the calender kept heading for the longest day in the year on the twenty-first of June. As far north as Montana Territory, the sun set after Nine p.m. as the fateful date approached.

Longarm explained to Maureen, and the good-natured bawd agreed he had good reason to behave more discreetly the last few nights before it came time for the big showdown. So Last Chance Charlene had Longarm all to herself after a late supper on the nineteenth day of June.

Reclining in bed together as the sun went down outside to paint the window curtains and bedroom walls a soft orange, the sofly curvacious brunette sharing a cheroot with him commenced to cry as, somewhere outside, a church bell tolled.

He knew better. But he felt obliged to ask her what was eating her.

She said, "Tommorow is the twentieth. The sun will set the last time before it rises on the longest day of the year."

He said, "That's how come they call it Midsummer's Eve. Ain't sure whether Empty Chambers was talking about sundown or midnight, when the longest day officially commences. For all the proclamations he and Honest John have been issuing as the day they chose approaches, it ain't too clear just which they might have meant."

She shuddered against him and said, "The thought of you and Dusty facing them gives me goose bumps, either way! Just how do you expect things to go, darling?"

He shrugged his bare shoulder under her pretty head and honestly replied, "Up to Honest John, I reckon. Like I told the law and that nosy newspaper man, we never issued any ultimatum to anybody. I told 'em both that we didn't mean to fire the first shot. We only meant to fire the *last* shots. As many as it might take to end any fight they choose to start."

She demurred, "Buck, you can't allow them to choose the time and place and fire the first shots. There are only two of you. Chambers may show up with a gang and . . ."

"He's a professional killer," Longarm cut in, adding, "He knows he'll hang for certain if he wins that dirty. He never ganged up on Bohunk Wojensky. He made it look like a chance meet-up where Wojensky wasn't expecting it. They won't come barging in downstairs with a gang. Empty Chambers has gone to a heap of trouble to set up a charade aimed at scaring us into running or, failing that, offering some justification for our demise. Honest John ain't about to elbow you out of this property before his gun waddie manages one or the other."

The next morning over ham and eggs Crown Sergeant Foster expressed as much concern about Longarm's apparant lack of concern.

Foster said, "We can't let the other side take the initiative. That's a sure formula for defeat!"

Longarm said, "Go teach your granny to suck eggs, pard. You think I never learned that much in the war they gave in my honor when I was a kid? Finish your breakfast, and I'll show you where I want you posted before sundown. I was saving it for later but I can't abide a whining kid who can't wait for Santa Claus to fill his fool stocking!"

"You *do* have something planned?" asked Foster with a relieved look.

Longarm snorted, "Hell no, I was waiting for Santa Claus to get us out of this at the last moment. Started planning as soon as I understood what we were up against."

"And you never told me?" his fellow undercover lawman said, scowling.

Longarm smiled knowingly and said, "I've been busting a gut keeping Charlene in the dark, knowing how worried she's been. I had not call to put you through the same torture with Martha. Wasn't anything either of you could do about it before this very day, in any case. Finish your eggs and I'll show you."

So Longarm did and later that afternoon, well before sundown, Crown Sergeant Foster was up in that dormer window with a high-powered scope-sighted rifle, grinning like a mean little kid.

And so it came to pass that after supper, with the sun still high, "Buck Crawford" was enjoying an after-dessert smoke out front, leaning against a lamppost, when under-sheriff Ebsen caught up with him.

Ebsen pointed with his thumb to say, "I just come from Honest John's, across the way."

Longarm said, "I noticed. What message might Honest John or Empty Chambers have told you to pass on to me?"

The older lawman flushed and said, "That was uncalled for. I come to warn you. Empty Chambers ain't there. Honest John swears he don't know where the murderous young cuss might be. He could be most anywheres out yonder, fixing to do you like he done Bohunk Wojensky!"

Longarm moved away from the lamppost, adjusting his gun to ride for walking as he replied, "Do tell? Reckon I'd best go looking for him, then. I'd hate to think of a child his age feeling lost with darkness fixing to fall most any minute."

Ebsen reckoned in that case he'd have a drink at the bar inside. So as Longarm stepped out into the suddenly empty street with everything in sight painted orange and purple by the setting sun, it seemed he had it all to himself. But he sensed the eyes watching from all around as he took a deep breath and muttered, "Shit like this reads silly enough in one of them Ned Buntline novels!"

As he started walking up the center of the street in the gathering dusk he had to admit to himself it felt even sillier in real life.

Chapter 12

Watching from on high through a telescopic sight, Crown Sergeant Foster couldn't make sense of what he was seeing. He'd been tricked by Longarm in the past and worked with him more often on the same side. So he knew what his friend and rival was capable of and he'd yet to see Longarm commit suicide. From his higher vantage point, with the crimson sunset rays sweeping across the flat rooftops more brightly as deep purple filled the streets below, Foster knew he'd be able to pick off any rooftop snipers, as Longarm strode down Main Street with his back turned to the doors of both rival saloons. But Foster had no way of spotting anyone in any of the dark windows overlooking Main Street from either side, and as the late Bohunk Wokensky had discovered too late, Empty Chambers was capable of popping out any doorway down below.

Yet nothing happened as Longarm strode on the the far end of the modest business district, turned as a barely visible blur in the distance and headed back toward the center of town.

Closer to the same, an old lamp-lighter had begun to make his rounds, reaching up with his long, flaming pikestaff to open the glass lanterns with a bill hook and light the wicks inside with his flickering open flame, until from the doorway of the Last Chance Undersheriff Ebsen called, "Leave them streetlights be!"

But from the farside Longarm called ahead, "Go ahead and light 'em. A body can barely see his way down this way, now!"

The old lamp lighter tore up the street the other way. He was still too young to die as, barely visible in the darkness, Longarm began to sing in a taunting tone . . .

"Oh, I'm looking for your bully.
The bully of your town.
I'm looking for your bully,
But your bully can't be found!
So bring me out your bully,
And I'll lay him on the ground!
I'm looking for your bully,
But your bully can't be found!"

That having failed to evoke a response, Longarm drew and fired a round in the air shouting, "Come out, come out, wherever you are, you yellow-livered son of a bitch!"

"Oh my God," said Crown Sergeant Foster, sighing.

But nothing happened as Longarm kept coming far enough to call up to him, "You still up there, Dusty?"

Foster called down, "I am. You're still on your feet down there. So there can only be one answer. But how did you know you'd run him out of town?"

Longarm called back, "Magic. Come on down, and I'll tell you about it as we drink to the fleeing footsteps of the famous Empty Chambers!"

The loud exchange was meant for local ears cocked all around. When Foster joined him down in the street with the high-powered rifle, Longarm murmured, "Later. Back at the Last Chance. Let's strut our stuff on the way back."

As they did they were joined by others who wanted to belly up to the bar with the men who'd rid them of some mighty sinister shadows, now that they studied on it. Along the way Foster muttered, "You knew all the time he'd leave town when you called his bluff, didn't you?"

Longarm said, "Close enough," as somewhere in the crowd a husky voice growled, "You boys go on and celebrate at the Last Chance if you like. Me and Honest John have matters to discuss!"

Another townee shouted, "I'm going with you! I can't wait to see how brave the cocksucker is without his Empty Chambers!"

And so, as most of the crowd followed Longarm and Foster into the Last Chance, a considerable minority hived off to enter Honest John's and there came the dulcet sounds of busting glass amid loud, rude laughter and somebody yelling, "Powder River and let her buck!"

Undersheriff Ebsen tore out the bat wings of the Last Chance as Longarm and Foster were fixing to enter. They sent him on his way with their blessings and led the procession to the bar, where the barmaids in low-cut bodices were already setting 'em up, on the house.

Last Chance Charlene had more duds on than usual, but still showed a heap of cleavage as she ran to meet her "Buck" with open arms and a radiant smile.

"You did it, you did it, you did it, and I'm so proud of

you!" she trilled as she crashed into him full tilt and threw bare arms around him to kiss him good whilst all the crowd whooped with glee.

So it was some time before Foster could ask him in confidence how in blue blazes he'd known a hired killer with a rep would run from a fight like a kicked cur dog without risking a parting shot.

Once it was safe to tell his fellow lawman, out in the yard on their way to the outhouse, Longarm drew the Mountie to one side in the dark and confided, "Empty Chambers didn't run away from a fight. He was the real deal. He was wanted, federal, for killing other federal deputies in other parts. It took me the better part of an hour. But I remembered who he was not long after he first stuck out his chest at me. The first night we were here."

"My God, why didn't you say so?" asked the Mountie.

Longarm said, "He wasn't wanted up Canada way. I couldn't arrest him without giving our show away. So I wired my home office about him. Took a brace of my fellow deputies called Smiley and Dutch until the seventeenth to get here. I hid them in that same room you just come down from with the help of local pals I've made more recent, until it was time for our move."

"*Our* move? I didn't know a damned thing about it!" protested Foster.

Longarm replied with no shame, "I told you why I felt you had no call to be burdened with secrets, earlier. I'm telling you the whole story, now, ain't I?"

Foster said, "Go on, I'm all ears. What was this move I was kept in the dark about?"

Longarm explained, "Last night in the wee small hours, Smiley grabbed Empty Chambers on his way back from the shithouse behind Honest John's. Might have been messy had they grabbed him headed the other way. Once they had him they frog-marched him to the ponies they had waiting in a nearby alley and by this time they'll have him well on his way to our federal house of detention in Denver."

Foster laughed, "Looking for the bully of the town, my sweet Aunty Fanny Addams! You never ran him out of town! He left town in handcuffs to stand trial in Denver."

Longarm said, "Not hardly. Judge Isaak Parker down to Fort Smith has first dibs on him. If Arkansas don't hang him, Texas surely will. So what say we take that leak and go back and join the party?"

They did and the party at the Last Chance lasted until everybody ran out front to watch the volunteer fire department as they tried in vain to keep Honest John's from burning down all the way.

Later, nobody could ever rightly say whatever might have happened to Honest John Jenkins. Some held he'd never gotten out alive. Others said they'd heard he was swamping a saloon in Cheyenne. He was never seen in the Montana gold fields again.

By the time anyone in Clarkside heard anything about swamping any saloons in other parts, of course, Buck Crawford and Dusty Rhodes were long gone, if not forgotten.

It was good old Maureen, not Last Chance Charlene, who put them back on the track to Natova, letting something about it slip to Longarm as he thanked her properly for sheltering his pals from Denver those few nights they'd had to hole up after they arrived from Denver.

Running a rooming house next door to a stage terminal exposed a gal to a more transient clientele than the gals around the Last Chance got to jaw with. Rambling men on their way from one neck of the woods to another were more likely to talk about what might lie over the far horizon, and so Maureen had heard more than one mention of a robber's roost up north in the glacier country. When pressed she allowed she'd heard the place called Medicine Valley and if Natova was Blackfoot for medicine, so be it. She'd heard it was run by a cuss called Saint Lou.

None of this meant as much to Longarm as her hazy recollection of some sinister young men with no visible means of support who'd been staying with her whilst they waited for some jasper they called Doc to ride over from Sliderock and show them the way to Medicine Valley. He didn't press her when she suddenly seemed unable to recall their names. She was a good old gal with her big old tits pressed to his bare chest, and he'd asked her not to gossip about Smiley and Dutch whilst they'd holed up with her.

He said he followed her drift when she said a lot of her business was dependant on her rep as a landlady who minded her own beeswax and never pestered her guests about where they'd really come from, where they were really headed or what their real names might have been.

Last Chance Charlene, in turn, was a woman of her word and a good sport about their leaving, with fresh ponies, new saddle guns and five hundred apiece in cash, leaving them well heeled indeed should anyone out ahead require proof about that payroll robbery.

Following Longarm's lead, the Canadian had already incorporated a sneaky money belt into his gun rig, seeing a gun belt was riding heavy on a man's hips, in contrast to a give-away load of twenty-dollar double eagles under his shirt.

They rode out of Clarkside the last week in June, and it was just as well they did. For Longarm's grandstand play, misunderstood as he'd hoped it might be, had already become another legend of the era and western newspapers in other parts had picked it up and added to its luster with details that might not even work when you studied on them.

But over in Helena, as His Copper Majesty Vance Larson was reading the papers over breakfast, descriptions of the hard cased Buck Crawford, who'd scared the notorious Empty Chambers out of some town, rang some bells. So he set his breakfast tray aside, sat up in bed, and rang for his bodyguard and *segundo*, Keystone Callaway.

Keystone had come by his handle in the Penn State coal mine country, fighting the Molly Maguires as a company dick. He'd gotten better at killing pests since coming west. He was going on forty, with the eyes of a man who'd lived longer. They were the eyes of a man who'd seen the valley and seen the hill and looked over the edge into the darkness beyond. He was dressed for town or country in a black undertaker's suit over riding boots and a brace of shoulder-holstered Detective Specials in caliber .38, with the bullets crosscut to dum dum and strychnine rubbed into the crosscuts. When the boss sent Keystone after somebody, Keystone did not mess around.

When Larson handed his *segundo* the paper, Keystone scanned the short article, handed it back with a puzzled smile and asked, "I'm not sure I follow you, sir. It's true Clay McCord lost the trail of that Omaha meatpacker along the way to Clarkside. But didn't you say his name was Weddington and he was dressed like a Fancy Dan? According to this wild west account of another unlikely walkdown, the hero's name is given as Buck Crawford, he's described as a denim-clad diamond-in-the-rough and the game was an invitation to a gunfight, not poker. So I fail to see any connection."

His copper majesty swung his bare feet to the rug as he smuggly replied, "That's no doubt why I'm so rich and you get to work for me. I'm so smart I sometimes scare myself."

Tossing the paper aside Kruger counted on his fingers,

"One: There never was no meatpacker named Weddington. Don't you think I've checked? Two: The rose by any other name was dressed for that occasion at that hotel. So fuck how he was dressed for a gunfight in a rough little mining town. Three: Our rose by any name is a trickster who pulls rabbits out of hats. I was watching for him to cheat. I know how to cheat, and I still don't know where the fuck he drew that royal flush from. How the fuck do you suppose an unknown stranger, dressed like a saddle tramp, might have scared a known killer and established bully of the town out of town, without doing shit to anyone in town?"

Keystone shrugged and said, "Maybe this Chambers cuss was yellow."

His boss snapped, "Maybe if the dog hadn't stopped to shit it would have caught the rabbit. Jesus H. Christ, Keystone, can't you add up a fucking row of dominos? Clay McCord trails the tall, dark drink of water with a heavy mustache most of the way to Clarkside and the bastard suddenly vanishes into thin air, mayhaps that same thin air he draws winning hands out of. McCord backtracks all the way home without cutting the rascal's sign. Mainly because he never came back here. You and your boys looked everywhere, right?"

The hired gun nodded stiffly and said, "If he ever came back to Helena he's sure been hiding under the rug."

His copper majesty nodded and said, "I believe you. That's how come I pay you. So number Four: If he never came back here as Weddington he went on to Clarkside and changed his name with his duds just about the time a hitherto unknown gunslinger called Buck Crawford rode in out of nowheres. Paper describes Crawford as tall, dark and sporting a heavy mustache. After that it turns out he's a magician. This time the table stakes are in control of the saloon trade along Main Street and the game is played with guns instead of cards. This time our rose by any other name is playing against an expert gun fighter instead of me and the professional gambler I hired to deal and help me watch for cheating. I'm still working on how he slickered me with that royal flush. Paper don't say where this Empty Chambers went when Buck Crawford called his bluff. Wouldn't you and your boys have heard if a famous gun-fighter had suddenly shown up here in Helena?"

Keystone said, "Not if he whipped through fast with his tail betwixt his legs. But now that I study on it, it does seem spooky a man with a rep and a brace of Schofields would just vanish into thin air."

His copper majesty nodded grimly and said, "Now you're commencing to see the light."

"How do you suppose this mysterious Buck Crawford did it?" Keystone asked.

Kruger said, "I've no idea. I only know things vanish or appear as if by magic when the son of a bitch who made me look so foolish is around. So take some of your boys over to Clarkside and make the sneaky son of a bitch vanish, *your* way. Won't matter how he made a fool of me if he never gets to make a fool of anyone again."

Keystone nodded soberly and said, "Consider him dead if we find him there, boss. But what if he's not there?"

His copper majesty said, "Find out where he went, track him down and finish him off wherever you may find him. Jesus H. Christ, Keystone, do I have to tell you how to do your job? I swear, sometimes I feel I'm surrounded by boobs and idiots! It's a wonder I don't have to go down in my mines and jack my own lodes!"

He rose to his bare feet to pace his bedroom rug as he grumbled on, "Like I told that mine foreman I fired last month, if I wanted to chase my own ore through the mountain I'd never hire anybody else to do it. Do I have to strap on my own guns and track that rose by any other name down my fucking self?"

Keystone shook his head and stiffly replied, "I said he was good as dead as soon as I catch up with him, and I'm on my way. Just one last question, boss?"

His copper majesty nodded and said, "Make it a short one."

Keystone did. He said, "I wasn't there when you played cards with this Armstrong D. Weddington. So how can I be dead certain we've caught up with the same cuss when we catch up with this Buck Crawford?"

His copper majesty said, "Don't bother a busy man of destiny with such petty details. If I'm wrong, I'm wrong. Pluck our rose by any other name, whoever he is, and let the devil sort it out!"

Chapter 13

The trail town of Sliderock was on the Clark, north of the Sliderock Mountain it drew its name from. There was no mine handy. The place had "just growed" like Topsy in *Uncle Tom's Cabin* after somebody built a sawmill powered by the Clark, logged off the surrounding trees to end up with a mess of well-watered grass, and everything else had mushroomed around the handy overnight stop along the riverside trail.

By the time Longarm and Foster rode in, the papers had commenced to compare Longarm's showdown with Empty Chambers to the famous confrontation betwixt John Wesley Hardin and Wild Bill Hickock, which had never happened, either.

His sudden noteriety as a famous gunslick on the side of law and order hardly squared with an outlaw on the run in need of a hidey-hole. So he and his Canadian sidekick had metamorphized into Shorty Sawyer and his pard, Mohawk Brown. Moe for short.

They found that as old Maureen had advised Longarm back in Clarkside, the erstwhile sawmill, with nothing much left to saw, had been converted to a trailside flophouse, with the cavernous interior honey-combed with small but private sleeping cribs, each coming with an army cot, bedding extra if you didn't have your own. So they hired a pair side by side to use for their own bedrolls and store their saddles and new Winchesters, boarding their new ponies at the municipal corral across the Clark. Not that much of a river that far upstream.

As they got set up they saw each of their compartments had lockable doors but, being neither eight-by-four-foot space had windows in its walls of vertical knotty-pine siding, the walls only rose eight feet to share such air and light as the higher, open loft might let in. If a guest stood on his bunk he could peer over the wall into the hired quarters of his neighbor. If he felt more daring he could swing a leg up and roll himself over to join him for some private vice or rob him if he wasn't there. So there were signs posted to the effect that any heads showing above the walls meant for privacy were subject to being blown off by the night watchman as he made his rounds.

They decided, seeing their hidden wealth would be tagging along with their gunbelts, their other gear was likely safe behind padlocks as anywhere else they could leave it in Sliderock. So they left it and locked up to take in the sights as, off to the west, the sun was already setting behind the Bitterroots.

That still left the sky above blue with only the town and its neck of the woods east of the range bathed in its shadow. The lay of the sky made for tricky lighting toward evening in Sliderock and they hadn't gotten around to streetlights yet. So there were lamps already lit in some windows, whilst interiors seemed murky blurs in others.

The town wasn't big enough to rate anything you'd call a main street. The cluster of trailside amenities had just grown so that they faced one another at angles odd or even. The folk who felt they belonged there knew their way through the uncertain spaces. Folk from other parts were on their own.

They'd asked at the flophouse and been told the Columbine Saloon offered warm meals as well as liquor and games of chance. When they found it none of its lamps had been lit yet. But it wasn't as black inside as it looked from outside the swinging doors. As their eyes adjusted they could see the big framed print over the back bar was that version of Custer's Last Stand with the Indians toting Zulu shields.

The barkeep was male, bald and fat, but amiable enough when they said they could go for some supper. He told them to have a seat at one of the tables, and he'd have somebody see to their needs. A card game was in progress at one table. None of the other five seemed occupied, so they took one in the other corner and the barkeep shouted, "Hey, Celestial? Get your Oriental ass out here and see to the needs of these gents!" Celestial, as in Celestial Empire, turned out to look like a middle-aged son of Han wearing blue pajamas and a pigtail down his back with the front of his head shaved back far as an imaginary line across the top of his skull from ear to ear. He didn't offer a menu. His English was surprisingly tolerable as he told them in a surly tone they had their choice betwixt fried hash or boiled stew. When Longarm asked if they might manage any lo mein, the Chinee brightened and allowed he'd see.

As he left, Foster asked what Longarm had ordered.

Longarm said, "Lo mein means pork with noodles. If the cook's as far from home as our waiter he'll have some on hand for the kitchen staff. Lo mein is an oriental secret code for grub. They call it chow. Show me a Chinee kitchen with no lo mein and I'll show you a whorehouse with no beds in it. They know how to cook our grub but left to their druthers they don't *eat* much of it."

The waiter came back, smiling uncertainly, to say the cook wanted to make sure they hadn't ordered chop suey.

Longarm said, "I don't much care for chop suey. Do you?"

The waiter laughed like hell and scampered back to the kitchen.

Foster asked where Longarm had learned so much oriental cunning.

Longarm said, "Holed up with refugees during those Chinese Riots we had a few summers back. Being a sworn peace officer, I could hardly let disturbers of the peace hang Chinee from lamp posts by their pigtails, could I?"

The Mountie in mufti said, "We heard about those race riots up our way. What were they all about?"

Longarm wrinkled his nose and said, "Human nature. The gut instinct to hate what we don't understand. This Frisco labor organizer, name of Kearney, having fled parts of this country where the signs assured him no Irish need apply, took it in his head to save us all from a Yellow Peril presented by Chinese labor out this way. There was Chinese labor out this way because there was more work to be done than men of any breed willing and able to do it. The Western Pacific Railroad brought most of the Chinese help from Canton. Couldn't have managed that Wedding of the Rail in Utah without 'em. Most of the Union Pacific crew that met 'em at Promintory Point were Irish. They were hard workers, too, in spite of what some say."

Their waiter came back with seperate plates and cutlery and one heaping bowl of lo mein, asking if they wanted tea or cofee with the same.

Longarm allowed they'd have coffee, adding with a smile he wasn't feeling quite *that* Oriental.

As the waiter left, Longarm served, saying, "Everybody knows the Irish are slovenly loud-mouthed drunks whilst Chinee smoke opium and hold white gals prisoners in them tunnels under Chinatown. But, like I said, being a peace officer sworn to uphold law and order, I was forced to defend some of the treacherous slant-eyed rascals."

The Canadian tried an experimental forkful and declared, "By God, this stuff tastes even better than it smells! But are you saying there's nothing to those tales of Chinese tongs and hatchet men?"

Longarm shook his head and said, "In spite of their odd looks, the sons of Han, as they call themselves, are just as human as the rest of us and just as inclined to grow up good, bad or in-between. Of course they've got outlaw gangs. Some as ornery as the Irish Fenians or the James and Younger boys. But as I was trying to uphold law and order around the Denver rail yards I noticed the mobs were more inclined to pick on the laundry men than any hatchet men."

He twirled some pork-flavored noodles into a handy bite with his fork, the way those Eye-talian folk had taught him, as he observed, morosely, "It seems ever thus. I understand that when them Russian Cossacks ride to save their country from the Jews they avoid some necks of the woods where Jewish bandits roam and tear through the more religous settlements where nobody packs a gun. I can't recall one so-called hatchet man getting lynched out our way yet."

The Canadian changed the subject to how they were supposed to go about meeting that mysterious "Doc" old Maureen had heard tell of.

Longarm didn't answer as the waiter came back with their coffee to ask if they liked the lo mein. He went back to the kitchen giggling when Longarm allowed it was good as they made it in Frisco.

By this time the aroma had spread some. A local teamster who'd been playing cards at that distant table rose to follow his nose like a bloodhound until he saw where the smell was coming from and paused to scowl down at them, declaring, "What's that you gents are eating? It looks like straw mixed with shit and smells like roast pork, only better by half."

Longarm smiled up at the rude cuss to say, "They call her lo mein. They make it with chunks of pork fried in this bodacious pan with soft noodles already boiled separate and some secret spices they refuse to discuss with us long-nosed devils. You want to taste some?"

The teamster edged foreward, uncertainly, observing, "I don't know. I've heard of alley cats going into a Chinee kitchen and never coming out."

Longarm twirled some lo mein into a spoon he hadn't had in anything, since he took his coffee black, and held it out to the surly stranger, insisting, "I understand they brag on it when they serve dog meat. You got to be rich to eat dog meat in China. They don't serve just any old dog, like Indians tend to. They raise a special breed of eating dog they call a chow dog, meaning a food dog. Chow being their word for grub. I promise you there's nothing but pork and noodles here."

The teamster tasted. He grinned like a child who'd just discovered chocolate and said, "Damn my eyes if this ain't something! What did you say it was and can I have some more, Mister, ah . . . ?"

Longarm said, "Call me Shorty. Shorty Sawyer. You call this dish lo mein and if you want some more I'll bet I can order you some."

So the teamster introduced himself as one Overland

Orville and asked if his pal, Shorty, could fix him up with some.

The waiter allowed he'd try, warning the cook hadn't been expecting to serve the general public the real thing. Overland Orville allowed he'd be a sport and wait some if he had to. The exchange had not gone unnoticed at the card table across the way. By the time Longarm and Foster were enjoying their desserts of regular apple pie with rat-trap cheese, the kitchen had served five more heaping bowls of lo mein and "Shorty and Mohawk, Moe for short," were in with the regulars as the after-supper crowd showed up.

Those who wanted to try some of them Chinese noodles were out of luck.

Chinese noodles, like Italian pizzas, were whipped up fresh for each occasion and fashioned mostly in midair by slight of hand. So the one skilled noodle-puller in Granite County was already hard at work on another batch of noodle dough. It would have to set some before he could pull it like taffy in a manner impossible for most to follow.

Not that the delighted sons of Han were upset with Longarm, whoever he was. His unexpectedly understanding nature, and the effect it seemed to have on the other long-nosed devils, was a refreshing change from the way some of their kind were treated in the gold fields. Leadville, Colorado, was only one major mining town where their countrymen were barred by statute law from setting foot in town.

Peeking out through the barely cracked kitchen door, one of the older hands of the kitchen crew declared, "I don't know. He fits the description, but the one of whom they speak, the one under the protection of the Ong Leong Tong for favors to our people is said to be an officer of their law. The one who joked with Chang is dressed like one of their cowboys."

The waiter said, "I don't care for their cowboys. One dragged me in the dust with his rope when I was new in this country."

They decided to leave well enough alone and say nothing to anyone about the oddly friendly long-nosed devil.

As the saloon filled up with regulars and tobacco smoke, Longarm and Foster hung on to their table, sharing a scuttle of beer with Overland Orville and two more permanent residents of Sliderock, a blacksmith and a younger cuss who clerked in the general store by day.

They were naturally curious as to where Shorty and Moe might have come from and where they might be bound for. When neither volunteered for more than one round, the store clerk asked.

Longarm said he wasn't certain. Foster allowed he'd clean forgot. As if to soothe hurt feelings Longarm, as Shorty, said, "We were expecting to meet up with a pal here. He knows the way north to this . . . job we heard about. Ain't seen him 'round town this evening. But what the hell, we just got here."

The blacksmith said he knew most everyone around Sliderock, seeing everyone as rode had to bring their mounts in every six weeks or less. When he asked if this pal they were looking for had a name, Longarm easily answered, "Henry. Henry Burquette. We call him Hank. He says he's French Canadian but he talk natural as everyone else."

None of the locals had ever heard of Henry Burquette. Longarm was not surprised. He'd just made the jasper up out of whole cloth. He had it on the good authority of a landlady catering to a transient trade that more than one rambling man had mentioned a gent in Sliderock called Doc, who could set you on the trail to safer surroundings up in the glacier country astraddle the border.

But it stood to reason anyone acting as a guide along the Owlhoot Trail would be shy around strangers and having established they were strangers who were shy about the recent past. Longarm had cast his bait well out from the bank to let it drift a spell and see if he might get a nibble.

He was still waiting as the evening wore on, with locals joining the conversation or drifting home to the little woman as everyone lost track of who'd introduced who to whom. Having been accepted as newcomers who'd been accepted, and having shown they were sports when it came their turn to spring for a round, the undercover lawmen stuck to their story about a French Canadian pal who knew the northern Rockies better than they did. Warming to his own mythology, Longarm let it be known old Hank was an old-timer who'd scouted all over the surrounding mountains for beaver before the first color was struck in Montana Territory.

But nobody seemed to know the old-timer, and as the smoke commenced to thin and the place began to clear out it seemed there might be no fish at all where he'd cast his bait.

Then, with no more than eight or ten men left in the place, counting the barkeep and the two undercover lawmen, they were joined by a rat-faced runt dressed like a cowhand in mourning, with a fresh scuttle of beer in his hand as he said, "Howdy. Name's Tyler, but they call me Doc. You mind if I join you?"

Chapter 14

Longarm never asked what Tyler might hold a doctorate in. Doc was one of those names such as Curly, Slim or Shorty that attached themselves to riders whether they deserved them or not. It was widely held the deadly Doc Holliday was a dentist gone bad. The Doc Scurlock who'd ridden for the Tunstall-McSween faction in that Lincoln County War had likely been guilty of no more than a good education and a tendency to read books in the bunkhouse. Longarm waved Doc Tyler to the empty seat across the table but said, "Ain't sure we got time to finish all them suds with you, Doc. Me and Moe, here, have set here swilling all evening and we were just now talking about packing it in for the night."

Doc Tyler nodded knowingly and commenced to top their schooners for them as he said, "I know. Someone made mention of some mountain man you gents were expecting to meet here?"

Longarm said, "Henry Burquette. They call him Hank.

He'll likely show up soon enough. We might have got here early. He said around the end of June and there's nigh a week of June left."

Doc Tyler said, "Can't say I've heard tell of a mountain man by that handle and I suspect I know all the mountain men left in these here hills. I come out here young and rid some trails since. Understand this old-timer was supposed to guide you gents somewheres?"

Longarm sounded deliberately cautious as he answered, "I disremember where they said Hank meant to ride with us? Do you know, Moe?"

Foster looked away and murmured, "I'm not certain. I'm waiting for him to tell us, once he gets here."

Doc Tyler soothed, "Far be it from me to pry! Where you gents come from and where you're bound ain't no never-mind to this child. I was only going to suggest, if you all are in a hurry and this other guide don't show . . . Well, I run me a horse spread just outside of town and I guide prospectors, pack supplies in or out of lonesome places or . . . show the way to some as ain't on no maps."

Longarm sipped some suds and tried not to sound interested as he replied, "Do tell? You must find your work interesting."

It wasn't easy, but he managed not to ask about hidden valleys or rumors of robber's roosts and faked a yawn, adding, "Bless my stars and garters if I ain't feeling a long day in the saddle and more beer than I usually put away when there's no women watching."

He turned to Foster to say, "I'm headed back to the sawmill to catch up on my beauty rest. You coming, Moe?"

Foster dryly replied, "Walk you as far as our separate quarters. Not drunk enough to be your beauty."

All three of them laughed as the two undercover lawmen rose. Tyler got to his own feet, saying, "I'll be at your service if that other guide don't show and you gents get to feeling anxious."

Longarm turned to scowl down at him, demanding, "Who said we had any call to feel anxious? You saying we look like riders on the dodge, to you?"

Tyler quicky replied, "Heaven forefend! I never meant to intimate nothing of the kind. I only met anxious to . . . get where you're going."

Longarm growled, "That's better. Anyone can see you're a good old boy, Doc. But accusing this child reckless can get a cuss in trouble."

Foster, as Mohawk Brown, soberly added, "Been known to take as much as fifty years off a man's life."

"You talk too much, Moe," growled Longarm as he headed the Mountie in mufti toward the door. Neither laughed until they got outside.

Doc Tyler hadn't followed them. He feared he'd overplayed his hand.

Heading back to the sawmill along the creekside path, Foster asked, "Do you think we sold him our charade?"

Longarm muttered, "I suspect he sold it to himself. He might have taken longer to decided we had to be those payroll robbers on the run if we hadn't chummed good old Hank Burquette where we cast the hook. An outlaw guide with no competition could afford to be more cautions. But like a whore with a sister in sin winking at a possible customer, Doc's likely more worried about our paying somebody else."

Foster had of course been thinking all the while and being a lawman in his own right he declared, "He has to be thinking we've still got most of our loot, and he's planning to charge us more than that bounty you had your office put out on us."

Longarm nodded and said, "That's how come there's

only five hundred posted on the pair of us. Upon conviction. Not dead on slabs. The man who first said there was honor amongst thieves never knew many thieves."

Foster smiled knowingly and replied, "Tell me about it. But Tyler knows, or thinks he knows we have more than five hundred to pay for his services and taking the two of us alive would surely strike any crook as a chore not worth the modest reward."

Longarm answered, "I just said that. Let's watch what we say from here on into the sawmill. Anything we talk about inside can be heard the length and breadth of the dump."

Foster said he knew the form and they went on without saying anything a pair of tired riders soggy with beer might not have said as they let themselves into their respective cubicles and called it a night.

Knowing anything they said in there would be overheard, neither said a word until they were outside the next morning, heading across to the municipal corral to check on their ponies.

Making sure they were out of earshot from anyone else, Foster told Longarm, "Somebody tossed my cubicle last night while we were over at the saloon."

Longarm said, "Mine, too. Missing anything?"

Foster said, "No. I might not have noticed if they'd put everything back exactly as they found it. But my bedding was rumpled and somebody had been at my saddle bags. Nothing was missing from them, but in the tricky light they failed to buckle up the same holes."

Longarm said, "Somebody had a look at my new saddle gun and put her back in its boot a tad farther. A common sneak thief would have held on to a new Winchester and they never took the Maryland rye I carry for snake bites. Must have been looking for something else, such as clues."

"Or the money we rode off with after that payroll robbery," his fellow experienced lawman decided.

Longarm said, "Meaning now Doc Tyler knows we got it on us if we're the birds he thinks we are."

Foster replied, "He thinks we are. He wouldn't have moved in so fast and eager had he taken us for less prosperous strangers. So what's our next move?"

Longarm kept walking as he replied, "We go on over to see how our stock has fared. Those two handsome standardbreds Last Chance Charlene bestowed on us have carried us well, but carried us some distance since we rode off on 'em. You heard me tell them hostlers to rub 'em down good and make sure they were watered well before they were fed. But if I had a dollar for every half-wit tending to riding stock I'd be dwelling in marble halls with Miss Ellen Terry and brushing my teeth with vintage champagne."

Foster said, "Amen. But assuming we still have mounts to ride, when do you expect Doc Tyler to make his next move?"

Longarm shrugged and said, "Can't say. It's up to him. Have you ever lost a fish by reeling in before the hook was set? We want him to think he's reeling *us* in, see?"

Foster did. They went on to find their two big bays with almost matching white blazes friskier than they'd seemed when they'd last seen them. Last Chance Charlene had bought them off the army remount service with a view to having them haul her carriage as a matched pair. They hadn't broken to harness worth shit, seeing they'd been broken in as cavalry mounts. Longarm had selected them from her *remuda* because in spite of being long-limbed standardbreds that could cover ground they were almost as nondescript as those corovan mules. The remount service sold off riding stock when it was seven years old with plenty of mileage left in it. So big bay saddle horses were common as cats in mining country, where the cutting and roping skills of the cow pony were not required.

Having seen their stock was ready and willing to go, they mosied on to see about a late breakfast at the saloon. They found it empty at that hour, save for the barkeep and another Chinese swamper spreading fresh sawdust on the floor he'd just swept. The barkeep allowed they could order some grub if they bought another scuttle of beer. So they did.

The same waiter came out to take their order. He said they didn't have any lo mein ready in the kitchen. Longarm asked if they could have *egg foo yung* and the waiter ran back into the kitchen, giggling.

Foster asked dubiously what egg foo yung might be.

Longarm said, "Just eggs, whupped up Cantonese style. They don't know how to just plain scramble eggs. Don't worry. Ain't no puppy dog tails or snakes in egg foo yung. If the truth be known, some of their habits are tidier than some of ours. I told you I got to know some pretty good during the Chinese Riots."

The waiter came back out to say the cook wanted to talk to them out in the kitchen. The two undercover lawmen exchanged looks. Longarm shrugged and said, "Likely aims to apologize for not having fresh eggs. Some of them are more polite than some of us, too."

They rose from their corner table and followed the waiter out to the kitchen, where an older gent of around sixty presided over a two-man kitchen staff as well matched as those two army bays they'd just left. Foster wrinkled his nose at the unfamiliar smells of a Chinese kitchen. Longarm was more surprised to see so many sons of Han at work back there, even if the helpers were a set.

But the sons of Han were a lot like Mexicans when it came to taking on out-of-work kith and kin. Good red-blooded Americans could hand a busted pal a silver dollar and send him on his way, figuring it was all one could do for a poor cuss down on his luck. Ignorant Greasers and Ching-Chong Chinamen tended to hire kith and kin on as dead wood paid *something* for whatever chores one could figure out for them.

When Longarm favored the old cook with a puzzled smile, the Oriental chose his limited English with care and said, "Suppose Mistah Tyler ask you go bye-bye with he, you no go."

Longarm was too polite to observe that the walls seemed to have ears in those parts. He asked, "Are you saying Doc Tyler is up to no good?"

The cook shrugged and said, "Fong no sayee what he do with men go bye-bye with he. Fong only sayee some he takee on pack train tip no come back."

Longarm exchanged looks with Foster, turned back to the cook and said, "Let me see if I get this straight, Mister Fong. You're saying Doc Tyler leads some parties off in the hills and brings them back, while others are never seen again?"

The cook nodded and said, "That what Fong say. Suppose you belong along Sliderock and hire he for pack train, you allee time come back. Suppose you from someplace else and ask to hire he. Sometimes. *Most* times, you no come back."

Longarm glanced at Foster. The Canadian said, "Makes sense to me."

So they thanked the cook for his well-meant warning and asked if they might have their breakfast. Fong said something in Cantonese to their waiter, who led them back to the scuttle of beer on their table, and when their order arrived Foster decided egg foo yung was tolerable, too.

Having eaten, and not wanting to finish all that beer,

they were about to leave when Doc Tyler slithered in. So they all sat down together.

Doc said, "I heard you gents were here. I missed you at the sawmill. I was wondering if that pal you've been waiting on here in Sliderock ever showed up."

Longarm dryly remarked, "You'd doubtless know if he had, Doc. But as we were just now saying, it ain't the end of June, yet."

Tyler said, "Yes it is. Almost, anyways. Reason I came by just now is 'cause I won't be here, come this time tomorrow, if you should change your plans."

Longarm said, "Oh? Where might you be headed, Doc?"

The local horse-trader and pack-train operator glanced about as if to make certain nobody was listening in before confiding, "Place they call Natova. Up near the border. Only not on the map. Ever hear of her?"

Longarm exchanged looks with Foster. The Canadian shrugged and said, "Might as well, seeing he knows, and Hank may not show up at all."

Longarm nodded and said, "Matter of fact, that was close to where we were headed. Are you saying you know the way to Natova, Doc?"

Tyler said, "A fellow traveler with . . . similar needs, is waiting out to my place as we speek. I've already agreed to carry him on up to that hidden valley where the birds sing sweet and there ain't no law. He's agreed to pay a thousand dollars."

"That's pretty steep, Doc," said Longarm, paying out a little more line.

Tyler shrugged and said, "So are some of the passes we'll be crossing and it's a ten day trip. Figuring a hundred dollars a day on the trail, I would say I'm offering a bargain."

"On what terms?" asked Longarm.

"Half now and half when I get you there?" asked Tyler.

Longarm glanced at Foster. The Canadian shrugged and said, "Sounds fair. If he was the law he'd have turned us in by now."

So they shook on it and Longarm said they'd pay the first installment when they were saddled up and ready to move out.

Doc Tyler said to meet him on the trail just north of town with their mounts and not to tell a soul in town they were leaving. Then he got up and sort of faded away. Things got slow around Sliderock after the Ice ages came and went. Rome fell and it seemed to take even longer before the evening sun went down.

Longarm and Foster met Doc Tyler a mile outside of town. Doc was alone on his darker horse. He asked if they'd brought the money.

Longarm said, "Of course. You think we'd leave it back yonder in that sawmill? Where are your packhorses and the rest of the party?"

Tyler said, "Off in the aspen a piece, of course. Show me the money and I'll show you the way."

So Longarm handed over the bag of gold coins he'd prepared, and, as if to show good faith, Tyler pocketed it without counting and told them with a smile to follow him.

So they did, up the slopes of Mount Sliderock, through ever thicker aspen groves, and it was almost dark when they busted through some thick second growth into a clearing, where two more ponies and two more riders waited. In the tricky light, Longarm could still see they'd dismounted and held shotguns cradled in their arms as they grinned up in greeting.

Longarm asked, "Where are the pack ponies, Doc?"

Tyler said, "They'll be along directly. We're supposed

to wait here for 'em. Let's get down and stretch our legs whilst we rest our brutes."

That made sense. So Longarm and Foster dismounted. It wasn't until they drew closer to the others that they could make out that big hole in the ground.

Longarm pointed at it with his chin and asked why they'd dug it. Doc said, "We dug it for you poor simps. Throw up your fucking hands and let us worry about your guns and the rest of that payroll money!"

Chapter 15

They both reached for the darkening sky. When a man's covered by two double-barreled shotguns and a six-shooter, he doesn't have much choice.

As Doc circled around behind them Longarm observed, "This is sort of raw, Doc."

Tyler chortled, "Ain't it ever? The boys covering you for me are my brothers, Caleb and Jethro. We like to keep the business in the family. Hold still. Hold very still whilst I relieve you of them sidearms."

The sneaky bastard knew what he was doing. There was nothing either lawman could do as Doc reached around to their fronts from behind, with a gun muzzle pressed between each one's shoulder blades in turn.

If he noticed the extra weight he never mentioned it as he unbuckled their gun rigs and tossed them aside in the grass. As he did so Foster grumbled, "God damn it, we were *warned*! But did we listen?"

Hoping to head his slip off at the pass, Longarm cut on,

"Aw, stuff a sock in it, Moe! That gal back in Clarkside only warned us to be cautious. She never said this skunk would double-cross us *pure*!"

"Who are you calling a skunk, Jailbird?" snapped Doc Tyler as he proceeded to pat them down with his free hand.

Longarm said, "If the shoe fits, wear it. Do you even know the way to that hidden valley up north?"

Tyler cheerfully replied, "Never heard of it 'til some lost loon said he'd give us five hundred dollars to show him the way to Natova. Like I said, we raise horses and run pack trains down this way. Never been north of Fort Missoula, but seeing birds like you keep asking, and money being tough to come by, events just followed one another natural as the night follows the day. Where's your fucking money belt?"

"Ain't wearing one," Longarm answered easily, seeing it was the pure truth. He was hoping Doc wouldn't find the double derringer he carried in a hip pocket when he wasn't wearing his vest. But Doc wasn't distracted when Longarm asked, "How many pilgrims have you boys pulled this on, Doc?"

Doc said, "You'll make it the seventh and eighth and what have we here, a pretty little ace in the hole?"

"What was it, Doc?" called the one named Jethro.

Doc laughed dirty and said, "Double derringer, with a nice pocket watch attached."

Then he poked Longarm in a floating rib with the muzzle of his bigger six-gun to demand, "Where's the rest of the money, Shorty?"

Longarm said, "Not on me," and that was the truth when you studied on those gunbelts yonder in the grass as it kept getting darker.

Doc was patting Foster down when Longarm said, "Let me guess. Once you boys knew Owlhoot riders were in these hills in search of Natova, one or more of you stayed at that rooming house over in Clarkside long enough to plant a detour sign, right?"

Doc sounded pleased with himself as he admitted, "That's about the size of it. Had Caleb and Jethro room there in turn, confiding in that Irish gal you had to ask for Doc in Sliderock. Where's the fucking money? It ain't on either of you and it wasn't in your saddle bags at the sawmill last night neither!"

"Your brothers just rolled over our padlocked doors whilst you kept an eye on us at the saloon, right?"

"Where's the money?" Doc replied.

Stalling for time, not knowing what he'd do with it if they gave it to him, Longarm said, "You never would have approached us if they'd found that payroll loot in our saddle bags. When one or the other or both signaled you they hadn't, you came over to slay us with your charm."

"I'll slay you this minute if you don't tell us where that money is!" the sneak snorted from behind them.

It's not smart to tell a man holding a gun on you that he doesn't want to shoot you just yet. So Longarm repeated, "It ain't on this child."

Jethro suggested, "Make the jailbirds drop their jeans and bend over, Doc. I hear tell jailbirds under lock and key hide kitchen sinks up their asses!"

Doc said, "I got a less disgusting notion. I'll bet they snuck the money back in their saddle bags. How did you know the boys were into your saddle bags last night, Shorty?"

"Trade secret," Longarm answered dryly.

Doc said, "You're right funny. I'll bet you die laughing. Get into that hole, the both of you. We'll pat down your ponies after we put an end to this pointless discussion."

Foster murmured, "What's the form?"

Longarm had nothing all that brilliant to suggest. He knew that Foster knew that once they were standing in that hip-deep hole they would have no chance to do shit. So, hoping the Canadian followed his drift, he said, "You jump in to the left and I'll jump in to the right."

But before either could make his desperate move a familiar voice called out from the surrounding tree line, "Moe Shorty *downee*!"

So the two lawmen dropped to the grass as the gathering dusk was ripped with blinding gun-muzzle flashes from two sides, and it was tough to say which of the murderous brothers was hit first, with all of them screaming in agony as hot lead tore through their startled flesh.

Then it got very still as the echoes faded away, with gunsmoke hanging like ground fog across the trampled grass all around.

As he heard soft footsteps coming out of the trees Longarm gingerly raised his head. He could barely make them out. But there was enough light to savvy the significance of white stockings betwixt low-cut cloth slippers and high-riding pajama bottoms.

"Could we order some of them fortune cookies with our chop suey?" Longarm asked as he got to his feet.

The old cook from the saloon kitchen laughed like a kid and called back, "No fortune cookie. No chop suey. No flied lice! This a noodle joint, not a dlagon joint, lound eyes!"

"What in the world?" marveled Foster as Longarm helped the shaken Canadian to his feet.

"I'm still working on it," Longarm replied as he peered about in the gunsmoke-scented gloom. The old cook's younger helpers had already moved to roll the bodies over and make certain they were bodies. Longarm had no doubt as to what they were saying as they gleefully reported to the cook in Cantonese.

The older man nodded at Longarm and said, "Bettah you two lide on, now. We clean up mess. Belly bad boys in hole they dig alleddy. Let ponies find way home. You no wully. Let Fong wully. Nobody ask dumb Ching-Chong Chinaman shit."

That sounded reasonable. As Longarm picked up his gunbelt and strapped his sidearm and traveling expenses on, he asked, "Might I know your from somewhere, Mister Fong?"

The cook laughed in a surprisingly boyish tone and said, "You all looky-like to us, too. Fong just one in clowd that night you save us all flum mob in Denvah. But Fong lemembah you and now we *even*, Longarm!"

To which Longarm could only reply, "We surely are, Mister Fong. But might you have any suspicion as to how those others who got past this bunch might have made their way to Natova?"

Fong called the younger waiter over and questioned him in Cantonese.

The waiter said in better English, "You people don't seem to notice us as we wait on you. I have heard talk about some Indian hideout far to the north. Some riders who passed through without meeting *that* Doc over there were talking about another Doc they were going to meet up in Fort Missoula, where the Clark meets Blackfoot River."

Turning to Foster, Longarm said, "There you go, pard. These murdersome brothers got started when some ignorant Owlhoot rider mistook a small-town sneak called Doc for the Doc he'd been told to look for!"

"I vote we go to Fort Missoula and see for ourselves," the Canadian grinned. So they shook all around with their unexpected rescuers and mounted up to work back down to the wagon trace.

It wasn't easy. They had to trust the better night vision

and steady hoofwork of their mounts, moving downslope in what looked like pitch blackness to human eyes.

But as they busted out of the aspens further down they saw a quarter moon had risen and by the time they found the wagon trace they could make it out well enough to see that it ran east and west.

Longarm said, "Fort Missoula's at least forty miles on. Ain't no way in thunder we'll make her in less than the rest of tonight and the day to follow unless we change mounts."

Foster said, "Speak for yourself. My spirit is willing but my bottom needs at least a few hours rest from time to time. There must be some place closer to turn in, up ahead."

Longarm said, "Likely more than one, seeing gold is where you find it and this is gold mining country. But we ain't about to find a place to rest up and swap mounts unless we ride on. So let's ride on."

They rode on, to the west, at a walk. Mostly out of consideration for their mounts. A good rider on a sure-footed mount could ride at a lope by moonlight. But not for all that many miles and they didn't know how many miles they had to go before they slept that night, if they got to sleep at all.

The wagon trace wound more or less west-north-west through tunnels of deep shade and open patches where they could see one another, over hill and down many a dale through the lower reaches of the Rockies. They had to ford whitewater creeks of uncertain depth in the tricky light. Such unexpected delights might have puckered their assholes in broad daylight.

From time to time they spotted the distant lamplight of widely scattered homesteads or stock spreads. None looked big enough to tempt them off the beaten path. It would have been less fuss to make camp and spread their rolls on the ground than it would have been to go through all the handshakes and jawings of a coffee-and-cake stop late at night.

They didn't want to skip out on open ground or in some settler's barn. They wanted directions and if possible new mounts. Longarm had opined and Foster had agreed they'd be sore put to swap two good remount bays for anything worth riding anywhere but a good-sized livery, and you only found good-sized liveries in fair-sized towns.

Foster grumbled and Longarm agreed the two of them, seeing they came with longer legs than most, could have walked afoot faster than their blamed bays were carrying them.

The Canadian got no argument from a man who'd lived through the war. Old soldiers who'd marched with Alexander the Great had observed legged-up infantry marched faster than the cavalry moved at a walk. But after that a horse carried a fighting man with all his gear and weapons farther than he'd ever want to march in one day and of course, once he put his spurs to his mount, he could charge in line faster than any infantry could advance, slashing down like a giant from overhead at a gallop.

Mounted lancers, even in war paint, scared the shit out of infantry on foot as well, and even if they never wound up charging anyone on horseback, Longarm and Foster had a long way to go with a whole lot of shit to carry, not counting their hefty gunbelts. So Longarm said, "Let's not and say we did," when Foster suggested they lope a spell.

The quarter moon rose ever higher without shedding enough light on the subject to matter and when Longarm consulted his pocket watch by matchlight and saw it was even later than he'd thought, he suggested they ride one more mile and rein in to make camp.

He was glad he had when they topped a rise to see

lights, a whole string of lights, across the trace ahead. So they rode more than one more mile and reined in out front of a saloon describing itself as the Proud Peacock, according to the lettering across its false front.

They dismounted, tethered their bays, and strode in to ask how come.

The jovial barkeep explained as he set up their boilermakers how the whole settlement was called Peacock, because it had grown up around the Peacock mine just up the slope. When Longarm complimented him on the originality of the lettering above the door outside he modestly admitted there were establishments called the Peacock's Nest and Peacock's Tail in town.

Longarm said, "Let me guess. Your hotel and your whorehouse?"

The barkeep nodded and reached under the bar to produce a fist-sized chunk of rock. Handing it over he said, "Hold it up to the light and move it to and fro. That's why they call it peacock ore."

Longarm had already seen the not-that-rare conglomeration of metallic salts. So he handed it to Foster. As the Canadian admired the shifting rainbow colors, mostly metallic green with winks of red, blue and gold, the barkeep said, "Mostly copper. Whilst they've been arguing over the ratio of gold and silver bullion in Washington, the market price of copper keeps going through the roof."

Longarm asked him how the prices at the Peacock's Nest might go.

Meanwhile, back up in Clarkside, Keystone Callaway had arrived by stage from Helena that afternoon, along with Clay McCord and a mass of muscle they called Turk Butler. Turk wasn't much for thinking on his own. But if you pointed him at someone they were in a lot of trouble.

Having fanned out to gather information, they had reassembled in a chili parlor near the stagecoach station to compare notes. Turk never had a whole lot to say because he mostly followed Keystone like a vicious pup and wasn't too interested in anything he couldn't eat, fight or fuck.

McCord had been working the liveries and stables of the county seat, pretending to be looking for work as a wrangler. As the three of them huddled 'round a table in the back, McCord was able to report, "Our hero and his sidekick, who calls hisself Dusty Rhodes, left town days ago on surplus cavalry bays they bought off a fancy gal. Headed west, likely to to Fort Missoula and the Blackfoot River. Should they backtrack yonder they could head most anywhere across the lone prairie."

Keystone said, "I'll wire the boss to that effect. Ain't no stage line to Fort Missoula. Already asked. Stage and telegraph lines run up into these hills like tree branches and dead end."

"How come?" asked Turk Butler in a rare display of curiosity.

Keystone looked disgusted and said, "Men working one mine, or sponging off the same, have no call to travel to or exchange trade secrets with rival outfits, Turk. Eat your chili like a good little boy and let Daddy worry about cutting the trail of those naughty boys the boss wants me to spank!"

Chapter 16

Between Longarm's cardsharpery and the handsome send-off from Last Chance Charlene they had more funds to flash than Dodge City pimps with the herds in town, and it was just as well. For the Peacock's Nest, the one hotel in town, was as up-to-date as the Cheyenne Social Club, and it charged accordingly.

The reasoning was self-evident. Most everyone in the company town built and managed or franchised by the Peacock Mining Company dwelt in company housing and had no call to stay in any hotel. The only folk who needed a hotel were investors visitng at company expense or, as in the case of the two undercover lawmen, transients passing through.

In the case of visitors, the company wanted to impress them, and in the case of uninvited transients, saddle tramps were not welcome in the town of Peacock. So rooms started at a dollar a night, with indoor plumbing and newfangled electrical lights to go with bed linens changed every day whether you checked out or stayed over. There was nothing slow about the Peacock's Nest, and it could have held its head up along Seventeenth Street down Denver way.

There was no town livery, but the hotel had its own stable out back, and they figured the matched bays they'd ridden so far would last them another etape after a full night's rest, seeing they were in no hurry with nowhere in particular to go, now that Doc Tyler had turned out such a disappointment. For until they met up with a real guide, their best bet was to flash more cash than their rough-hewn appearances warranted and look sort of lost.

They each paid a dollar and a half in advance for rooms with baths. As they supped on Welsh rabbit in the hotel taproom under a moose head outfitted with Edison bulbs wired to the tines of its antlers, with their riding stock secure out back and their possibles upstairs under lock and key, Crown Sergeant Foster said, "This is pretty posh, but I'd feel safer if we were a few more miles from the scene of the crime."

To which Longarm replied, "I've been studying on that. If Fong and his boys covered up after themselves worth shit, nobody ought to figure anything happened to Doc Tyler and his trash brothers. After that, seeing Doc wasn't the real thing, the real thing can't be stationed too far up the road to Natova or nobody would have ever found him, and we know some did."

Foster nodded but asked, "Why should we expect to find anyone in particular here in this little company town? Wouldn't it make more sense to set up an . . . outlaw travel agency somewhere more substantial, such as the river crossing at Fort Missoula?"

Longarm rinsed some melted cheese on toast down with lager before he said, "Told you I've been studying . . .

Moe. A bottleneck such as this with one saloon, one whorehouse and this one hotel makes it easier to hail ships passing in the night. I vote we give our mounts a day or so more to rest up as we sort of stand out from the company crowd as trail-weary travelers able to pay our way if only we knew just where we were bound for."

"Do you think it's wise to hang on to those army horses?" asked a Mountie who always got his man by tracking sharp.

Longarm said, "We ain't on the run from where we got 'em and they're good old brutes. Why swap 'em before they tucker out under us?"

Foster asked, "Have you forgotten that sinister sorrel whose rider tailed us west from Helena?"

Longarm shook his head and said, "Not hardly. I was braced for him to show up all the time we were back yonder in Clarkside. But we were stuck there for nigh a fortnight and he never. So he likely bought our ruse of pretending to backtrack from that stagecoach stop east of the county seat."

"Who do you think he was riding for?" asked Foster, cutting himself another morsel.

Longarm said, "Like I told you at the time. Likely the sore loser I took at poker back in Helena. Copper kings with money to burn and mean dispositions can be risky to play cards with. But by now he's no doubt sore at somebody else, and, like I said, nobody riding for him came after us in Clarkside."

Foster decided Longarm was likely right and suggested they finish their snack and mosey to see if there was any other action in Peacock.

He said, "It occurred to me back in those aspenwoods, wondering how we were ever going to get out of there alive, and doubting we ever would, that Martha, back in the

Last Chance, would be the last piece I'd ever have, and, if the truth be known, Martha was only so-so in bed. So as I stood there, more certain by the minute I would never see another sunrise or another pretty girl, I had this raging erection by the time we were saved at the last moment by Fong and his lads!"

Longarm said, "Professor Darwin never put things that earthy in his theory of revolution, but it stands to reason that's how come buffalo bulls and hanged men shoot their wads as they die. Trying to the very last for the survival of their species. I was fixing to whirl on Doc and see if I could gouge out at least one eye before he killed me. But I know the feeling. I have felt it on calmer occasions I thought might be my last. But why are we dwelling on events that happened hours ago? The clock has yet to strike midnight and they got electric streetlights outside!"

The not-yet-middle-aged lawmen who'd grown up in a world illuminated by flaming fuel of one sort of another stepped out into what the newspapers kept trumpeting as the dawn of an age that would banish darkness. The banishment had a ways to go, yet. But since that Belgian inventor had come up with the electric dynamo right after the Wedding of the Rails the earlier sputtering British arc lights and the more recent sort-of-spooky Edison bulbs had lit up full furlongs of Chicago's State Street, New York City's Broadway and a bodacious stretch of Paris, France. So Longarm was less uneasy with an eerie effect of electric light that more than one journalist had noted.

Nobody in their right mind left a candle, oil or gas lamp untended and still lit when they called it a night. So everyone who'd grown up whilst darkness had still been banished the old-fashioned ways was used to figuring nobody was up, if they were even there, when they saw nothing lit inside.

But as the new arrivals in Peacock walked its electrified main street late at night, they passed padlocked shop after padlocked shop, closed for the night, with their confounded innards lit up as if for business, and nothing going on in there under the silent sort of brooding glow of Edison bulbs.

Foster decided, "It's going to make burglary more complicated as the fad spreads, but I must say the effect is creepy!"

Longarm said, "I follow your drift. You never think of how quiet and still a shut shop feels, late at night, when you can't see it plain as day. Sort of like them ghost towns you pass through when the sun is really shining."

Pointing ahead he added, "The worse part is that you can't tell when things are open or shut for the infernal night! We have to traipse all the way to that blamed saloon to see it she's open or shut!"

As it turned out, and as he'd hoped, the Proud Peacock was open 'round the clock like any other saloon in any other mining town. For the mine would never shut down as long as the lode was there to be worked.

There was another barkeep on duty and none of the other customers remembered them from earlier. It gave them the chance to introduce themselves all over, and each stood a round in turn. But none of the mining men they'd treated offered to buy a round, and it was hard to say whether they were sullen or just tired. Men coming out of the shafts after midnight were unlikely to know the way to Natova in any case.

As they nursed their own drinks in more privacy than they'd had in mind, Foster suggested the Peacock's Tail, seeing it was doubtless open in spite of the hour.

Longarm said, "You go ahead if you feel the need, pard. I feel the need but not that much."

"Are you idealistic or cheap?" laughed the Canadian.

Longarm said, "A little of both, I reckon. I know money won't buy love, but I'll be damned if I'll pay for hostility, and there's so much of that going around when you pay for pussy."

Foster allowed Longarm's depressing observation had spoiled the mood for him as well and they both headed back to the Peacock's Nest to pack it in for the night.

As Longarm hung his hat and gunbelt up, alone in his hired room, he had to shake his head at his self-imposed restrictions. For now that Foster had mentioned it, he did feel sort of horny, and it wasn't as if old Maureen back at that rooming house or less inspiring gals than her he'd had in his day had been visions of loveliness. The kindly old philosopher who'd described a stiff dick as an appetite with no conscience had no doubt had a stiff dick in his day, and it was a simple fact of nature that a heap of whores good enough to work in high-toned houses of ill repute with electric lights and all were better looking than your average librarian.

But he knew he'd still take a plain librarian or, hell, a homely chili waitress before he'd pay to get on like he was boarding a merry-go-round.

He wryly conceded that that long stay in Clarkside had spoiled him, some, with Jo and Last Chance Charlene being semi-retired whores he hadn't had to pay and good old Maureen putting out as if she'd been a pure old maid, as long as you didn't study on it.

Unbuttoning his shirt, he decided that was the snag when it came to out-and-out whores. By just not asking, a man could enjoy a widow woman who'd been laid a thousand times during one or more happy marriages way more than he could forgive a spanking new whore who'd only laid a hundred men or so.

He was fixing to switch off the overhead bulb and finish undressing in the dark when there came a gentle tapping on his chamber door. It didn't sound like Foster, and he doubted it could be that raven from the poem. So he got his gun and moved over to the door to see who it was.

It was a gal of about thirty, more sedate in appearance than Last Chance Charlene but a hell of a lot better looking than Maureen. Her head was bare. She'd let down her taffy-colored hair, but she was otherwise presentable in her summer frock of beige shantung.

Lowering the gun muzzle with a sheepish smile, Longarm allowed he was the lady's servant, hoping she had at least a dragon for him to slay for her, but she just said she was embarrassed.

When he asked how come, she said she'd been fixing to get undressed and turn in, across the hall in her own hired room. Longarm started to ask if she needed help with her bodice, seeing it buttoned down the back, but he somehow doubted that was it. So he just stood there with a puzzled smile until she said, "It's the elecrical lighting in this hotel. I can see how you put the *bed* lamp out. It has this little chain you pull like a . . . never mind. I can't seem to put the bulbs in the middle of the ceiling out. There are four of them. They just stay lit above my bed and how am I to ever sleep with them shining in my eyes all night?"

Longarm pointed out his own ceiling fixture to ask if they were talking about the same problem. She glanced up to say, "Not really. Yours are out already. You only have that lamp by your bed to worry about and I see it has the same sort of chain."

Longarm moved to the wall switch near the door and turned on the overhead lights. She gasped, "How did you do that?"

He showed her, flipping the switch on and off. She

asked if she could try and laughed girlishly when she found she could turn lights off and on with so little effort.

She said, "Well. I never! But how does it ever work? I mean those bulbs are up there and this thighamabob is over here on the wall . . ."

He said, "I ain't no expert, but I suspect there's electrical wires running up inside the wall and across the ceiling. Don't ask me where they might come from. But there must be a powerhouse somewhere here in town, Miss . . . ?"

"Oh, dear, where are my manners? I'm Theda Barnes!" she replied, adding, as if he needed to be told, "I'm new in town. I came in answer to their advertisement for an accountant. They say they need someone to better supervise their payroll operations."

Longarm dryly replied, "I've always found payroll operations interesting. They call me Shorty Sawyer. I just got here with my sidekick, Mohawk Brown. He's always been interested in payroll operations, too."

She looked up at him uncertainly to observe, "You don't look all that short to me."

Then she flustered, "Oh, dear me, that's supposed to be a joke, isn't it? You westerners have such . . . droll manners."

He asked if she wanted him to tag along and show her how to flip her own light switch. She flustered some more and allowed she felt sure she had the hang of it, now, thanks to him.

Then she said good night and left him standing there with a foolish smile on his face and a raging erection in his jeans.

He wasn't the only one feeling frustrated as he shut the hall door with a sigh. Foster was jerking off in the dark next door and down in Slide-rock Keystone Callaway was not looking forward to a flop in the sawmill as he huddled at that same corner table with Clay McCord and Turk Butler. McCord was for riding on, seeing none of the locals had laid eyes on the fondly remembered Shorty and Moe all evening.

McCord said, "They've rid on, with new names but them same army bays we heard tell of up in Clarkside. They say the next place up the trace worth stopping is a mining-company town called Peacock. They say there's a fine hotel in Peacock, which is more than this wide spot in the trace has to offer!"

Keystone shook his head and said, "It's after midnight. If they stopped there they've turned in by now. If they rode through they ain't. In either case I want to be bright-eyed and bushy-tailed when we catch up with the sneaky sons of bitches and leave us not forget they doubled back on you one time already, Clay."

He stared down into his suds for a time and declared, "It's them army bays we want to talk about with somebody awake and cold sober. We'll catch up on our beauty rest in that infernal sawmill and ask about them army bays at the municipal corral in the morning, when somebody might know more than that half-ass night man who couldn't tell us shit."

He finished his beer and rose, adding, "Let's go. I aim to get an early start, come morning."

Chapter 17

Having tossed his shirt aside, Longarm was seated on the bed, shucking his boots by the light of the bed lamp when there came another tapping on his chamber door. He rose in his socks to reach for his shit, decided he had no call to slow things down, and went to open the door once more to his sleepless neighbor across the way.

She said, "Oh, dear, I hope I didn't get you out of bed!"

He dryly remarked, "Not yet. I still got my pants on. Is there anything else I can do for you, Miss Theda?"

She said, "I was hoping a . . . nightcap would help me sleep out here in strange surroundings. I think the altitude may have jangled my nerves as they warned me it might."

He was too polite to say the thinner air of the high country usually tended to make pilgrims sleepy-headed. He said, "I have some Maryland rye in my saddle bag, along with running water and hotel tumblers."

She said, "Oh, I was considering the taproom downstairs. But of course it would never do for me to enter even a hotel taproom without an escort and . . . Do you think it would be proper if we were to imbibe up here all alone, seeing you'd have to get dressed again and I'd need my hat and gloves downstairs?"

He opened the door wider, suggesting she let her conscience be her guide.

She demurred, "I don't know. It's so late. We've barely met. What sort of a girl might you take me for if I behaved so boldly?"

Longarm said, "An up-to-date woman of the world who knows her own mind. A woman in a strange town where nobody knows her, facing a night alone in a strange bed with nobody to talk to."

She flustered, "I'll have you know I'm not in the habit of talking to strange men in bed when I'm back home in Ohio!"

He shrugged his bare shoulder and said, "I stand corrected. In the meantime it's after midnight, and if you mean to make it to that job interview in the cold gray dawn you'd best let your conscience be your guide one way or the other, Miss Theda."

She hesitated, said, "They told me to come in after noon. But it does seem awfully late to shilly-shally. So maybe just one little nightcap before we call it a day."

He let her in and shut the hall door after her. When she demurred he asked if she wanted to explain her sharing a highball with a man with no shirt on to others passing in the hall.

She flustered that she wasn't used to the customs of hotel life. He was too polite to say he'd be the judge of that once he got some of his snake medicine in her.

There were two thick-bottomed hotel tumblers handy to the sink in the bath next door. The Peacock's Nest was an up-to-date hotel in every way. He built them hefty highballs with rye whisky and tap water and noticed when he joined her in the bedroom that she was seated on the bed. As he sat down beside her to hand her her drink she flipped the bed lamp off, but then she flipped it back on, marveling at the wonders of modern science.

She said she'd never stayed in such a modernistic hotel, even back in Columbus, and said that checking in downstairs they'd bragged on being modeled after a famous new hotel in Paris, France. She made a wry face as she added, "I'm not certain I hold with all their fancy French notions. One of their French chambermaids popped in on me this afternoon to catch me in my all-together, just stepping out of my bath! I mean, the little snip came in from the hall without knocking!"

Longarm set his own drink aside and got back to his feet, moving to the door as he explained, "The maid likely thought you were out, Miss Theda. Check-out time is three in the afternoon if you don't mean to stay another night. If you don't want the help barging in on you early you take this DON'T DISTURB off the inside knob, hang her on the outside knob and bolt the door from inside, like so."

She watched him assure they'd not be disturbed, making no objection when he threw the bolt and rejoined her on the bed. She didn't move back when he had to reach across her for his glass. She didn't seem to have any corset stays holding her grand breastworks in place. So he knew they were natural, and, seeing she didn't seem to flinch from his copping a feel, he put the fool drink back on the table, switched off the fool lamp, and got a better grip on the subject as they fell backwards across the covers with her tongue in his mouth.

After that things went natural enough, with her protesting now and again that she didn't usually do such things, even as they got to doing them. It sure beat all how a gal who'd knock on a strange man's door after midnight with nothing on under her skirts thought she had to bullshit him about her social habits. But he never let on she might be overdoing it, seeing that once he had her shucked all the way out of that shantung she wanted to get on top.

They finished old-fashioned, on the rug, and that was sort of high-toned Bigelow carpeting, pretending to be Oriental.

But, thick-piled as it was, the floor underneath was a tad firm for smoking and cuddling. So he helped her back in bed and lit them a cheroot to share as she flicked the lamp on and off, laughing like a kid.

She allowed she found the on-and-off flashes of naked flesh sort of exciting. But when he suggested she just leave the Edison bulb on she said, "Oh, I couldn't. We look so naked."

He allowed he'd thought that had been the general idea. But in the same way he rode a pony with a firm but gentle hand on the reins, Longarm let a gal have her head, as long as she didn't come up with anything that might hurt.

As they shared a smoke with the lights out, most of the time, she asked how long he and Foster meant to be in town.

He honestly replied, "Ain't certain, now. We only meant to stay this one night. But Peacock offers . . . possibilities to riders in our . . . situation."

Theda said she didn't follow him, asking what he and his friend were doing in Peacock if they couldn't say whether they were just passing through or meaning to stay. He snuffed out the smoke and kissed her good to change the subject. Something about the way she'd taken to questioning him had the hairs on the back of his neck disturbed. As a man who enjoyed pillow conversations, Longarm was used to the light banter and natural curiosity of the head on the next pillow. It stood to reason a new gal in town who'd just met up with some slap and tickle would want to know how long it was likely to last. So what was there about the way she'd taken to questioning him that inspired him to choose his answers with more care than usual?"

After he had it in her some more and she was responding as if she was enjoying it without a care in the world, he decided it might simply be he was on his guard because he'd met her under a false name, living a lie since he and Foster had left Great Falls.

They caught a few winks and when next he woke she was getting dressed by the cold gray light of dawn, and when he asked how come she said she'd just die if anyone else in the hotel found out she'd been such a shameless wench. Then she showed no shame when she bent to kiss his limp manhood and playfully ask if he cared to invite her to supper that evening.

They agreed to meet after sundown in the lobby, as if by surprise, after she'd gone for that job interview and he'd taken care of . . . whatever he and Moe were up to there in Peacock.

So there it was again, he thought, as she let herself out, leaving his DON'T DISTURB sign in place.

What might she suspect him of, seeing she seemed to suspect him of something, and what sort of gal consorted with gents she suspected of something?

Longarm finally decided that she likely suspected a wife and kids back wherever in thunder he really came from. If she suspected they were on the run from robbing that other payroll down in the Anaconda Range . . .

He decided he'd sleep on it. He hadn't gotten enough sleep to matter, starting so late with such a frisky bed partner, and it wasn't as if he had to worry about anyone really being after them for that robbery down in the Anaconda Range.

To begin with, it had never happened. Billy Vail had just put it on the wire so's he and Foster could pretend to be WANTED. If push came to shove and they got picked up by anyone for a robbery they'd never pulled off, they'd never stand trial for a crime that nobody had committed. The plan was to go along with whatever happened for as long as they could manage before any prosecuting attorney worth his salt caught on and threw them out of jail.

With any luck, a night or two in a holding cell with other riders of the Owlhoot Trail might put them on to something. They hadn't managed to meet up with the real thing, so far, over here in the high country.

So he turned over and went back to sleep, knowing nobody would pester him with that DON'T DISTURB sign out in the hall and figuring he'd meet up with Foster around noon.

It was already getting light out. So not too far to the south, in the less up-to-date community of Sliderock, Undersheriff Hamilton Forbes had lit his kitchen lamp the old-fashioned way, with a match, and raked the banked coals of his kitchen range awake and put a morning kettle on by the time a senior deputy was pounding on his back door, as if it was important.

The lawman assigned to Sliderock Township by the Sheriff's Department in the county seat went to the door in his nightshirt as, off in their bedroom, a sleepy she-male voice called out, "What's going on out there, Ham? What are you doing out of bed at this hour?"

He called, "Go back to sleep, old gal, I'll bring you some coffee and a wake-up kiss when you and the coffee are ready. Got to answer the damn door now."

When he did, his senior deputy stepped inside to ask, "You know that fat breed gal as cooks and keeps house for Doc Tyler and his brothers out to their Triple T, Ham?"

The older lawman made a wry face and said, "That

ain't all she does for the three of them, way I hear. What about her?"

The deputy said, "She came in before dawn, all flusterpated and teary-eyed. Seems they left her alone out yonder, last night, saying they'd be back by midnight. Only midnight came and she was still waiting."

The undersheriff shrugged and suggested, "Something came up. Might have been prettier than her. Might have been something else. I can think of a dozen things those three could have gotten into. I've warned Doc I have my eye on them."

The deputy nodded and said, "That's the way we saw it and that's the way she saw it, 'til three or four this morning. She says she heard their ponies out back and figured they'd come home. But as she waited, she was sort of vague on which one she was waiting for, nobody came in from out back. She allows it got sort of spooky."

Forbes nodded and said, "I get the picture. Never mind which one in particular she was expecting, if not all three. What happened next?"

The deputy said, "She called out, waited some, and commenced to cry before she screwed up her courage, loaded a ten-gauge Greener and crept out back to challenge whoever was out there with the ponies."

"And?" asked Forbes.

"And nobody was there," replied the younger lawman, adding, "Just the ponies all three of them, tuckered out but shying some, as if they'd been through a lot."

He shrugged and opined, "They likely had. They'd drug their reins a piece through tall timber and tanglewood to wind up lathered and all scratched. She had a time unsaddling them and getting them back in their stall, even offering 'em water. Then she got dressed and rode in on her own palfry, like I said, all teary-eyed and scared. She thinks something must have happend to the Tyler boys."

The undersheriff nodded soberly and said, "She's likely right. Like I warned Doc, the ringleader of the trashy clan, I've been expecting them to get in trouble. Doc has this way of buttering up to saddle tramps passing through. Rode off one time in the company of a hard case I'd ordered to leave town."

"How come?" asked his deputy.

The older lawman shrugged and said, "You get so's you can sort of feel trouble riding in with the hairs on the back of your neck. Doc Tyler seemed inclined to buy such strangers a drink. When I asked him why, he said he was interested in travelers' tales, and, come to study on it, wasn't Doc drinking with those odd birds who ate Chinese noodles the night before last?"

The deputy nodded and said, "Shorty and Moe, they called themselves. They seemed all right. Shorty said he'd found out about Chinese noodles out Frisco way. Had a heap of droll traveler's tales and the boys had a pleasant evening with him and his less talkative sidekick. Doc would have been only one of the regulars who shared draft beer and Chinese noodles with old Shorty and Moe. I don't think his brothers were there."

"Doc and his brothers are the only ones missing," said Undersheriff Forbes, "so see if you can find them strangers Doc took up with. If they ain't around Sliderock. See if you can discover where they might have headed. Oh, and posse up a search party to ride out to the Triple T, and see if they can backtrack them three riderless mounts to wherever they might have left their riders."

The deputy allowed he knew how to look for lost children. But as he turned to leave, the older lawman had another thought and called out, "Wait up. You know that old-timer, Dad Shriner, hunts wolves and mountain lions for bounty money?"

The deputy nodded but said, "If the truth be known, he enjoys hunting stock killers just for the hell of it."

Forbes said, "Whatever. My point is that he hunts the varmints with them redbone hunting hounds that can track good as bloodhounds. Go see if old Dad would like to help us out with them redbones he tracks other varmints with. If he's willing, and that old breed gal can let 'em smell some dirty duds of Doc's . . . Shoot, why am I telling you how a hunting hound backtracks kids lost in the woods? Just go ask him."

The deputy said, "I'm on my way. I know what Dad Shriner will say. So wherever Doc and his brothers may be, them redbone hounds are sure to find all three of 'em."

Chapter 18

Longarm slept nigh to noon, and when he got dressed and stepped out in the hall he found Foster still slugabed, or hiding out behind his own DON'T DISTURB sign. Longarm was about to give Foster's chamber door more than a gentle tapping when he heard the creak of bedsprings and the muffled gasps of a gal trying not to cry out as she was coming. So Longarm moved on with a puzzled smile.

He visited their two army bays. When the colored hostler admitted they had a corral out back, Longarm bet him a quarter the bays couldn't laze about outside with other stock, lest they stiffen up from too much time in their stalls.

After he'd lost, the hostler asked how long he and his pal and their ponies might be staying there. Longarm said he honestly didn't know but added, "You do have poles around that corral, don't you?"

Having assured himself that their riding stock would be in shape to ride when such a time might come, Longarm stretched his own legs along the short main street to see shops did seem less spooky with their electric lighting off and folk moving about inside. At the saloon they told him all the lights that burned all night were powered by one steam-driven dynamo near the mine adit up the slope. The same engine house powered the cable cars hauling ore out of the mountain and stamping it to refine it some before it was hauled off to the smelters in Phillipsburg. They'd been talking about a narrow-gauge railroad. They said it depended on the price of silver and copper after the next election.

The western senators in Washington were forever arguing that silver bullion was valued too low, next to the gold standards of the international bankers. Copper kept edging up on its own, even though copper coins were only small change. Longarm was just as glad he didn't have to worry about such figures.

He ordered steak and potatoes in the taproom to start, without old Foster. But the Mountie joined him there, looking as if butter wouldn't melt in his mouth. Longarm said, "I've been studying on how long we want to stay here. Her name's Theda, and she may or may not be working for the mining company by this evening."

Foster sat down to say, "I seem to have lucked out with my limited grasp of Québécois. Chambermaid seems to be one of our *Métis* rebels, on the run down here in your Montana Territory. I feel it my duty to Her Majesty to investigate the matter further. I mean, she may know all sorts of things about Louis Riel and his future plans, eh?"

Longarm smiled thinly and said, "I can tell you his plans. He means to set up a separate half-breed nation on the Canadian prairie. What's the difference betwixt regular French and that Quebby-Quash?"

Foster said, "A French revolution and an imperial court

presided over by an upstart with a Corsican accent. French Canadian is French the way it was spoken under Louis XVI."

Longarm cut his steak as he soberly intoned the doggeral verse to the effect that . . . "Louis was the king of France before the Revolution . . . Then the Frogs cut off his head and spoiled his constitution?"

Foster said, "Exactly. With the working-class accent of the Paris mobs, followed by the so-called French of Corsica now the official French spoken in France, to the chagrin of Québec and Montreal. But we were talking about our stay here in Peacock."

Longarm said, "We were. Like I said last night, a nice little town with one saloon, one whorehouse and one hotel would be about where I'd set up an outlaw travel agency. On the other hand, we don't know for certain anybody has. Directions to Natova may just be passed about the way tramps pass the word on mean or friendly housewives. Nobody could hope to make a regular *living* by showing riders on the run the way to that robber's roost to the north."

Foster said, "We know somebody must. How else would all those outlaws from other parts find a hidden valley nobody else can?"

The waiter came to take Foster's order. Longarm waited and once they were free to talk again he pointed out, "Whoever may be offering such directions has to be doing it as a sideline. The way a more commonly honest pawnshop keeper makes a deal to fence stolen property. Crooks who don't do anything else 'round the clock are caught in no time. So we have to find some pillar of some community who only helps out fugitives from justice on those occasions they ride through, see?"

Foster did, but spoiled it all by asking, "Very well. Assuming our . . . travel guide to Natova has some local position not even the local law might suspect, how in blue blazes are we supposed to find him?"

"Ain't certain we have to look that hard," Longarm replied with a bemused expression. He explained, "Ever since I woke up all the way this morning, late and feeling mighty smug, I've been pondering on the laws of probability."

Foster naturally wanted to know what he was getting at.

Longarm said, "I ain't one for boasting of my bedroom conquests. I've always felt a man who'd kiss and tell would eat shit. But rules are made to be bent some. So answer me this. What would you say the odds were a gal who claims she's just shown up to work in the payroll department of a rich mining outfit would wind up in bed, her first night in town, with a stranger answering the desciprion of a payroll robber on the dodge?"

Foster cocked an eyebrow and asked, "*She* moved in on *you*?"

Longarm nodded and said, "I didn't know she was in this hotel. She came to my door. When I behaved like a gent she came back to try again, harder. I can't swear for certain she even booked a room of her own the way she said. For a gal who seemed too country to flick an electric switch, she sure turned out worldly enough about slap and tickle. Forgive me if I sound like a green hand bragging on his first night in a trail town, but she screwed with considerable experience for her age and when we got to talking, she questioned me tight for a gal who wasn't supposed to know all that much."

Foster almost made a dumb suggestion. Then he nodded soberly and declared, "If she was working for the county, or some bounty hunter, we'd have heard from them by now, right?"

Longarm said, "Too soon to say. I never told her right

out we were outlaws on the dodge. Thinking back, and hoping I remember everything we talked about last night, I tried to leave the impression we were sort of at loose ends, not certain where we meant to go from here and mayhaps waiting for an offer."

He washed down a morsel of steak with black coffee and added, "I've been trying to give that impression all along our way, hoping some damned somebody would step foreward to show us the way. I don't see how those others could have made it past Fort Missoula without pals who knew the way putting them on the right track to Natova. Owlhoot riders who ain't headed somewhere tend to get picked up in strange country, acting strange."

The waiter brought Foster's sausage and eggs. As he dug in, the other lawman mused, "You've raised some disturbing questions about chambermaids who just happen to have a lot of free time on their twats, as soon as one considers the odds. So what's the form? Wouldn't we be running for it, about now, if we were the real thing?"

Longarm said, "Not if we were fooled. And if we get up from the table now we'll never be sure about the name of the game. I figure we can risk paying out a little more line. The one who may or may not be playing games with me is supposed to meet me here after sundown, with supper some more slap and tickle in mind."

He sighed and added, "If she don't show up, I'll know it was all an act. Then all I'll have to do is figure out what she was really up to.

Foster said, "I can come up with an easy answer, whether she meets you for supper or not. What if her game is simply to hold you here in Peacock?"

"Until what?" asked Longarm.

The Canadian manhunter said, "Until whoever she wired about us can get here, of course. Say she recognized you as a mysterious stranger in a company town, having no business there, but answering the description of a man prone to rob mine payrolls. Say she contacted somebody like the Pinkertons, and they wired back, asking her to see if she could keep you here until they could arrive?"

Longarm shrugged and said, "Sounds a tad complexicated when you study on it. We never really robbed any mining company. So no private company guns would be after us."

He was wrong, of course, albeit the company guns that were after him rode for a copper king just as certain he'd been robbed.

That morning, back in Sliderock, it hadn't taken Keystone Callaway more than the tinkle of silver in the right ears to determine that those jovial strangers riding matched army bays had been seen talking to Doc Tyler, a local slippery cuss steeped in local lore, before mounting up to ride uncertainly into the woods instead of either way along the east-west wagon trace. The same hostler, once he'd studied on it some, was able to recall Doc having similar conversations with other strangers on their way from somewhere uncertain to no place in particular.

After consulting in private with Clay McCord and the dim but dangerous Turk Butler, Keystone had declared, "This Doc Tyler reads like a guide along this stretch of the Owlhoot Trail. That so-called meatpacker out of *Omaha gets curiouser and curiouser as you study his ways and means*. Boss had him down as a more-clever-than-possible crooked gambler. Then McCord, here, noticed he seemed to perform magic tricks with horses, and now he's hired him a local guide to the surrounding hills."

"What could he be up to?" asked McCord.

Keystone had thought the sensible answer to that was, "Let's go find out. Hostler back yonder says this Doc Tyler breeds riding stock and runs pack trains out of his home spread just north of town. They call her the Triple T. We'll start from there and see if anyone can tell us where the boss went or when he said he'd be back."

McCord had been the one to suggest a local guide might have no more to show magical riders than a secret trail up to the next town. McCord had pointed out, "We figure that's how he got past me that time outside of Clarkside, remember? You were the one figured out how he and his pal never backtracked to Helena at all. I know they never rode past me into Clarkside for that famous showdown with Empty Chambers. So they must have gone *around* me, through the *woods*."

Keystone had suggested they simply catch up with Doc Tyler and ask the son of a bitch. So they'd ridden on to the Triple T, where everything went to hell in a hack.

"What are you talking about? Returning to the scene of what crime?" Keystone Callaway had blustered as he found himself facedown in the dirt of the Triple T dooryard with a county deputy warning him to hold still and let them cuff him, damn it.

Clay McCord had whirled his pony when he sensed a trap and been blown out of his saddle to writhe nearby in the dust like a wriggle-worm caught by daybreak on a brick walk.

Turk Butler had landed on his feet and kept going with buckshot in his burly back when they'd blown his pony out from under him. They knew he wouldn't get far, wounded and afoot. So they gathered around the obvious leader, hauling Keystone to his feet, with one eye swollen shut and blood running down his chin from his split lip.

Feeling good about the way things had gone, the deputy in charge of that modest posse chortled, "Thought we'd never come back here once we found the bodies, did you?

Thought you'd look for hidden treasure with the Tyler boys dead up the mountain and their poor scared housekeeper cowering in town?"

Keystone sputtered, "What are you talking about? What treasure? Whose bodies? We just got here! We didn't know shit about any treasure or any bodies!"

The local lawman snorted, "Why sure, stranger. Anyone can see the three of you just stopped by for coffee and cake. Let's just see what caliber this gun you were packing might be."

As he hunkered down for the six-gun they'd knocked out of Keystone's shoulder holster when they'd jumped him, ripping his frock coat all to hell, he casually asked one of the other riders gathered 'round what caliber their deputy coroner had dug from the remains of Doc Tyler.

When the answer was .38, Keystone sputtered, "Well, shit, most everybody who doesn't load .44 loads .38! That doesn't mean anything!"

The deputy holding Keystone's six-gun calmly answered, "Means Doc Tyler was killed mostly with a .38 along with some number-nine buck, and here you are packing a .38 as well as trespassing on the property of three murdered local boys."

He turned to ask the deputies standing over McCord whether that one was in shape to ride on back to town. The answer came, "Not hardly. If he ain't breathed his last there's not much left of the murderous son of a bitch."

"We didn't do it! You've killed the wrong man, you idiots!" Keystone protested. He was too upset to consider his words with more care.

The deputy in charge of the bunch who'd grabbed him calmly replied, "Sure we killed the right man. Wouldn't be right to kill the *wrong* man. You better watch them wild accusations, stranger. Wouldn't make sense to take you in to the county seat with you accusing us of being idiots."

Another posse rider growled, "Why bother hauling him all that way when anyone can see he's guilty as all get-out? I say hang him here and get it over with!"

There came an ominous growl of agreement from the dozen Sliderock riders assembled.

Keystone bleated, "Hold on! You can't be serious! I'm a licensed company dick! Look in my damned coat for my damned wallet!"

"Bounty hunter, eh?" The local lawman smiled. It was not a nice smile. Then he added, "It all comes clear, now. Doc and the boys had their faults but they was *Sliderock* boys! Let's string the stranger up!"

So they did, and as Keystone thrashed his legs and crapped his pants that seemed to be the end of it.

But off among the aspens, still on his feet and hurting like hell, the totally bewildered but still armed and dangerous Turk Butler was trying to make sense of what had just happened as he staggered on.

Turk had never been one for heavy thinking and nothing that had just happened back yonder made a lick of sense to him. But with every step he ran he put more distance between himself and whatever had just happened and, no matter what had just happened, Turk Butler was mad as hell about it and somebody, anybody, was going to pay in blood.

Chapter 19

Bellied up to the bar in the Proud Peacock that afternoon, Longarm felt better about the apparant coldness he and Foster had felt the night before as Theda's story about the need for new bookkeepers began to make more sense. Nobody had been paid at the recent end of June. Nobody figured to get paid until after the Fourth of July, and it was just as well Peacock was a company town, with the saloons and shops extending lines of credit to somewhat pissed-off employees. Old boys who wanted to avail themselves of the services at the Peacock's Tail on credit were out of luck.

The reason for the hang-up, according to a Cornish Cousin Jack with a month's worth of drilling owed him, was the regular paymaster coming down with something in May and his assistant getting the payroll all wrong at the end of the month, with some workers getting too much whilst others were short-changed and sore as hell.

The regular paymaster was still in the hospital at Fort

Missoula. That fool who'd messed up had been let go. The company had promised to get it right with the June payroll, if the boys would hold their horses until the Fourth of July. Longarm didn't tell anybody in the Proud Peacock they'd only hired Theda that morning, if they'd hired her at all. He had no idea how long it would take even a sharp accountant to straighten out the mess.

Foster, as Mohawk Brown, had been working the stable hands of Peacock in hopes of getting a line on the trail to Natova. Short of outright asking for directions to a robber's roost, they'd both given any local volunteers every opportunity to come forward. Anyone could see they were well-heeled strangers with no connection to the mining company or other visible means of support. They'd stayed out of card games lest somebody take them for traveling tinhorns. They'd stayed away from the Peacock's Tail lest they be taken for pimps. If there was anyone in town acting as an outlaw travel agent he was a piss-poor judge of likely prospects.

When Longarm met Theda in their hotel taproom near supper time, she'd changed to a new summer frock and a perky straw boater with fake cherries atop it. She said she'd been hired and to celebrate she wanted to have supper at this fancy French tearoom she'd just heard about.

He apologized for showing up in clean but faded denim and pointed out it was late in the day to hire formal duds. She dimpled and assured him he cut a handsome enough figure "to those who admire cowboys."

So they both laughed and he escorted her no more than a city block down Main Street to where she pointed at a lady's notions shop and said that was where they were fixing to dine. Then he saw the steps leading up to a restaurant on the second floor. So they went on up and the

French-looking cuss who met them at the head of the stairs seemed a good sport about cowboys and led them to a table by the front window.

Crown Sergeant Foster was already seated there, in his own cowboy outfit, with a pretty little thing who had to be that *Metís* chambermaid from the hotel. The French *Metís* and Mex *Mestizo* had the same meaning.

Foster was as suprised to see his pal "Shorty" there with a taffy blonde. Things got less surprising when the gals both giggled and Theda said "Dear Louette" had told her about the place and they'd meant to surprise them.

So they gathered 'round one table overlooking Main Street as the sun was setting and electric street lamps switched on outside as if by magic. Nobody switched on any Edison bulbs in their restaurant. The help commenced to light more romantic candles. The effect was darker than the oil lamps in most old-fashioned beaneries. But the gals seemed to feel it was more romantic to dine by candlelight. So they did. And by the time they were ready for dessert it was hard to tell just what was on the table in front of them.

Longarm had asked for the dessert menu, but it never came. What came to their table was an uncertain blur in a business suit with a flower in his lapel. Theda introduced him as her new boss, a Mr. Garner or Will Garner as he liked to be called. As he sat down the two gals got up to go powder their noses or whatever. From the way Theda brushed his face with her fingertips as they were leaving, he wondered whether she meant to come back.

Will Garner sat in the seat she'd just risen from. With his face a tad closer to the candle you could see he lived well and paid for his shaves. Longarm asked if he'd care for some coffee. The paymaster shook his head and soberly replied, "Let's get down to brass tacks. To begin I know who you are. Been expecting you. Had you figured from the moment you checked in at the Peacock's Nest."

"Is that why you won't drink coffee with us?" asked Longarm, dryly.

"Who do you think we are?" asked Foster with an eyebrow cocked.

Garner said, "You answer the descriptions of the boys who robbed that payroll down in the Anaconda Range and you've been acting, frankly, weird. You haven't applied anywhere in town for work. You obviously have money to burn. You don't know where you go from here, do you?"

Longarm quietly suggested, "Why don't you tell us where we go from here, Will?"

Will Garner said, "Off down a fork to a much smaller mining camp called Redeye. I have the number of the miner's cabin you'll want to stop by. It will look like a dozen others. You don't want to knock on any other door."

Longarm palmed the slip of paper the chubby paymaster slid across the tablecloth to him, asking, "Then what?"

Garner said, "Then you follow the directions they'll give you in Redeye to the letter. Nobody will be riding along with you to Natova. Nobody will lay out the whole route for you in advance. You'll be passed along from one stop to the next, as if you were mail pouches on the old Pony Express."

Longarm nodded and said, "Meaning we can't get out of paying as we go by passing any relay point up."

It had been a statement rather than a question, but Garner replied, "I've always admired a man who can think on his feet."

Longarm asked, "What are *you* charging for directions to Redeye, Will?"

Garner said, "A favor. Nothing but a little favor. The few

dollars I've made from time to time up to now as a mere signpost suddenly strike me as penny ante, since they put me in charge of the payroll safe instead of merely guarding the office from outside."

He shook himself free of his self-admiration to explain, "You boys are going to ride off with another big payroll. Just like you did down in the Anacondas."

The two undercover lawmen each knew what the other was thinking. They could only push their outlaw act so far.

Longarm said, "I dunno, Will. Sticking up a payroll office we've never laid eyes on sounds . . . exciting."

Garner chortled, "Nobody's asking you to go anywhere near the office. Let us worry about any tales of woe we tell. At five minutes to midnight I want you mounted up in the alley behind your hotel and ready to ride. When you get our signal I want you to ride down the center of Main Street at full gallop, firing your pistols in the air."

Longarm smiled thinly and asked, "Is that all? What's the signal for such a dramatic stage exit?"

Garner said, "Our own staged fusilade of gunshots, fired at more distant followed by every electric light in Peacock winking out. One master switch in the one powerhouse will cut the current to the whole town. Nobody will be able to see you. But a lot of them will hear you and come to think, long after you've left town, no doubt bound for Wyoming, didn't the two of you answer to the description of those riders on the dodge for another payroll robbery and . . . hell, do I have to draw the rest of it on a blackboard?"

Longarm said, "Not hardly, and so much for the wonders of modern science. How do we know you won't double-cross us?"

Will Garnet easily replied, "How do you know I don't aim to cut my nose off to spite my face? If *you* get caught *we* get caught. It's in our mutual self-interest we all get away with it. You with your freedom and me and mine, with more money than you can shake a stick at."

He let that sink in before he asked, "Well, are you in or out?"

Longarm shrugged and said, "Reckon we're in. I take it you mean to just hang tight, here, as a robbed and outraged loyal employee on the lookout for other wayward riders in need of directions?"

Garner said, "You let me worry about my own future plans. I frankly don't give a shit about yours, as long as you don't get caught."

"What if we do get caught?" asked Foster, knowing from his own experience how much honor there really was among thieves.

Garner said, "We've considered that, of course. It will be your word against ours. With you still flush with the cash from that other robbery, and me and mine upstanding citizens with stories that back each other up. That's why you've only been told the little you need to know to carry out your part of the plan."

"You're all heart," said Longarm, adding in a more sober tone, "How can we be certain you don't mean to shut us up for certain after we've provided you and yours with your devious distraction? That's what stage magicians call it when they get the audience to look the other way as they stuff the rabbit in the hat, a distraction."

Garner said, "Our little sideshow here in Peacock has nothing to do with the overall operations of what you might describe as a syndicate of extended adventurous clans. Our associates in Redeye won't know what you boys did here in Peacock before they read it in the papers like everybody else. How long do you suppose Natova would remain open for business on the sly if nobody showed up to check in?"

Since Garner likely hadn't heard of Doc Tyler and his brothers short stopping some of the cash flow, Longarm felt no call to enlighten him. He said, "Sounds about as safe as a relay race with lit sticks of dynamite. We got to get somewheres before our money runs out. You said five minutes to midnight?"

"Make certain nobody spots you leaving the hotel while you're robbing us up the slope and for God's sake don't knock on the wrong cabin door in Redeye!"

He got to his feet, adding, "Give me a head start. I don't want to be seen in your disreputable company. Your tab here's been taken care of. You might want to leave a tip. All *they* know is that a Miss Smith came by earlier to arrange a surprise party. Don't tell them anything else."

Longarm started to ask which of the whores Garner had set them up with had been Miss Smith. He decided he didn't want to know. If Theda was in deep she'd be in deep shit when the county and the mining company were tipped off. If she was only a spear carrier in the grand opera she might get off with a warning.

He couldn't help hoping she'd get off with a warning. She'd played him for a sucker, but he suspected some of what she'd said she was feeling had felt real to her as well.

After Garner left, Foster glanced about to make sure they were holding a private conversation before he asked, "Do you think they'll have a telegraph office in Redeye?"

Longarm said, "Doubt it. If they do I vote we pay out a little more line before we set the hook. Garner and his confederates will still be here a spell. If anyone along the relay route gets picked up before we make it all the way to Natova we may never make it to Natova. Crooks are a lot like cockroaches. They tend to vanish into the woodwork when you walk into the kitchen with a candlestick."

The Mountie in mufti said, "Tell me something I didn't

know. Most of the ones up the line shape up as part-time petty operators, like that bucket of slime who just left. Didn't you admire the big-shot airs he's put on since they entrusted something like a company dick with the keys to their payroll office?"

"Leave us not forget the combination to the safe. That'll be a point the prosecution will have fun with at his trial," said Longarm.

They left the fancy French restaurant, feeling better about the future for Mr. Know-It-All Garner as long as even one of them made it back from the field alive. They celebrated their good fortune and killed some suddenly heavy-hanging time at the nearby Proud Peacock, admiring the overhead electrified lights more than ever as they marveled at the way their world kept changing.

Longarm said, "I was reading in that magazine, the *Scientific American*, how common Edison bulbs and Bell's telephone may be in a hundred years or less. This writer predicts a world free of crime, once crooks have fewer dark shadows to hide in and most everyone will be able to call for the law without leaving their electrified houses."

The Canadian lawman said, "They'll find new ways to be crooked. It's the nature of some misfits to live crooked lives. I was reading about this respected doctor they just caught over in Scotland. Pillar of the community. Money in the bank. No reason at all to rob his neighbors. Yet rob them he did. Creeping about like a common cat burglar until they caught him in the act."

Longarm grimaced and said, "When you're right, you're right. It was ever thus and no doubt it always will be. But look on the bright side. Gents like you and me will always have steady jobs."

They drank to that and drank some more. Then Longarm decided they'd best get on back to the Peacock's Nest and check out, quietly.

They moved up the back stairs and saw nobody in the electrified hallways at that hour. Foster ducked into his own room to gather up his saddle and such. Longarm was about to do the same when he spied the bit of match stem on the rug outside his door. He'd wedged a match stem in the crack below the bottom hinge with just such a visible alarm in mind.

He drew his .44-40 and tried the knob gingerly with his free hand. It turned silently. The door wasn't locked, so he threw it open to follow his gun muzzle in, snapping, "Freeze!"

Then he saw it was Theda. The taffy blonde stood frozen but fully clad in a poplin travel duster and veiled riding derby. She gasped, "Where have you been? I've been waiting up here for hours, Shorty!"

Lowering the muzzle to a friendlier angle, Longarm dryly asked, "How come? Were you expecting an extra tip for services rendered?"

She said, "Don't be cruel. I came to warn you. You have to take me with you. Now. By way of the south road to Phillipsburg. Will Garner means to have you killed before you make it halfway to Redeye!"

Chapter 20

Longarm wasn't ready to put his pistol away. But he held it politely as he asked, "How come the sudden change of heart?"

Theda shook her head and said, "I only thought I was in on a robbery. Lovette recruited me just yesterday and assured me that was all they had in mind. She's Will Garner's girl. He likes to show off his high-school French with her. Neither knew I speak better French than he does. I saw no reason to tell them I could listen in on his mostly bawdy remarks. So earlier this very evening, after Will rejoined us here at the hotel, they had no way of knowing I knew what they were really saying when she said she was worried about you both getting picked up and spilling the beans. You'd have been proud of the poker face I managed as he assured her you'd never make it as far as Redeye."

Longarm replied, "I noticed last night you had some acting ability. Where did that other . . . lady recruit you, the Peacock's Tail?"

She flushed and snapped, "I should have let them kill you! If you must know I've been stranded here, owing two weeks rent and . . . all right, a girl may be easier to lead down the primrose path when she's really desperate. But I swear I never knew they planned on *hurting* anyone!"

Longarm's bridle and saddle gun were naturally fixed to the stock saddle draped over the foot of the bed. As he holstered his six-gun and hefted the heavier load he said, "We can continue this conversation on our way to the stable. Where's your baggage and what were you expecting to ride tonight?"

As he peered out the doorway to make sure the hall was clear Theda told him, "My things are with my own mount, out back. I was going to ride out of this den of thieves in any case. But I thought it best to warn you, if only for . . . sentimental reasons."

Figuring Foster had already left by then, Longarm led the way on the balls of his feet. Theda made no noise on the thick carpeting trailing after him. Neither dared to speak as they made it down the stairs and out the back way to the dark stables, where a familar voice softly called out, "That you, Shorty?"

Longarm said, "Not hardly. I'm the Ghost of Christmas Past and I've brought another spirit along. Where's the night watchman?"

Foster said, "Under the haystack, fast asleep. The nightcap I offered him when I came out to see to our army bays worked faster than you said it would. Why did you bring that . . . guest along?"

Longarm said, "She just told me Garner means to do us dirty on the way to Redeye. They didn't spell the whole murdersome plot out for her in detail. But I suspect they mean to hep themselves to our money as well as the contents of the company safe and allow us to just sort of vanish from human ken."

Foster sighed, "Whom can one trust in this wicked world? What did you have in mind to turn the tables on them?"

Longarm said, "We play dumb and go along with the first instructions. They'd be sure to wonder if we failed to go along with Garner's stage directions. So we'd best lead our mounts along the alley outside and mount up to ride out whooping and shooting in the sudden darkness."

"Into a perishing trap?" asked Foster.

Longarm said, "Not hardly. Garner won't want his boys, likely company dicks, dropping us handy to town as the rest of Peacock posses up to ride after us. So here's what we're going to do."

Theda said he was mad, mad, mad and Foster expressed some doubts until Longarm allowed he was open to a better suggestion.

When none were forthcoming he said, "Right. Let's get cracking."

So they did. Theda's roan Tennessee Walker was sidesaddled with her carpetbags on board. The three of them led their mounts along the alley and mounted up just outside the artificial dawn provided by Mr. Thomas Alva Edison to those few in town who could afford it as yet.

It seemed to take longer. Then every light near and far in Peacock winked off, to plunge everyone and everything into a deep pit of total darkness.

Longarm shouted, "Powder River and let her buck!" as he tore out of the alley, shooting up at the stars at full gallop.

Foster followed close behind, making just as much noise, while Theda rode blind, screaming fit to bust as she clung to the leg brace of her sidesaddle at full gallop.

They never would have made it down the middle of Main Street on foot, running that fast, blind. But horses see almost good as cats in the dark having revolved from grazing critters preyed on by lions and such.

No serious lamplight appeared at any dark window they tore past in the dark, albeit here and there a match sputtered and above the general babble they heard somebody shouting, "Who turned off all the fucking electricity?"

Then they were out of town with empty six-guns, reining in and laughing until Longarm said, "All right. Simmer down and show some damned poise as you follow my lead."

Theda sobbed, "It's not going to work," but she fell in between her male companions as the three of them rode back the way they'd just come at a sedate slow trot.

As they rode back into town Main Street was crowded with folks milling in the darkness and abuzz with conflicting suggestions. Slowing his bay to a walk, Longarm asked anyone who might be listening what in blue blazes was up.

Somebody yelled back, "Ain't certain! Nobody can get the damned lights back on. Somebody just said something about a robbery! Gang rode out of here just minutes ago! Headed north-west towards Fort Missoula!"

"Is *that* who just tore past us as we rid in the other way?" marveled Longarm, calling out to Theda, "You hear that, old woman?"

She didn't answer. She sat frozen mute in her sidesaddle as Longarm led them south along the crowded thoroughfare. Nobody challenged folk coming *into* town and by the time they were headed *out* of town, to the *east*, that wasn't the way those outlaws had been headed. The streetlights switched on as if by magic as the two men and a gal passed the last shop windows on Main Street. A bewildered older man with a shotgun came out of a suddenly lit-up doorway to ask them what on Earth was going on, dad blast it.

Longarm called out in an uncertain tone, "They say there was a robbery up the other end of town. Gang tore out of town to the west. That's all we know. We've been riding around in the dark a spell."

The man with the shotgun tore north along the walk to get in on the excitement, whatever it might be. They rode east past the last street lamp, with the windows of private homes to either side still glowing with that same newfangled shade of artificial light. It was Foster who said, "You Yanks are so quick to discard older toys. I'll bet you can't find a common coal-oil lamp in any of those new homes."

Theda made a noise midways betwixt a sob and a laugh before she said, "You had no way of knowing that for certain before you took such a terrible chance back there!"

Longarm said, "Six or eight lit lamps wouldn't have made much difference. Might have added to the confusion, as a matter of fact. Farther along in the future someone better invent electrified lights you can switch on without having to draw current from a wall plug. I doubt Will Garner will be the only crook who spots that weakness in the wonders of modern science. Somebody always does. The Reno brothers never could have invented train robbing if nobody had invented trains."

As they rode at a walk their eyes began to adjust to the light of a low quarter moon. It sure beat all how electric shocks blurred your night vision. As they rode, Longarm wasn't really listening to the tale Theda spun about an adventurous young thing having more adventures out west than she'd bargained for. He was watching the trace ahead for a brook they'd forded, coming up from Sliderock. He wasn't certain, but he thought there'd been a pony track following her downstream.

By the time they got there, Longarm had been counting coins in the dark with his fingers. Once the three of them were safely across, Longarm called a halt and handed the adventurous Theda five double eagles as he told her, "This is where we part company, Miss Theda. Phillipsburg is too far south for you to ride alone. Ride upstream to Clarkside, where you can catch a stage or ask for a job at the Last Chance. Say I sent you."

She protested, "I can't take *money* from you, Shorty! Don't you see what that would make me?"

He said, "Ain't paying you for last night. This is partly because you likely saved our hides *tonight* and, well, let's say you could use it."

She asked where they were headed.

He said, "You let us worry about that, Miss Theda. It's been good to know you and we all have some riding ahead of us. So *vaya con Dios* and *mucho gusto*, hear?"

She softly asked, "Do you have a real name I can . . . remember you by, Shorty?"

He soberly said, "Think of me as Percival and now you know why I like to be known as Shorty."

She sighed and said, "I'll never forget you, Percival!"

Foster waited until she'd ridden out of earshot before he snorted, "Percival? Can't you ever be serious?"

Longarm shrugged and asked, "What'll you bet she made up 'Theda'? This creek has to run into the nearby Clark. This pony track along it has to mean a handy ford. If we don't drown fording her in the dark we ought to be able to work our way 'round Garner's ambush, which figures to be east of that fork out of the way to Redeye."

As they moved single file along the creekside pony track, Foster called out, "I can see how we might make it to

Redeye the long way 'round. But what happens when we never ride into Garner's ambush?"

Longarm said, "I'm hoping he'll figure we smelled a rat and never tried for her. If I'm right about these jaspers, Garner has no way to get in touch with any relay in Fort Missoula, even if he wants to. He has no call to want to, once he sees that posse never caught us."

"Or so you hope," muttered the Mountie, adding, "Why go to Redeye at all? What if they're in on Garner's plot?"

Longarm said, "They ain't. If he let anybody else up the line know he was in business on his own as a payroll robber they'd want a slice of the pie. The two-faced cuss is acting as they'd expect one of their travel agents to act. The address he gave us in Redeye is likely the one he'd be expected to give us, in the unlikely event we made it past his ambush so let's get past his ambush."

They did, but it wasn't easy. Fording the whitewater Clark in the dark felt spooky, even at a clearly oft-used ford. On the far side, as they'd hoped, another, albeit less traveled, wagon trace served the needs of homesteads and stock spreads on the north bank of the Clark. During a trail break, with the help of a carefully cupped match, they could see by a survey map from Longarm's saddle bags how the alternate trail grew in time into a right handy route to Fort Missoula near the junction of the Clark and Blackfoot Rivers to their west–north-west.

But first they had to make it to Redeye, south of the infernal Clark. So with the help of the same match-lit map they worked their way west of that fork Garner had told them about, forded the Clark the other way, and got themselves good and lost in the tangle of secondary trails upslope and south of the east-west wagon trace everybody had expected them to follow, they hoped.

It was getting harder to navigate by the stars above as

said stars commenced winking out against an ever-lighter sky.

Summer dawns came early in the high country at that latitude. But a few stars still winked down at them as they spotted brighter lamplight through the trees ahead.

Longarm called out, "Hello, yonder homestead!" as they rode closer, lest they ride undeclared into proddy buckshot in such uncertain country.

Closer in, they saw the lamplight spilled out an open barn door and a yard dog was barking fit to bust until the old-timer who'd been milking the family cow appeared in the doorway in silhouette.

The homesteader hushed his hound and called out, "Who's yonder?"

Dismounting just outside of easy pistol range, Longarm called back, "Grub line riders bound for Redeye. Might this trace run that way?"

The old-timer said, "Sooner or later. Must be going on twelve miles. Stick with me out here and I'll see you on your way with some breakfast in you. Old lady's still slugabed in the cabin."

As they joined him in the doorway, on foot, he turned back to his milking, muttering, "Durned old cows. You'd think they'd keep natural hours, like chickens."

They were country enough not to ask dumb questions. Anyone who didn't have milk delivered to their city door knew cows were milked at three or four in the morning and three or four in the afternoon. They liked to graze some after their afternoon milking.

As he milked, the old-timer naturally asked where they'd rid in from.

"Phillipsburg," said Longarm, which was close enough when you studied on it. From the easy way the old-timer swallowed that, they figured nobody had been by spreading gossip about them, yet.

Once he'd half filled his bucket and picked up his lantern to lead them to his cabin door, the homesteader observed, "No offense, but I'd say you've rid them bays a piece. You ain't likely to make Redeye this side of hell freezing over on them jaded horses."

Longarm said, "We were just talking about that. It ain't as if we're on the run, you understand, but we do have important business in Redeye. What did you have in mind?"

The old-timer said, "First we'll eat and then we'll talk. I got a few cow ponies I've been meaning to sell or swap. Got 'em off others in a hurry to ride north. They're a tad frisky for me and the old woman. I can show 'em to you after breakfast, if you like."

So they enjoyed an early breakfast of bacon and sourdough biscuits and rode east at first light aboard a buckskin and a chestnut with a white blaze and four matching stockings. They both seemed full of vinegar but neither stood more than fourteen hands at the withers.

Foster, riding the buckskin, grumbled, "I hope you know that old gypsy got the better of us by half. Those were good cavalry brutes we parted with back there!"

Longarm said, "Jaded cavalry brutes, and leave us not forget Garner will have told an uncertain number of assassins we don't know they're to watch for two poor suckers riding army bays."

"Along this other route?" mused Foster.

"Along any damned route we choose," said Longarm, adding, "It ain't as we're set to recognize them on sight. So let the bastards guess who we might be if they're laying for us in Redeye!"

Chapter 21

Redeye was an ominously small as well as out-of-the-way detour. Knowing how strange hands fit in to the local saloon crowd at high noon, and seeing the old-timer who'd swapped them cow ponies had allowed he'd had 'em a time, they stopped by a smithee open for business on the one street of Redeye you could call a street to ask for a professional opinion.

The smithee was less curious and anxious to do business than anyone at the saloon might have been. He said Foster's buckskin needed to be reshod for certain and added it wouldn't hurt the chestnut to renail that off hind shoe. So Longarm left Foster there with the riding stock as he mosied up among the miner's cabins clinging to a bodacious slope to see if that old pal of theirs still lived in Redeye.

A once-pretty drab with eyes too old for her thirty-year-old face came to the door in a thin, threadbare shift to tell him her man was on the day shift, down in the mine. When

Longarm told her he'd been sent by a pal in Peacock—Garner had said not to offer any names—she told him to come on in and set a spell.

When he followed her inside she pointed at a corner cot and asked him, "Want to fuck, seeing my man won't be home before six?"

Longarm took a seat by the deal table instead as he soberly allowed that whilst her offer was sure tempting he had a pal waiting down the slope.

She said, "Have him come on up and I'll fuck you both. I fuck good and I only charge four bits a jiggle. Fuck you both for one dollar extra. Be a sport. My man don't give me none of the money you traveling men pay him for directions to Fort Missoula."

As the penny dropped Longarm got out a shiny golden eagle and snapped it flat on the greasy pine, saying, "That hardly seems fair, ma'am. You keeping house so fine for him. Would you like to make an easy ten dollars for yourself?"

She nodded without thinking, then thought a moment, and asked suspiciously, "I don't have to do nothing that might hurt, do I?"

He said, "Not hardly. My pal and me are in a hurry and like you said, your man won't be home until supper time. So why don't I pay you to tell us where we go from here?"

She cackled like an old hag and said, "You must think I was behind the door when the brains was passed out! You know full well my man charges riders like you fifty dollars, each, to steer them on to the next stop."

Longarm quickly recovered his edge by soothing, "I only meant we'd give you ten dollars *extra* for saving us all that time. I wasn't out to *cheat* nobody. A hundred and ten dollars it is, for you to send us on our way. You said the next . . . relay station would be in the county seat up ahead?"

She nodded but said, "I ain't supposed to know such things."

"But you do, don't you?" he insisted.

She said, "Well, sure. I got ears and there's only these four walls. But I ain't *supposed* to know and did I offer my man all that money he'd know I knew, wouldn't he?"

"If you gave him the money," Longarm soberly replied.

The still fairly young woman with an old woman's eyes stared off into what a drab stuck in her position might do with 110, or more than an honest mining man made in a month. Longarm didn't press her. He knew what she was thinking.

She licked her lips and pleaded, "You won't tell, will you? He only beats me when he finds out I've been fucking for pin money. Lord knows what he might do if he thought I was interfering in *his* sideline."

Longarm answered, simply, "If you steer us straight he'll never know we stopped by. If you give us a bum steer we'll be back. It's not that hard a cup of tea leaves to read, ma'am."

She said, "There's this boarding house in Missoula, run by a sweet old Dutch widow woman they call Mother Kelly, Keller, some Dutch name like so. They say her boarding house is on the old officers' row by the municipal corral. That's all I know for certain, and he'll kill me if he finds out I told you that much!"

Longarm said in that case they'd best not tell her man and as he counted out the hundred and ten dollars in eagles and double eagles her eyes got younger, and she asked if he was sure he didn't want to fuck her before he left.

He gallantly declined in the interest of brevity and left her to her own sudden options, idly wondering if she'd be there when her man got home expecting supper.

Rejoining Foster at the smithee, he found both ponies

were ready to go. Foster had already settled up. Casting a thoughtful eye at a grayer sky than they'd planned a day with, Longarm said, "Looks like we're in for some rain."

The friendly smithee volunteered, "I admire understatement, or mayhaps you boys are new to our hills. When she rains in the Rockies, this time of the year, you ain't talking about *rain*. You're talking about thunder, lightning, wind and hail. How far you boys fixing to ride this afternoon?"

Longarm said, "We were headed for your county seat across the Blackfoot. Reckon we'll make her by sundown. Mayhaps a little after?"

The blacksmith shook his head and said, "Not if she gullywashes this afternoon. The Blackfoot's only one of the whitewater streams that cross your path from here. When they're running high you just don't try to ford 'em. If I was you I'd hole up and wait her out."

The two undercover lawmen exchanged glances. Longarm asked if there was a hotel there in Redeye.

The friendly local shook his head and said, "Your best bet would be the Bar Four spread just out of town to the north. Cattle outfit as offers grub and a roof overhead to passers-by at reasonable rates. I understand they got plenty of spare bunks betwixt roundups, when they do take on extra hands. Tell 'em I sent you and they'll treat you right. I shoe a lot of their ponies and I always treat *them* right."

They shook on it and parted friendly. The blacksmith had said the Bar Four was just outside of town. They'd both broken out their oilcloth slickers by the time they rode in under a darkening sky with rolling thunder coming ever closer.

It started raining as they dismounted in the dooryard. The blacksmith's observations about Rocky Mountain thunderstorms had not been off by much. If they hadn't donned their slickers in time they'd have been soaked to the skin by the time they made it to the long veranda running along the front of the main house. Two Indian kids stripped to their waists ran out to gleefully lead their already waterlogged mounts somewhere. As the two undercover lawmen stepped up on the veranda, both beating their soaked-through hats against their thighs, a handsome ash-blonde in calico came out to make them welcome, saying, "Come right in and shuck those slickers, boys. You look like you could use some hot toddies!"

It would have sounded dumb to remark on hot toddies being a usual dead-of-winter drink. When you got soaked at high altitude it felt cold as Christmas any day of the year.

They shucked their slickers just inside the door and hung their hats with them on pegs driven into the wall of peeled logs. The obvious lady of the house took in their trail-worn denim and six-guns without showing approval or disapproval and said, "Come on back to the kitchen with me. I'd be Fran Moorheart. I keep house here for my dad and uncles. We'll have plenty of room at the supper table if this storm lasts the night. Most of the outfit's in Fort Missoula, at the courthouse. Our sheriff is such an old fuss."

Back in the kitchen the grinning cook was already mixing the hot toddies he'd been told to. Longarm didn't ask if he was any relation to his old pal, Fong, down Sliderock way. You found Chinese cooks and laundry men all over the west for the same reasons you never found them working in a mine. It was widely held nobody could beat a Chinese at cooking or washing most anything. So he was welcome to work at tasks the good Lord had obviously intended for the sons of Han. Just so long as he never unfair advantage of white men by working harder at mining or construction.

Longarm had read somewhere about the British discovering hot toddies in India, where they were made with ice-water and the same rum with brown sugar. They tasted way better hot, when you needed a quick warm up.

As they gratefully accepted her hospitality Fran Moorheart reminded them she hadn't caught their names.

Longarm said he was called Blacky, whilst they called his sidekick Curly. Foster didn't ask how come. It seemed obvious Shorty and Moe, like Buck and Dusty before them, had ridden far enough along the Owlhoot Trail.

To change the subject "Blacky" asked how come their hostess found the local sheriff an old fuss.

She said two of their riders had been arrested. Her dad and his brothers, along with their foreman, had naturally ridden in to the county seat to go out on bail or, failing the judge granting bail, to see the boys got a quick, fair trial.

It was Foster who asked what her riders were charged with. He was new to West Montana cattle customs.

Longarm's hot toddy suddenly lost some warmth as she easily replied, "They had to shoot a Flathead. Caught him red-handed, butchering one of our steers. Some of them can't seem to get it in their flat heads we're not raising elk on the Bar Four."

She sighed and went on in a tone of sweet reason, "Even if we were raising elk they know perfectly well they're supposed to wait until we sell stock to their agency before they eat it."

Each undercover lawman knew perfectly well what the other was thinking. So neither answered as they buried their noses in their toddy mugs.

The so-called Flathead Indians on the western slopes of the Continental Divide had been there first and had perfectly natural-looking heads. They were more accurately described as Chinook. They were natural-born traders who acted as middlemen betwixt more stay-at-home nations of the Pacific North West and those on the Eastern slopes of the divide. Their dialect, classified as Penutian by the Bureau of Indian Affairs, had been larded with the words of French, English and other Indian dialects into a commonly used trade pidgin known as Chinook. They were blamed for the so-called Chinook winds blowing weirdly warm some winters because they were the ones who'd first warned early mountain men about that freakish and dangerous winter wind they called "the Snow Burner" in their own words. Professors who studied freak weather explained the fortunately rare mid-winter "Chinook Winds" as heavy moist winter air moving off the Pacific to drop tons of snow on the western slopes of the divide and then spill over the Rockies dry and thinner, to warm up as it compressed at ever-lower altitudes. The effects were more awesome than scientific.

The wide-ranging Chinook traders had been dubbed "Flatheads" by their Penutian cousins, who followed the odd custom of binding their newborn infants' skulls betwixt their cradle board and a flat plank to distort their bitty skull into what they regarded as handsome points that added some to their standing height as adults. They'd naturally regarded the Chinook who'd failed to follow this sensible custom as runts with flat heads and early mountain men and traders had passed the endearment along.

Since Chinook were known as wandering, usually friendly traders north and south of the Canadian border, Longarm and his Mountie pals shared warm feelings toward so-called Flatheads. Since it was still raining fire and salt outside, neither thought this was the time to lecture any cattle woman on tolerance and Christian charity, and, in fairness, anybody with a lick of sense, red or white, knew better than to let people catch you butchering beef on their own range.

Hoping in vain for a break in the storm, the undercover

lawmen wound up having supper in the bodacious dining room with the ash blonde in charge, some household staff of varied gender and ancestry and of course their octet of top hands.

Common cowboys got fed back nigh their bunkhouse. Top hands did not consider themselves common cowboys. They tended to quit when you treated them as such. It was understood a top hand worked only at chores he could manage on top of a horse. Asking him to dig a post hole was like calling him a Mexican, while asking him to pile manure was considered worse than calling him a pathetic accident born out of wedlock. "They handed me a shovel" was the top hand's way of saying he'd been fired. No owner who wanted a top hand to stick around ever treated him like common hired help.

The current wages of a top hand were forty dollars a month with food and shelter fit for a white man. It was easier to let him dine with the owner and household staff than cope with the complaints one was certain to hear if one couldn't see for oneself what the boys had been fed every evening on the home spread.

That evening they got served noodle soup, steak and potatoes with collard greens, along with serviceberry pie with rat-trap cheese and Arbuckle brand coffee. It was still blowing wet and wild outside when Longarm and Foster turned in for the night with the boys in the bunkhouse.

The summer storm front hadn't extended as far south as Helena, but His Copper Majesty was rumbling like distant thunder as he stayed up past his own bedtime, going over the survey maps he'd had them bring to his den.

As Vance Larson grumbled and rumbled, another company security hand who was paid to put up with His Copper Majesty's temper tried to convince him in a more reasonable tone, "I don't see how that Omaha cardshark you're so concerned about could have inspired those Granite County lawmen to kill Keystone and McCord by mistake, sir. Even if he could have, it was days ago and by now he and that other rider we don't know at all could be most anywhere on the far side of the divide!"

Vance Larson rumbled, "I don't care where the tricky bastard might be. I want his head on a stick. You don't know what we're up against, Nutmeg. You've yet to see him wave his magic wand. Those possemen who mistook our riders for other killers were somehow slickered by our Mr. Armstrong D. Weddington, and they were only out that way in the first place on my orders to bring me his head!"

"When do you want me and mine to ride, sir?" asked the killer from Connecticut by way of Texas.

His Copper Majesty growled, "At daybreak, with me, in my private coach, swapping teams every chance we get. I'm tired of sitting here like a patient orb spider in its web. I mean to go after the bastard in person, like one of those hairy, poison wolf spiders!"

Chapter 22

A Bar Four rider brought word to Fran Moorheart the next morning that her dad and uncles were still trying to bail the boys out and meant to stay in the county seat a spell. So Fran decided that since the storm had blown over and Lord only knew what they served for dessert at the Drover's Rest in Missoula, it behooved her to deliver some of the fresh baked serviceberry pie she was famous for.

Longarm and Foster would have been proud to take care of the chore for her, seeing they owed her. But she allowed she was overdue some shopping in the decomissioned army post that was not the county seat.

That summer storm had blown over, but the white-water Clark joined up with the brawling Blackfoot a bend upstream from Fort Missoula to leave the ford in full flood, due to all that recent rain.

So fording the saddle-high whitewater as a soggy nightmare, with Fran Mooreheart blessing her stars and "Blacky" when he got her across only soaked to her hips by holding her down on her sidesaddle whilst Foster led her mount by its reins, with the foaming current washing across their ponies' spines.

Once they got her to her Dad's hotel across the old parade from all the fuss, Longarm and Foster tethered their own new ponies out front of a nearby saloon to wet their whistles, get their bearing, and ask directions to Mother Kelly, Keller or whomsoever's boarding house.

The fort was the county seat, but it was a small county seat on the west slope of the divide, and strangers riding in drew notice. So even as they stepped up on the plank walk in front of the saloon, one of the Missoula County deputies lounging across the way observed, "Did you see how close them strangers match the description we just got on them birds who robbed that payroll over to Peacock? Same description we've had a time on a tall, dark drink of water with a mustache and a lighter smooth-shaven sidekick!"

The calmer deputy at his side snorted, "You surely are observant, old son. Anyone can see one of them Bar Four riders has a mustache whilst the other one don't. After that the birds who flew off with the payroll of the Peacock mine were riding matched army bays, not fool cow ponies, and one doubts either was on the payroll of Big Malcolm Moorheart."

The more hasty man-hunter flustered, "They ride for Big Malcolm?"

His overconfident pal said, "Saw 'em ride in with Big Malcolm's daughter, Miss Fran, not more than twenty minutes ago. That's how come all three of them are still soaked from their hips down. You can tell when anyone crosses the Clark, right now."

And so neither Longarm nor Foster would ever know how close they'd come to some tedious explaining, if they'd been lucky. But with a view to just such an interview down the road apiece they'd decided to call themselves Pat and Mike for the time being. Nobody would have told Mother Kelly, Keller or whomsoever to expect anyone by any name that morning.

It turned out to be Krieger. Longarm learned this on the sly by just asking the friendly barkeep to list boarding houses in the neighborhood. When he got to the Krieger place across from the municipal corral, Longarm didn't see who else worked as well.

Mother Krieger had a slight accent and a pronounced limp. She had white hair and favored her gimp leg with a cane. She allowed she'd been expecting them, by any names, and added with a toothless smile, "You two have so busy been. What took you so long from Peacock to ride?"

Longarm knew better than to deny the story their murderous pal, Will Garner, had doubtless told more than one newspaper reporter. He shrugged modestly and asked, "Where do we go from here, Mother Kreiger?"

She said, "No place, for a time. Around to the coach house take your ponies and tell my stable boy I said to make nice. Then to the back door come and I will you to your rooms show."

Longarm asked, "How come you expect us to stay awhile, ma'am? Me and Mike, here, are riding sort of anxious."

The old Dutch landlady replied, "Here nobody will bother you and on the trail it's dangerous to ride. The army is in force out to the north. They are every trail patroling and signaling back and forth with those things that flash."

"Signal Corps heliographs?" marveled Longarm, who'd patrolled some in his time. Foster asked whatever for.

Mother Krieger said, "Indians. Sioux. Back down from Canada, some say."

Before Longarm could stop him the Canadian lawman

mused out loud, "Sioux refugees camped on the Alberta plains on this side of the border again, west of the continental divide? Makes no sense. Friendly Chinook would never side with them and even if they would, those hostiles would have to get through their deadly enemies, the Blackfoot!"

"So much about Indians you know?" said the old woman, smiling.

Longarm said, "He reads too much. Let's get our ponies under cover and leave such worries to the army, Mike."

Once they were out of earshot Foster murmured, "Sorry. Lost my head. But it still makes no sense. Who could your cavalry be hunting?"

Longarm shrugged and offered, "El Dorado or the Big Rock Candy Mountains. Some greenhorn spied a cloud on the horizon and reported it as yet another hostile smoke signal. You Canadians didn't share in the Great Sioux Scare of our Centennial Summer. After Custer went under at Little Bighorn, settlers scattered in smaller numbers under a suddenly bigger sky got to seeing hostiles in every shifting shadow and hearing war cries with every shift of the wind."

As they gathered the reins of their ponies out front he added, "Your cantankerous prime minister sheltering Sitting Bull and his boys didn't cheer folk up down this way. I wish I had a dollar for every newspaper article warning us all those bloodthirsty savages are about to descend on us across your border!"

As they led their mounts around to the carriage house, Foster asked how such rumors might apply to their situation."

Longarm replied, "It wouldn't, if Mother Krieger wasn't fixing to steer us on to Indian country. Or there was another relay this side of the so-called Flathead Reserve. If

I've got the survey map straight in my own head, we're about one cavalry etape south of Arlee Agency."

Foster frowned and asked, "That far south of the border?"

Longarm nodded and said, "We're west of the divide. Not much of this side settled, yet. So the B.I.A. in its infinite wisdom has set aside enough Indian territory to qualify as a modest state, back east. Half or more ain't been surveyed yet. Nobody worried about Chinook getting lost in the hills."

He thought and added, "I reckon there's a hundred and seventy or eighty miles of Indian territory betwixt the Arlee Agency and the border. Of course, there's other agencies and trading posts scattered across the same. I suspect they'll be spread out more as we follow directions north."

"You mean these relay stops along the Owlhoot Trail are being operated right on reservation land, under the noses of your Bureau of Indian Affairs?"

Longarm shrugged and said, "I doubt anyone in Washington's all that interested. As you'll see, all sorts of so-called improvements are run by licensed white folk across reservation lands. That famous gunfight at Blazer's Mill took place on the Mescalero Reservation, down New Mexico way. Tunstall-McSween riders shot it out with Buckshot Roberts, a Murphy-Dolan rider, at a sawmill run by a dentist named Blazer. Not one Indian had a hand in the shootout. Judge Parker, over to Fort Smith, keeps hanging white outlaws hiding out in the Indian Territory. Met this old bawd called Belle Starr, running a regular outlaw hotel at Younger's Bend on Cherokee land. But that's another story."

They handed the ponies over to the stable boy who in point of fact admitted he was pure Chinook, and headed back to the house.

Mother Krieger served them coffee and cake in her kitchen, but turned them over to another Chinook, this one she-male, so she wouldn't have to lead them up the stairs on her gimp leg.

The Indian gal said her name was Marie and proudly added she was a good Roman Catholic, educated by the Black Robes at their mission to the Chinook named for Saint Ignatius Loyola. After that she looked to be around twenty and could have been considered pretty by anyone who cared for smiling moon faces and slanty eyes.

The separate rooms she showed them to were modest in size but clean-smelling, with narrow but soft enough beds. Marie didn't have to tell them the rooms were meant for single occupancy. She said they'd be serving dinner downstairs at noon and added that they'd hear the dinner bell if they paid any attention at all.

Once that was settled they both went back out to the carriage house to haul their saddles and possibles upstairs where they'd be tougher to mess with. That left them with time to kill. So they went out on foot to explore the neighborhood some.

There wasn't much to explore in what there was of Fort Missoula. They'd already wet their whistles enough before noon, so they got back before anybody rang a dinner bell.

Longarm had taught Foster his matchstick-under-the-hinge trick so they both knew at a glance, as soon as they were back upstairs, that both rooms had been tossed while they were out.

Nothing had been taken, but their saddle bags had been emptied out and then repacked by somebody trying to remember where everything went and not quite managing.

Foster suspected their landlady had meant to skim some of the profits from the two robberies she'd chided them about. Longarm wasn't certain. He said, "Other riders of the Owlhoot Trail wouldn't be as anxious to ride this way if word got around your property wasn't safe. Like I said before, the crooks passing us along in turn are smarter playing square."

Foster cocked a brow to ask, "Like Doc Tyler, Will Garner and that cheating drab in Redeye?"

Longarm smiled sheepishly but insisted, "Doc Tyler wasn't a member. He'd horned in on his own. Will Garner never robbed us. He asked us to rob his boss."

"Before he set us up to have us killed," the Canadian pointed out.

Longarm said, "Only to cover what he'd done from others up and down the line. Had we been dry-gulched on our way from Peacock to Redeye it would have looked like we'd been given the right steer but ran into trouble with road agents. Nobody could have said Will hadn't done right by us in Peacock. As for that pathetical gal with the mean husband, she ain't supposed to be a paid-up member of her man's gang, and, what the hell, it ain't as if she done *us* wrong."

Shutting his bedroom door with a fresh matchstick under its hinge he declared, "Let's go eat. It was just as likely one of the other boarders staying here, and, what the hell, nobody tumbled toward our sneaky gunbelts when they had the drop on us."

Foster pointed out that the dinner bell hadn't rung. Longarm said, "Gives us a chance to scout the other boarders as we await the magic moment down in the front parlor."

So they went down the stairs in single file, resisting the impulse to fiddle with their gunbelts. Both held a considerable number of gold coins pressed flat with rims touching between thin layers of what appeared to be one thickness of heavy hide. Only some of what seemed to be decorative nickel-plated studs were snaps that held what amounted to long leather envelopes together, threaded through their holsters and buckled securely as any other gunbelts.

They didn't get to wait long with the motley group in the front parlor. They'd barely said "Howdy" when the dinner bell rang in the next door dining room, cutting conversation short.

But once they'd all filed in and taken their places around the long table, Longarm was able to sort two fair-looking gals from the seven all told, and the other eight strangers were male. Five dressed like they worked in town, with three dressed more cow.

Nobody there was citified enough for small talk while they ate dinner. But Longarm was able to establish that the two good-looking gals were called Edna and Gert. The two gents in riding dugs worked at the nearby municipal corral. The others held clerical or sales jobs in town. None of them were connected with government or law. Longarm did not find this surprising.

Mother Krieger presided as hostess at the head of her table. They were served by Marie and a younger breed gal with more white blood. She wasn't any better looking.

Mother Krieger's menu was Franconian Dutch, but nobody noticed. That tidal wave of High Dutch immigrants that had worried some so at the time of the Mexican War had melted in better than some, and by their second generation in the melting pot most everybody thought of High Dutch baking as American as apple pie, whilst everyone but visiting Englishmen knew regular draft beer was supposed to taste like foaming lager.

After their American pie dessert Mother Krieger got "Pat and Mike" aside to sweetly ask both not to wander about outside anymore whilst they waited for the coast to clear to the north.

She said, "Stronger than beer we have to serve you,

here. So no need have you to mix with ruffians in the saloon around the corner."

She hesitated, then slyly added, "If girls you like you don't away from home need to look. Girls also lonesome become, so far from their home town they work, now. If you like I can see if I can to such lonesome girls introduce you, ja?'

Longarm asked how lonely Gert or Edna might feel.

She shook her head and asked, "Such girls you think I would have as *boarders*? Just promise you'll stay home like good boys and let me worry about who you may later be introduced to, ja?"

Longarm allowed he'd pass on her kind offer, saying he'd noticed she had a swell bookcase in her front parlor.

But Foster said, "Speak for yourself! You did say we faced a hundred and eighty miles of thinly populated Indian country to the north, did you not?"

Mother Krieger grinned like a dirty old woman and asked him, "You want a lonesome pretty girl to call on you after supper?"

To which Foster soberly replied, "I'm hardly in the market for a lonesome pretty *boy*!"

Chapter 23

In spite of the way she'd switched sides, Longarm was still vexed about the way Theda had led him on in Peacock. So he whiled away the afternoon in his room upstairs with books selected from the well-stocked parlor. They were all in English in spite of what Mother Krieger said about her late and High Dutch husband reading every one of them. Longarm wasn't all that surprised. Western travelers as early as the days of the Texas Republic had remarked on how settlers from the Prussian kaiser's ever-growing and ever-stiffer Germanic Empire seemed more ready than some to adopt American ways, even as they influenced the hell out of them.

The old immigrant had been interested in natural history and geology, with some of his books about the makeup of the very mountains all around. So Longarm applied himself to the same. You could never know too much about the Rocky Mountains.

Nobody knew that much and each new survey turned up

hitherto unknown peaks, parks, watersheds and glaciers that would have stuck out like sore thumbs if they hadn't been mixed with so much of the same. Those folk who studied mountain ranges by postcard tended to picture the Rockies as a sort of giant backbone running from Alaska down to Central America. But they were really a confusion of lonesome peaks and ranges long enough to rate their own countries, running every damned way to either side of the uncertainly defined continental divide. The whole shebang could be three to five hundred miles or more across. The Scotch Highlands or the Swiss Alps could have hidden in stretches not yet mapped. Trying to guess where he'd hide that robber's roost of Natova where the divide and the piled-up jumble draining east or west crossed the international border would have been nigh impossible with detailed contour maps. All Longarm could see for certain was over three hundred miles of torn-up planet to hide it in, mostly west of the divide, like Foster had said, and most likely east of still-active Fort Colville near the border, if the route ahead led north through the vast Indian country. Foster had made mention of that one poor cuss fleeing across glaciers. That at least put his escape route closer to the divide, higher where it crossed into Canada than further south.

Longarm gave up and settled on a novel about Eastern Indians by Fennimore Cooper. It made more sense than "Hiawatha."

When he got to go back down to supper neither Gert nor Edna were at the table. Gentlemen callers had taken them both to supper at fancier restaurants in town. Plainer gals paying for room and board got to eat in boarding-house dining rooms.

After supper Longarm smoked a cheroot out on the front porch as the sun went down. When that didn't work he went back in the parlor where one of the plainer gals was browsing at that bookcase. Her hair was the color of those fuzz-balls you see under beds. There were no scars or serious distortions to her undistinguished features and her figure wasn't bad if a man hadn't had any for a spell.

He asked if she'd read either of the Jane Austen novels in the bookcase. She had, along with everything on tap by the Brontë sisters. She allowed with a sigh she was bored, bored, bored by her career as a manicurist in a two-chair barber shop in a one-horse town.

He'd promised Mother Krieger he wouldn't go out on the streets of Fort Missoula, spoiling one easier way to get started. When he asked if she'd like to set out on the porch swing and see if she might spot a wishing star in the darkening sky, she said there were night-flying bugs and bats inclined to tangle their wings in a maiden's hair.

He felt no call to argue. Gals who believed bats gave a hang about their hair were inclined to hold out for Prince Charming on a white horse. Nothing a man might manage with a plain and simple gal who'd read all those books by the Brontë sisters was likely to be worth the discomforts of waking up in bed with one in the cold gray dawn.

He said something about not wanting to stink up the parlor with his tobacco fumes and went back out on the porch. He sat on the steps instead of the swing. No bugs bothered him. No bats got in his hair. When he went back inside the plain gal with dust-bunny hair wasn't there.

He met Mother Kreiger in the hall. She said she'd just received good news. Someone riding in from the Arlee Agency had told her that army column had packed it in and were headed west to Fort Colville. She said, "That Indian fright everyone has been listening for includes night riders, *nicht wahr*?"

He asked how much he owed her. She said they'd settle

up after breakfast in the morning. He didn't argue. He went upstairs and turned in, wondering if he'd missed anything by turning down the dirty old lady's offer to fix him up.

Out in the loft of the carriage house, Crown Sergeant Foster would have said Longarm had. Her name was Lilo, she'd said, and after that she was a pneumatic natural blonde with a thicker High Dutch accent than Mother Krieger's. She said she rented the loft. She might have been telling the truth. If their landlady had sent out for Lilo, Foster didn't want to know. She'd assured him she'd been desperately lonely and hadn't had a man for an *Ach Gott*. She certainly acted like it between the sheets, at first, and then on top, stark naked in the soft romantic light from outside a skylight over the bed.

The one large chamber had been fitted out as a lonely lady's quarters or the workplace of a dedicated professional, with cheap but frilly furnishings, an unlit globe lamp of Bavarian ruby glass, and a Boston fern in a hammered brass pot in a dormer window. When Foster had asked about financial transactions Lilo had told him not to behave toward a maiden so fond of him in such a callous fashion. So Foster decided she was on the level or included with room and board. He and Longarm had already resigned themselves to paying dearly for their stay there.

The healthy Canadian lawman was a meat-and-potatoes man when it came to fornication, as a rule. Blessed with healthy appetites for all natural pleasures, and virile enough to please most natural women, Foster considered some of the customs his French Canadian compatriots were said to follow as childish piggery.

Foster held that just as a sensible dinner satisfies his hunger and pushes away from the table when he's full, or an adult with a craving for chocolate eats no more than a box of chocolate at a time, a man with a virile member wilted by satisfaction ought to simply stop, assured the ruddy thing would rise to the occasion again in due time. Blighters who tried to wake up the dead with unusual practices were like children with no control making themselves sick in a sweet shop to Foster and so, after he and Lilo had climaxed together three times, or so she'd said, Foster suggested they call it a job well done and catch a few winks before morning and perhaps a bit more innocent fun.

Lilo confessed he'd about worn her out and snuggled naked in his arms, replying to his polite attempts at small talk with sleepy bubbles blown against his bare shoulder until Foster sighed in satisfaction and closed his eyes.

The mistake Lilo made was in assuming a healthy man of muscular build and supurb physical shape could fall asleep before ten p.m. just because he'd come a few times. Foster wasn't even pretending to be more than considerate as he cuddled her quietly, before she softly asked if he was awake.

That struck a man accustomed to questioning suspects as a very odd question. So he didn't answer. Lilo snuggled closer, kissed his bare shoulder and softly breathed, "Mike?"

Foster was beginning to find it interesting as he modulated his breathing to seem out of the world.

The big blonde rolled smoothly out of bed without bouncing it a hair. She rose in the dim light in all her naked glory as Foster watched with his eyes only *almost* shut. It wasn't easy, but the disciplined Mountie didn't alter the rhythm of his breathing as Lilo picked up his pants and went through the pockets with one eye on his softly heaving chest.

She of course showed no interest in the gunbelt draped over the back of the same chair. Like Longarm, Foster had been keeping a few dollars handy in his pants to avoid having to open his secret money belt when paying his way along the Owlhoot Trail. So he knew the naked lady could expect no more than forty-odd dollars in coinage as she helped herself to the contents of his pants.

Forty dollars seemed a bit steep for a roll in the hay with even a slut of such generous proportions. On the other hand it hardly seemed worth the dramatic scene that was sure to take place if he confronted her as an armed and dangerous outlaw would be expected to.

Watching through slitted eyelids, Foster saw Lilo tiptoe over to that potted fern with his money, lift the fern's clay pot out of the bigger brass container and hide his money in the bigger pot before she put the smaller pot back in place.

As she tiptoed back to bed Foster shut his eyes completely, lest she get wise to his being wise to her. He knew how it was supposed to go when he noticed his missing money in the cold gray dawn.

She was banking on his not missing it right away and not being sure how much he was missing as she helped him hunt for it.

She'd pouted and said that he'd insulted her when he'd implied she might charge for her favors. He could already hear how she'd sound when he accused her of being a common thief.

He decided he'd better not accuse her of anything. As she slipped back into bed and snuggled against him, Foster yawned, hauled her in closer and reached for her fundamentals with his free hand, growling in a sleepy voice, "Oh, yes, acres and acres of it and it's all mine!"

Lilo giggled and began to play with his sated shaft, as if she, too, wanted more, or wanted to soothe her conscience.

So they were soon at it hotter and heavier than before, with Foster putting his back into it, inspired as much by anger as by passion, albeit once a man gets going in a beautiful pneumatic blonde he begins to feel sincere.

Lilo gasped, "*Mein Gott*! What has over you come, *mein Tiger*?"

Foster growled, "Lust, pure animal lust! You *have* turned me into a tiger with your adorable little pussy and I'm going to come in you until I drown it!"

The buxom blonde responded to his savage thrusts like a sport, but moaned, "*Sich Zeit lassen! Immer mit der Ruhe*! You are hurting me!"

Foster didn't stop. It wasn't hurting *him*. He came in her, feeling it down to his toes, and took her collarbone in his mouth to gnaw as he growled, "That felt grand, but enough of this prim and proper fucking, Let's get French!"

She asked if they could rest and recover their breaths before she served him that way. He wasn't sure he'd ever get it up again with a block and tackle. But he didn't want her to get her breath again, and, attending a fancy school his parents could ill afford, he'd heard of a vulgar bit of bedroom athletics guaranteed to make Her Majesty come whether she wanted to or not.

Knowing Her Majesty would not approve and his mother would faint, he went down on Lilo, who didn't complain if she found it vulgar. Foster found it less revolting than he'd imagined and as he recalled the old saw that went, "By the time you get used to the smell you'll have it half licked!" he repressed a chuckle as he was kissing her clit and Lilo gasped, "*Ach du lieber*!"

So he inserted two fingers and commenced to quickly crook and uncrook them in a "come hither" gesture as he tongued her, with results that surprised them both. He felt her contractions around his teasing fingers and when she gasped she'd had enough and begged him to stop he kept on and on until the helpless Lilo took the only way out and simply fainted.

He made certain she was out by kissing his way back up to her lips. As he Frenched her and felt her up Lilo moaned, "*Nein! Loslassen mich*!" and struggled loose to roll over on her face for some well-earned shut-eye.

Foster rolled silently out of bed, quickly dressed in the dark and tiptoed over to that potted fern to scoop out all the coins Lilo had hidden there and put them back in his pants where they belonged.

He tiptoed out and made his way back to the main house. He tried to sneak silently into his own room. Longarm heard him and joined him in the hall to tell him to keep it down.

When Foster told him what he'd just done and asked if Longarm thought Mother Krieger was in on it, Longarm said, "I doubt it. But we'd best be on our way, in any case, before the night is rent by the dulcet sounds of screaming, either way!"

He added, "Meet me in the kitchen with all our shit. I have to get the next relay stop out of Mother Krieger."

They both moved down the back steps like cat burglars. When they got to the old woman's door Foster went on and Longarm went in, without knocking.

Moving over to the barely visible figure in the four-poster Longarm touched a blanket-covered toe to murmur, "It's me, ma'am. Pat Smith."

As he'd hoped, as with most elderly souls, she was a light sleeper. She sat bolt upright with her white hairs on end to gasp, "*Nicht mir schmerzen*! Everything I have is yours!"

Longarm gently repeated, "It's only me, ma'am. Me and Mike just got word someone's asking around town for us. So we're moving on out!"

She protested, "Not at night so late! The army to the north yet is on patrol!"

He said soothingly, "We'll do well to make the Arlee Agency before sundown. I wanted to settle up, here, and ask you who we want to scout up when we make her to the Indian country."

As he'd hoped, mention of money gained her attention and put her in a more receptive mood. She allowed they owed her a hundred for room and board and another hundred if they wanted to know where they wanted to go from Fort Missoula.

He'd already taken more than that out of his money belt, and they both knew she was sure running an expensive boardinghouse. Once she had the ten double eagles in her eager claws she told him they wanted to ask further directions from Big Al, nobody else, at the Arlee trading post.

So a few minutes later he and Foster were leading their saddled mounts out of the carriage house as Lilo sawed wood up above.

They left town riding at a walk, got a little trotting in by cock's crow and reined off the northbound wagon trace for a trail break as the dawn was breaking.

Dismounting, Foster removed his gun-toting money belt to put some of the load in his pants away. That was the first time he'd had a good look at why he seemed to be packing so much coinage. He blinked, recounted it and commenced to laugh like a loon being tickled with a feather duster.

Longarm naturally asked what was so funny.

Foster said, "I told you how I reached under Lilo's potted fern for my money. She'd taken forty-odd dollars from my pocket. I seem to have a hundred and sixty in gold and silver at the moment."

It was Longarm's turn to laugh like a tickled loon as he considered how Crown Sergeant Foster of the Northwest Mounted Police had pulled a pretty slick burglary.

Chapter 24

They made good time in spite of having parted company with the east-west stage and Western Union lines. The weather held as good as it got that far north in the Rockies, and by a seeming paradox of geology the narrower pony tracks ran straighter and more level as they followed the lay of the land.

Complex as they might rise, the mountains of the far west, all the way out to the High Sierras of California, crested mostly north to south as they broke like infinitely slow waves from east or west against the granite spine of the continental divide, running all the way from Alaska to Central America and, some said, on down the west coast of South America as those even higher Andes. So the north-south trails got to mostly run along the troughs between such waves, seldom having to climb more than fifteen to twenty degrees through the wide meadowlands called "parks" in the high country or along the shorelines of many an alpine lake or mountain stream. The sun-silvered poles of the B.I.A. telegraph line to their Indian agencies, scattered widely across what they defined as their Flathead Reservation, kept them company, even though Longarm had no way of availing himself of this modern wonder without giving away his true identity as another government employee.

The Indians got to keep so much land between Fort Missoula and the Canadian border because the outcrops of gold, silver, copper and such that had scattered white towns like fallen leaves blown by a whirlwind across the high country to the south seemed to peter out as one prospected north. Foster said there were indications of color in the Canadian Rockies, north of the Peace River, but that cut no ice in Montana Territory. So whilst they passed a few abandoned try-holes and prospector's cabins, the less beaten track to the Arlee agency was sort of lonesome as well as mighty pretty at that time of the year.

With the last snows of winter falling late as May and the first snows of the next blowing in early as September, the greenery adapted to the high country, even where it ran lower, got in a heap of growth and most of its flowering in July, needing the remaining warmth of August for the flowers to go to seed and drop the same before the first frosts.

So as they rode they were serenaded by buzzing bees and surrounded by carpets of orange poppies, blue colombines, the pretty but pesky larkspur that could poison cattle, and less certain wild flowers of most every color but black, strewn like confetti across grass green enough to be growing in Ireland.

The slopes to either side were still timbered, this far from uncertain benefits of "civilization," with island groves mostly of aspen dotting the lower parklands. Pine, spruce and juniper favored the higher windswept slopes above. Where the trail rose betwixt one park and the next they rode through a sort of high chaparral of dwarf conifers and more thorny brush.

It was a grand day for riding, but they'd been up all night and by noon their mounts were getting tired, too. So Longarm suggested they pull off out of sight of the trail and make camp.

The Mountie in mufti was for pushing on to Arlee before they called it a day.

Longarm said, "Ain't never going to make Arlee today aboard these half-jaded ponies. Ain't sure we want to. Those cavalry patrols we heard about ought to be but may not be north-west of Flathood Lake about now. They'd have no call in the first place to patrol far south as the Arlee Agency. But I say better safe than sorry and thanks to you and your horny way I am overdo some beauty rest. But I'll meet you halfways. I'll ride you far as one p.m. or the next good patch of high chaparral, whichever may come first, so's we can spread our bedding without worrying as much about ticks. I don't know what draws ticks to aspen, but something seems to.

Neither got his way in the end. A little after noon they rounded a bend to see a hamlet of log and frame structures spread across the trail in welcome. So they rode on in.

It only got sort of spooky up close. Ghost towns were like that when they'd been recently abandoned. This one, being so far off the beaten track, had hardly been picked over worth mention and only a few of the already dusty windows had been shot out.

When Foster speculated on the oddly out of place mountain town Longarm suggested, "Somebody struck color up this way during the boom of the late sixties. There was enough to justify some mining. Not enough to keep going when the frosting petered out. That's the way color lies in these here hills. Take a geology professor to say why, but whatever sends veins of color upwards through granite basement rock works sort of like them rock-oil refineries of Mr. John D. Rocky Feller. The metal salts settle out at different levels as they cool, with gold lying near the top, sometimes as golden carpets just under the sod, with silver contaminated by lead, and copper and such deeper underground. As far as this ghost town lies from any sensible place to haul ore, I'd say they skimmed the gold or silver and never bothered to drill deeper. Let's see if we can find a working pump to water these ponies."

They dismounted in front of what had been a saloon, where a hand pump stood by a dried-out watering trough. As Foster held the reins for both of them, Longarm pumped the handle, to be rewarded by the complaints of rusty metal. Foster said, "It's gone dry."

Longarm said he'd noticed and moved over to unlash a canteen from the swells of his saddle. The Canadian started to ask a dumb question, but Foster caught on and kept quiet as Longarm poured canteen water gently but generously down the pump rod into the depths below. When he'd used up the canteen Longarm put it back in place on his saddle and fished out a brace of cheroots, allowing, "Take a few minutes for the leather to swell, if it means to swell at all."

Foster waited until both their smokes were going before he asked what the form would be if the leather washers and flap valve of the long-abandoned pump had rotted away instead of drying out like prunes.

Longarm allowed they'd have to find water somewhere else and added in a cheerful tone, "It ain't like this is Arizona, you know. Let's see if priming that pump did any good."

As Longarm worked the pump handle with his cheroot gripped in bared teeth, the fingernails-on-a-blackboard screeching gave slowly way to hollow moans, burbling farts, attempts to puke and at long last an expectoration of ever-thinning muddy slime, until he had what could be described as muddy water coming out of the spout to collect, or try to, in the long-dried-out water trough.

A lot of it leaked out about as fast as he could try to fill it. But he didn't care. The first ten gallons or more were too muddy to consider. The cleaner water to follow leaked out slower as the sun-dried planks of the street trough swelled to nearly seal the gaps between them. Foster warned him not to work his lungs so hard in such thin air. Longarm said he was used to fucking every chance he got in the mile-high city of Denver and suggested Foster lead the damned horses to drink instead of just dammit standing there pretending to be his damned doctor.

So with Longarm still pumping, Foster watered both ponies and refilled all their canteens so Longarm could, damn it, cease and desist, panting just a mite for a Denver fornicator.

Moldy hay or any other fodder they found in the remains of a deserted livery being dangerous, they turned both cow ponies into a paddock out back, now long gone back to grass and forbs with a sassy aspen sprouting like a sunflower along the fence line. The gate was still in good shape and neither pony had any place better to go. So they left them to graze, bareback, and toted their saddles on to what looked like private quarters attached to the barn-like livery. When they got inside they found the cabin bare of furniture. The ghost town had been deserted in an orderly fashion, with the livery owners likely among the last to leave.

They spread their bedrolls on the floor planking. It was after noon in high summer, outside, but the interior of the cabin smelled of damp wood and the so-called dry rot that went with the same. Foster moved over to the stone fireplace where, noting that someone had prepared a night fire they'd never lit, he struck a match to set the tinder and kindling under split-cedar firewood alight. The experienced Canadian frontiersman was not surprised to see more smoke than flame at first. When you got damp tinder to do anything but just sit there and sulk, you didn't bitch about it.

Longarm was already getting into his bedding in shirt and jeans without his boots, gunbelt or hat. He'd dumped the contents of his pockets in the crown of his overturned hat. As Foster sat down to shuck his own boots he explained, "Damp wood ought to get to blazing more as it dries. If nothing else, the scent of smoldering cedar has dry rot beat, if you ask me."

Longarm rolled over to sit up, frowning, and decided, "If you ask *me* you've provided too much of a good thing. Did you open the damper on that Rumford fireplace?"

Foster asked what he was talking about, even as his eyes began to water, too. So Longarm sighed, said, "I thought not," and rolled out of his bedding to pad over in his socks, muttering to himself.

A few moments later Foster marveled, "What did you just do to my fire?" as the air began to clear as if by magic.

Seeing they were visible to one another again, Longarm jiggled the wrought iron rod sticking out from one corner of the sizable but shallow fireplace to explain, "Folk who mean to winter-over at this altitude put some thought into fireplace design. Back around the time of the American Revolution a New Englander who liked to be called Lord Rumford designed this breed of fireplace with a view to saving on firewood whilst providing heaps of warmth. He'd be famous as Ben Franklin if he hadn't stayed on the losing side with King George and you Canucks."

His Canadian sidekick sniffed, "You mean Lord Rumford was intelligent about politics as he was about fireplace design. How did you make that example of his genius stop smoking?"

Longarm replied, "Oh, she's still smoking, thanks to that damp wood you now see burning bright. Sending up a smoke plume you can see for miles as we, down here, enjoy such warmth as it has to offer. It's all in the way a Rumford fireplace moves hot and cold air and smoke. There's a good-sized smoke-step just out of sight up the flue to catch any downdrafts as might blow smoke in at us. After that there's this long, cast-iron damper built into the narrow slit betwixt the smoke-step and the front wall of the chimney. This rod, here, opens or shuts her part or all the way, depending on how hot the smoke is rising. When you shut her all the way, as you just found out, no cold winter air can come down the flue to chill your bones in bed, and no smoke can go up until you open the damned damper before you light another fire."

Foster finished shucking his boots as he muttered, "How was I to know? Of course we have dampers in the fireplaces of our more *civilized* parts of the Dominion. But you Yanks are so . . . casual about things out this way."

Longarm sat back down on his own bedding, saying, "I just now told you how you can freeze to death up in these mountains anytime twixt early fall and late spring. Folk out our way do what they need to get along. A roof that don't leak beats fancy trim and white washedsiding. Comfortable boots beat spit and polish. Guns as shoot straight beat silver inlay or pearl handles. Go to sleep."

"To what purpose? Now that we've called it a day at this hour in the middle of nowhere? A full eight hours sleep will see us up and about with no place to go before ten in the evening, and I thought we'd agreed it would be unwise to ride late at night during an Indian scare."

Longarm lay flat atop his bedding as he declared, "Thanks to you and Lord Rumford it feels warm and dry in here, now. I never suggested we ride late at night. We can cover nine or ten miles before midnight and with any luck we'll stumble over someplace more populated. I could go for some relaxation in what stands to be the last saloon we'll see for a spell, thanks to picky B.I.A. regulations about trading posts dispensing liquor in Indian country, and, after that, I'd like to get us some real riding stock."

Foster asked what he called the cow ponies grazing outside.

To which Longarm calmly replied, "Cow ponies. Texas-bred, from Mex stock or Arab stock, if I'm any judge of horseflesh. Nothing better for working with cows. Not so grand for covering ground cross-country. You been riding aside me since we swapped for 'em, Sarge. Ain't you noticed how they seem to come with two gaits, slow-walking and hell-for-leather full-gallop?"

The Mountie in mufti conceded, "They have struck me as spirited."

Longarm said, "That's the way serious cow ponies are trained to move. Poking along at the speed of an ambling herd or running all-out to head off a stray or circle a stampede. I've been trying in vain to get my mount to trot steady. It won't. I can get a furlong or less at a trot before the brute slows to a walk or breaks into full gallop. Can't ask any mount to run more than four miles. Can't cover ground worth a damn walking slow as a cow. Let's try for some sleep. Ain't no horse traders around here."

So they both lay flat and, thanks to not having slept for a spell, were both sound asleep in no time.

Longarm didn't recall falling asleep, nor did he know he

was asleep as he trudged to school on saddle-sore legs. He felt increasingly confused by the snow-covered peaks rising to either side of the West-By-God-Virginia hollow the old schoolhouse lay on, or was supposed to lay on. He didn't want to be late for school again. He'd promised he'd try harder after giving in to that mumbly peg game with those trash kids who never went to school. His pa had assured him, in the woodshed, that boys who skipped school grew up to draw water and hew wood for smarter folk.

But how was a willing lad going on nine supposed to get to school on time when the country lane that usually led to the schoolhouse seemed to end at the dooryard of that honky-tonk roadhouse the minister had warned all young boys to stay away from? What in blue thunder was a honky-tonk roadhouse doing where they'd built the prim and proper schoolhouse? He knew something wicked had to be going on inside because somebody was at a tinny piano in there, playng it like a minstrel-show man, real dirty.

So Longarm opened his eyes, still confused until he saw he'd been asleep in a mountain cabin a good piece from West-By-God-Virginia, all grown up and not about to be late for school after all.

It was getting dark outside. So it was around eight of a high summer's eve and that piano tinkling in the distance didn't sound so dirty, now, as it went on playing "Aura Lee." It sounded more like sad and sweet as a matter of fact.

Longarm softly sang along,

"Aura Lee, Aura Lee,
Though she was pledged to me,
The angels came down in the night,
And stole my Aura Lee.

Then Longarm sat bolt upright, wide awake, to nudge the sleeping Foster and hiss, "Wake up! We ain't alone in this here ghost town! Some ghost or worse is playing some damned piano!"

Chapter 25

The undercover lawmen played by ear as they moved afoot behind the muzzles of their saddle guns through the gathering dusk, past gaping doorways and dark windows staring friendly as the eye sockets of long dead skulls. The piano music haunting the seemingly deserted town seemed to come from somewhere up the gentle slope to the east. That made some sense. That side of town would get more of the low winter sunlight and snow didn't drift as deep on higher ground. They rounded a corner to see lamplight ahead. More than one lamp aglow in more than one window. The music got less mysterious as they followed it to a still well-lit-up saloon, open for business to the handful of holdouts left in town.

The middle-aged but still handsome brunette tending bar didn't act surprised to see them as they came in with their gun muzzles lowered at a more courteous angle. She asked what they'd have to wet their whistles.

As they bellied up to her bar they could see by the back-bar mirror that a small crowd of men, and more women than you usually saw in a saloon, had gathered 'round the old-timer playing the piano. By that time he'd buried poor Aura Lee and gotten to celebrating Sweet Betsy from Pike.

Longarm allowed they'd both settle for draft and asked how come there was anybody else in town.

As she poured, the friendly old gal said, "Copper. Copper sulphide as green as an Irishman's dreams. When the silver mine bottomed out in a base metal lode the Bonanza Boys pulled up stakes and cleared out, a lot of 'em owing bar tabs. They said, and who am I to argue, it took tons of copper ore to match pounds of horn silver. In the meanwhile they left a whole mountain of copper sulphide just waiting to be worked by anybody who'd work a little harder and haul a little further. So, as you see, some of us elected to stay."

Longarm asked if anyone was working the mine at the moment. She said, "Lord no. Be our guest if that's what you're here for. We'd be the sort of folk who *follow* mining booms, most of us getting a little long in the tooth for such tumbleweed ways, as you've no doubt noticed."

She sighed and confessed, "There was a time, not too long ago, I'd be down in Butte, where they've more recently struck gold and, some say, a whole lot of copper under it. Copper is the coming thing. You mark my words. Gold and silver are mighty pretty. But when you get right down to it, copper is more useful than either. Alloyed with baser metals it's as strong as mild steel and nothing carries that new electric juice half as good as copper."

Longarm could have argued silver was the better conductor, but silver cost too much to wire motors with, so she had a point.

Changing the subject to one he found more interesting, Longarm told her they were looking to engage in horse trading. He explained that they had two fine cow ponies down the slope and said, "We'd like to swap 'em for more leggy saddle stock. At least fifteen hands and trained to a steady trot. Elderly army mounts or rangier Chinook ponies would be worth our pretty-good cow ponies with a few dollars thrown in."

She leaned closer to ask, "Are you boys on the dodge?"

Longarm didn't answer.

She smiled and said, "I like that in a man. I lost my cherry to a band of Confederate raiders, down New Mexico way, when me and the world were young and frisky."

Foster blinked and asked, "Confederate raiders, *plural*?"

To which she demurely replied, "Don't knock it 'til you've tried it. I got married up within the year and, somehow, it wasn't the same. But he got killed in the war and why speak ill of the dead?"

Longarm nudged the Canadian and suggested he find out if the old piano man knew "Oh! Susannah" by his cousin, Steve.

As Foster left the two of them to talk in private, the bartending gal fluttered her lashes and asked how Longarm felt about a pair of Indian war ponies, bigger than most at fifteen hands and spotted pretty as firehouse dogs. When she added, "Funny thing about those spots. You can *feel* 'em with your fingers in the dark."

Longarm brightened and asked, "You have a pair of Appaloosa for sale, Ma'am?"

He said, "Don't call me ma'am. I don't feel *that* old. What might they call *you*, handsome?"

She said, "Call me anything but late for breakfast and let's talk about those Appaloosa war ponies. How did you ever come by them?"

She said, "If you feel shy about names call me Sweety. Got those odd, spotted Indian ponies off Indian traders, or a trail-dusted pair who said they were Indian traders and need fresh mounts in a hurry. As I said, I like that in a man. They'd ridden both those Happy Suzies lame, but after new shoes and a few days' rest you could see they were spunky warhorses all right."

She topped his beer and added, "Only trouble is, I don't go to war that often and when we tried to hitch them to my carriage as a matched team they didn't like it much. After one of 'em kicked in the dashboard we gave up and run them in with the other stock for future reference."

She beamed and said, "So the future is here and if you're in the market for big old frisky Apple Pussies we'd best get down to brass tacks. You say you want to swap me two cow ponies and sweeten the deal with hard cash?

Longarm said, "I figure the two ponies we have to offer are worth say forty a head. Saying an Appaloosa would be worth a hundred . . ."

"Let's say this child was not born yesterday?" she cut in with a wistful smile, adding, "You likely know more about horseflesh than I do. I've admitted I don't have that much use for those restless Indian war ponies. But the boys I got them from assured me they were worth as much or more as thoroughbreds."

That was stretching things, Longarm knew, albeit Lewis and Clark had cited the superior qualities of the big spotted mounts bred by the far west Palouse cousins of the Chinook, hence the name, sometimes spelled Appalousian by fussy purists. The various bands who spoke the Chinook trade jargon most easily were among the few Indian groups who understood the basics of animal breeding. Most Indians were better at breeding wild weeds to corn, tobacco and such. But however the Palouse had done it, they'd come up with a breed to rival at least the standardbred if not the thoroughbred in a dead heat, whilst some said the Appaloosa could outlast either across rough country.

He said he just didn't have more than two hundred to throw in with their cow ponies, hoping she'd believe him.

Whether she did or not, she called out to one of the gents over by the piano and, once he joined them, told him to take over at the bar whilst she and "Handsome" did some horse trading.

As she came around from the back of the bar Longarm assumed they'd be heading outside to look over the war ponies she had for sale. But she led him for the stairs as, over by the piano, everybody else got to wail,

"It rained so hard the day I left,
The weather was so dry,
The sun so hot I froze to death,
Susannah don't you cry!"

The rest of the refrain was muffled as "Sweety" led him into a dark, perfumed chamber and shut the door after them. He could tell by the click of the barrel bolt behind him she didn't mean for them to be disturbed as they discussed business.

She took him by one hand, saying, "Stick with me and I shall lead you to the light, Handsome. I know my way 'round up here like a wise old owl."

As she led him through the darkness she softly muttered, "Us owls get so soon old and so late smart. We're almost there."

She opened another door. Thanks to his eyes having had time to adjust he could see fairly well by such light as came through her upstairs windows as that waxing moon smiled down, outside.

She said, "If I lit my bed lamp we'd need to pull the shades and I don't have any shades up here. Us owls get used to moving about in the dark after sundown, dwelling alone and seldom turning in until after closing hours, downstairs."

Longarm gently asked, "What happened . . . Sweety?"

She turned to face him, looking less elderly by soft moonlight, as she said, "What happened to which one, just when? Things happen. Then they happen again as every love story ends in tragedy or as a dirty joke and things don't happen either way as often and you do find yourself sort of wondering what happened. Are you going to kiss me or might you be planning to write a book about me?"

He kissed her. He really wanted those war ponies. And when she kissed him back, natural, without the cynical cracks and knowing eyes, it felt a tad like kissing a princess. A lonesome princess who'd been waiting in a ghost town for, if not her Prince Charming, *some* damned cuss to come along and do her wrong.

So Longarm did her wrong, which was all right by her, before they'd finished undressing one another atop her bedding in the dark. If a man checked his memory at the bedroom door it was true enough that all cats were gray in the dark whilst all willing women seemed pretty enough.

Womenkind could no doubt say the same about most willing men. But as he entered her, pleasantly surprised by her tight wet warmth, she let out a gasp and sighed, "Oh, my lands! To think I went all these years without ever knowing they could come this big! Have you ever measured that bodacious dick you've shoved up me, Handsome?"

Longarm modestly replied, "Sounds like kid stuff to me. Who's about to whip his old organ-grinder out of such pleasant surroundings to stretch it out on a yard stick, for Gawd's sake?"

She tittered at the picture and said, "I can understand why you're not curious. You know full well you have little or no competition and . . . why are we *talking* about your lovely love tool, Handsome? Shove it to me! Shove it to me fast and deep and make me feel like a skittish but hot and horny bride again!"

He could try. So he did and whether he really made her feel younger or not she felt young enough to him where it counted, and a gal kissing you French was a gal kissing you French when you were fixing to come in whatever she might really look like.

Meanwhile, back in Slickrock, His Copper Majesty Vance Larson had made her that far in style. Most everybody in the trail town gathered 'round to admire the blue-and-scarlet coach built to a copper king's specifications back in Concord, New Hampshire, by J. Stephens Abbot and company—The same outfit that built the famous Concord coach at a starting price of thirteen hundred dollars, with trimmings extra.

Vance Larson had paid extra for a heap of trimmings.

As she rolled out of their shop on her hickory-spoked Lewis Downing wheels, the best stagecoach money could buy weighed twenty-five hundred pounds. His copper majesty's private coach weighed more, calling for double thoroughbracing to spare His Copper Majesty's royal ass. The interior seating was thicker, softer, but not as filling as the three regular seats of a standard coach. The removable center seat had been left in New Hampshire, replaced by a folding table for meals along the way. A commode built under a lift-up foreward seat allowed his copper majesty to crap without stopping as well. The part he liked best, even if it didn't show, was the pull-down Pullman berth allowing him to sleep or, if he so desired, fornicate on the fly behind his team of eight, rather than a pokey six. Vance Larson wanted it known there was nothing slow about him.

Feeling above the common herd in every way, His Copper Majesty had been able to change teams at every stage stop along the way from Helena, because he paid cash on the barrelhead like mamy another self-styled man of destiny.

Dismounting grandly from his wondrous transportation and treating everyone who could crowd into that same saloon, Vance Larson shot a hole in the pressed tin ceiling for silence to declare, "To those of you who may not know me, I am Vance Larson the copper king and I own the men who think they own Montana Territory. I am after those birds who chased Empty Chambers out of Clarkside and gunned your own poor Tyler brothers. I understand they pulled another payroll robbery over in Peacock more recent. Me and my personal bodyguard are after the sons of bitches. Who rides with us out of here?"

There came no answer. His copper majesty smiled knowingly and said, "Perhaps I should have phrased that different. I'm paying five dollars a day for men with their own horses and guns, provided they can show my *segundo*, Nutmeg Waterman, here, they can hit four out of five bottles with their six-guns at fifty feet."

There came a low, thoughtful whistle from the crowd assembled. Hitting most of the time at fifty feet was tolerable shooting with a pistol. His copper majesty knew that. He wasn't about to pay five dollars a day to a tag-along who couldn't shoot. Dropping your man from, say, across the street was the least one expected of a hired gun.

He added, "I ought to mention the bonus I'm offering for anybody who drops the darker cuss with the mustache. I don't know his real name. I don't much *care* what his real name is. I want him *dead*. Any rider who kills him gets one thousand dollars before the bastard cools off. I'm offering a hundred for his sidekick. He ain't done nothing to me personal but let's kill him before he can."

As the laughter calmed down a sallow-faced individual in a high-peaked hat of dusty black felt called out, "I'm with you, Mr. Larson!"

A stubbier local boy in a fringed buckskin jacket yelled, "Take me! If this pathetical cuss is riding with you, I'd best come along to keep him from crying when it gets dark!"

Others clamored to ride along as the sallow-faced rider suggested his stubby associate try something physically impossible.

Turning to his *segundo*, Nutmeg Waterman, Larson chortled, "We'll stay the night, separate the wheat from the chaff and roll on over to Peacock to see if they have a line on which way those devils rode with the Peacock payroll."

The erstwhile New Englander who'd learned a lot about killing at a place called Gettysburg softly asked, "Are you aware, sir, this is the same neck of the woods where Keystone and McCord were lynched?"

His copper majesty replied, "I am. What about it?"

Nutmeg said, "Some of the riders you're asking us to ride with may have been the very ones who murdered our fellow employees!"

His copper majesty shrugged and said, "All the better. They share our distaste for those bastards they were really after. Why should we let an honest mistake stand in the way of cutting their trail in the company of of really dedicated bastards who've proven they know how to kill?"

When Nutmeg didn't answer, his boss punched him on the shoulder and insisted, "Wipe that sulky frown off your face, Nutmeg. I know what I'm doing and good help is so hard to find these days!"

Chapter 26

By the cold gray light of dawn indeed a suddenly older-looking gal who still felt mighty young allowed she didn't want her Handsome to recall his Sweety as the sort of woman who took money from a man after a roll in the feathers with him. So they agreed on an even swap and sealed the bargain dog-style with her best features presented to him.

As Longarm and Foster rode out to the north aboard the handsome, spotted war ponies, Foster was too considerate to ask how Longarm had managed such a swap. The well-rested and spunky Appaloosas were all Lewis and Clark had written about their ancestors, and this pair had been broken to the white man's ways of riding, likely by early Chinook traders who knew better than to sell a white customer a pony who'd throw him if he mounted from the left instead of right, as Horse Indians were more inclined to. Chinook left surprising dried berries out of the pemmican they sold white men, knowing white men thought what seemed a mixture of sausage and raisin cake grotesque, whilst by the same token they added all sorts of shit to the trade tobacco they provided their Indian customers, knowing they felt tobacco mixed with pungent sumac leaves, red willow bark or even cedar bark had more medicine than the sissy shit cowhands smoked, if they were low on cash.

The two undercover didn't give pet names to their high-stepping war ponies as they agreed to stick with Pat and Mike as easy to remember.

They rode some at a lively walk and trotted some at an easy, mile-eating gait that didn't hurt as long as you stood in your stirrups. As an experiment before their first trail break, they heeled their fresh mounts to full gallop, to discover that both ran faster than your average cavalry mount, without heaving as much when you reined 'em in. Had the pointy-headed Palouse taken it in their pointy heads to ride a war path against the whites aboard such horseflesh, they'd have no doubt wound up more famous than the Lakota Confederacy. Chief Joseph's defensive and misunderstood Nez Perce had skirmished with and ridden circles around assorted cavalry columns, only partly mounted on Appaloosa stock they'd traded for with Chinook. The war department was still talking about the confusion of '77, when no more than a score of Nez Perce had given overwhelming odds a riding lesson.

In the end, as always, the run-ragged Indians with no place left to run had given up, and the far more numerous Palouse and their "Flat-headed" Chinook cousins had never ridden their dappled war ponies against the U.S. Cav. For which the U.S. Cav felt eternally grateful.

"It hardly seems fair," Longarm mused aloud to Foster as they downed some canned beans during a trail break, "but our *smarter* Indians have never gotten top billing in our history books. I mean, the Pawnee are tough or tougher than their Dakota enemies and the same can be said for the friendly Ojibwa or Chippewa who named the Sioux for the rest of us after fighting them to a stand-still for generations."

The Canadian wearily asked Longarm to explain the difference between Nakota, Dakota and Lakota.

Longarm said, "The ones the Ojibwa named Sioux call themselves *Nakota*. The biggest central bands call themselves Dakota. We know western bands as Lakota. Indians I know tell me none of those spellings are right. Us *Washichu* can't pronounce the words the way the Indians say 'em. So we do our best with our own alphabet. Not having any letter with the sounds *they* use, white experts have settled for an N, a D or an L as the first letter for their word for friends or allies, east to west. I've read missionaries have done much the same to the Kanaka lingo spoken in the South Sea Islands. With a gal being called a *wahini* in the Sandwich Islands or a *vahini* down Tahiti way. I understand Kanaka folk say both words for the same gal. Ain't that a bitch?"

"How far are we now from that Arlee Agency?" the Canadian asked.

Longarm crushed his bean can and dug a hole for it with his boot heel as he decided, "Hoping to ride in well before sundown, taking it easy, because we'll want to stay there overnight. The crook they call Big Al ought to know whether the cavalry's still patrolling, as well as the way to our next relay point."

"Somewhere on the reservation lands ahead, right?" asked Foster.

Longarm bit back a sardonic retort as he buried the can, saying, "I doubt he'll steer us towards the *Mexican* border. Unless some Indians are in on it, I'm betting on a string of trash whites, connected to or just hanging 'round agencies, missions, trading posts and such. Down in the Indian Territory west of Fort Smith they have whole shantytowns of outlaws and other trash spread across what's supposed to be an Indian reserve. Some of them, like the slatterly Belle Starr, are married-up Indians who ought to be ashamed of themselves. There's a mess of bad colored boys pretending to be Black Seminole, taking advantage of the fact some Seminole are descended from runaway slaves. Other outlaws or just plain squatters don't bother to explain what they're doing there. It's up to the Indians to complain, and when white trash camped downwind of you offer hard liquor the Great White Father says you can't have, you don't have much call to complain."

Foster said, "I hope you won't think I'm trying to be unkind, Yank, but your Indian Policy was written by blithering idiots!"

Longarm kicked dirt in atop the crushed bean can as he replied in a weary tone, "You'll get no argument from this child about that subject. You ain't the first who's noticed. George Armstrong Custer, himself, was only one among many who allowed our Indian Policy was written by idiots or, as Custer charged, crooks out to take advantage of illiterate wards of the state. Let's ride."

As they mounted up, Foster marveled, "Are you trying to tell me your General Custer felt tenderhearted to those Indians he slaughtered on the Wachita?"

Longarm heeled his mount foreward as he replied, "Not hardly. He shot Indians out on the warpath and slept with an Indian some say was pretty as his wife, Miss Libby, depending whether he was in the field or back home on Officer's Row. Custer got along fine with Indians who didn't want to lift his hair and he charged troublemakers in writing for inspiring those Indians who did. He warned more than once the so Sioux were sure to rise again if we broke the Red Cloud Treaty of '68."

Foster snorted, "Oh, come now, wasn't it your General Custer himself who led that military expedition into the Black Hills that started all that fuss in '76?"

Longarm said, "Sure he did. He wasn't a general. He was only a lieutenant colonel, following orders from generals, when he led that army column, like you said, where he as well as the Indians knew it wasn't supposed to go."

He fished out a cheroot as he explained, "The newspapers described him as General Custer after Little Bighorn because he'd been a brevet brigadier, or temporary acting general, during the war back east. They say he and his brigade backed Grant's play at Appomattox. He should have quit whilst he was ahead."

He lit his cheroot to add, "So should the Lakota Confederacy. How long do you figure Queen Victoria will let Sitting Bull's bunch hide out up Canada way?"

Foster, who had his own views on Indian Policy north or south of the border, shrugged and said, "As long as they behave themselves, as far as our Yankee-baiting prime minister is concerned. They'd have left for the States to face the music by now if Her Majesty was the sole authority I'm sure she'd like to be. Do you suppose there could be anything to those rumors of border-jumping Sioux on the reservation ahead?"

Longarm shook his head and said, "I doubt it. Two reasons. The cavalry would hardly be headed home to Fort Colville if they'd cut any sign at all and, after that, I thought we'd agreed you can't hardly get to the Indian country ahead from Canada."

The Canadian protested, "That's not what I said at all! I said you can't seem to get to that robber's roost called Natova from our side of the line. There are pleny of trails leading north and south between our wilder wests and did I forget to mention rivers, starting with the Columbia you lot are so proud about? It would be perfectly possible for experienced warriors to slip south across the border east or west of the divide."

Longarm grimaced and said, "Some have already said Sitting Bull's hunting buffalo along the Milk River, south of the border, even as we speak. Scouted for him over yonder, a spell back, but that's another story and, what the hell, they can't be *everywhere* out this way. You want to lope down that grade ahead?"

Foster did. It would have been fun if they hadn't been going anywhere. The spirited, spotted war ponies enjoyed it, too, as they thundered single file down the pony track, precluding further conversation for a time.

By the time they were walking their mounts again they'd lost interest in speculating in circles about possible hostiles ahead. They walked some, loped some, and broke trail some until along about quitting time back in Denver, they rode into the hamlet of Arlee, built around the "Flathead" agency there and inhabited by assimilated Indians, breeds, and the sorts of whites who bred with them, mostly with some connections to the B.I.A.

You weren't allowed to shack up with Indians right in front of their appointed agents, as such supervisors were politely described.

They tethered their still-lively war ponies out front of the trading post to be admired mostly by Indian and breed kids. They went in to find business slow at that hour. The burly, bearded white man behind the counter said they were fixing to close and suggested they say right out what they might be in the market for.

Longarm said, "We were looking for Big Al."

"You're talking to him," said the bearded mass of lard behind the counter, adding, "Who sent you?"

Longarm easily countered, "I ain't good at recalling names. Suffice to say we were directed here and told to ask for you by mutual friends in Redeye. Before that we were steered to Redeye by another helpful soul in Peacock. How much are you asking for them three-for-a-nickel cheroots I see on the shelf behind you, Big Al? Lord knows when I'll get a better chance to stock up."

Big Al glanced at Foster to ask, "What about you? You want some smokes, too?"

The Canadian dryly replied, "I reckon."

Big Al turned to take two bundles of three cheroots from the shelf. He turned and placed them both on the counter, saying, "That'll be fifty dollars a pack, friends."

Foster asked, "Isn't that a little steep for cheroots marked three for a nickel, friend?"

Big Al calmly replied, "They'll charge you as much at the trading post I'll be sending you on to, if I send you on to any trading post at all, that is."

Longarm, having counted out the hundred in gold in advance, laughed and said, "Let's not get our bowels in an uproar, gents. Fifty dollars for three smokes sounds fair enough when one considers the alternatives. Is this other place we can buy smokes so cheap far from here, Big Al?"

The relay man shrugged his massive shoulders and replied, "That's for me to know and you to find out, at our going price."

Longarm snapped five double eagles in a tidy row across the counter as he reached for the cheroots with a smile, confiding he was all ears.

Big Al swept the gold coins out of sight as Foster picked up his own expensive purchase. Longarm nudged him to hold the thought as the other lawman took to looking sort of tense.

Knowing the game they were playing better, Longarm waited a bully out with an assured smile. Big Al said, "You want to ask for the Old Sarge up at Poison. Old Sarge don't really work there. He helps out a mite at the Poison trading post when the old widow who runs it gets to feeling tuckered. Try to scout Old Sarge up about this time at night. It ought to take you no more than a damned hard ride to enjoy Poison the Fourth of July and you'll love it. They put on a swell fireworks display up at Poison. The Chinook consider themselves American, you know."

Longarm said, "So I've heard. This Poison is the name of another town, I hope?"

Big Al nodded and said, "Good-sized town for Indian country. Growed around the agency, yonder. Don't ask me what's poisonous about the place. Poison is situated on the south shoreline of Flathead Lake. Big lake. Too big to see across, albeit you can see mountains rising above the far horizon, of course. They shoot the fireworks out over the lake at nightfall. Pretty as hell and the Indians think it's heap big medicine. Try to catch Old Sarge before dark, though. You want to get him alone at this awkward hour, no sooner, no later, see?"

Longarm saw indeed. It was Foster who asked if this Old Sarge would relay the east or west around the big lake. Big Al looked pained and suggested they take that up with Old Sarge, adding, "I hardly know the cuss. He hardly knows me. We like it that way."

Longarm allowed they followed his drift. Then he asked what Big Al had heard about cavalry patrolling for hostile border-jumpers up to the north.

Big Al said, "Not as far south as Poison. Can't say

they're still on the reserve at all. Last I heard they's made her north-west of Whitefish Lake. That's still on the reserve but not by much."

Longarm asked what Big Al and his Chinook customers had made of that great Sioux Scare and how word got around so sudden across such rough country.

Big Al explained, "B.I.A. and War Department both use the old army telegraph lines strung between Forts Missoula and Colville in tenser times. Us civilians don't get to use her. But the military posts and agencies are mostly hooked up by wire and . . . we have friends in a heap of places."

Longarm declared, "That's the way Sioux Scares get around, I reckon. Somebody spotted a Chinook kid playing Peeping Tom or picking berries out back and put it on the wire as hostiles on the warpath. I wish folk would cut that out. Come along, Mike. We got us some riding to do if we mean to make Poison by the Fourth."

Outside, Foster asked, "Are you off your chump? The evening sun is going down and even if I was up to night riding with army patrols out looking for strangers in the night, I am damn it to hell *tired*! So are those poor ponies ahead. Look at the listless way they're standing, and you expect to push on tonight?"

Longarm said, "Don't cloud up and rain all over me, pard. I only had the Jesuit mission at Saint Ignatius in mind. I make her ten miles. Hard enough on tired horseflesh, I know, but we have to ride at night because I don't want anybody else to know we're stopping there, see?"

Foster said, "I'm beginning to. What's the plan?"

Longarm swung around the hitching rail as he replied, "Let's mount up and ride. I'll have plenty of time to tell you all about it on our merry way."

Chapter 27

As Longarm and Foster rode north by twilight, something unwholesome awoke from feverish dreams in a patch of high chaparral to their east–south-east. Turk Butler neither knew nor cared where he was as he rose to his feet and staggered on, hurting like hell and mad as a wolverine with turpentine under it's tail. The shallow but festering buckshot wounds across his broad back burned and itched at the same time. He'd torn off and discarded his bloody shirt. That had served to dry the blood and puss on the outside of his hide. But puss still seeped out from under the itchy scabs and when he went to scratch the itching he felt hot pokers where his fingernails usually went. From time to time Turk threw back his head to bay at the moon like gutshot coyote. His screams rose as the mindless howling of any other tortured, large and dangerous animal. They could be heard for miles. Nobody that heard them felt reassured by the distant sounds. More than one settler a good ways off sent his wife and kids on to bed but stood watch by the windows with his scatter gun, long after Turk Butler had passed on to the north.

It was ever to the north because one of the few things the hurt brute recalled from his human past was his Uncle Nick pointing out the North Star one coon-hunting night and showing a younger Turk how you could always find it because those two stars of the Big Dipper always pointed at the North Star no matter how the Big Dipper cartwheeled across the night sky. Finding the North Star was important, Uncle Nick had explained, because she was the one star who never went noplace. She was always in the same position, night after night, summer, winter, spring or fall. So a lad could never get lost at night if he knew where the North Star was.

Turk Bishop howled like a wolf and gasped, "I'm coming, North Star. I see you, yonder, winking down at me as ever. I know that do I follow you long enough I'm sure to wind up . . . somewhere."

So the feverish Turk Butler staggered onward, ever northward, over hill and dale, through tanglewood and open parklands as if he wasn't aware of them, because he wasn't. He only knew he had to get . . . somewhere, if he ever wanted this nightmare to end.

Meanwhile, to the south in Peacock, his copper majesty was being lied to by another mining man with a bone to pick with the outlaws he'd taken Longarm and Foster for.

There was no way Will Garner of the recently robbed Peacock Mining Company could steer Larson and his considerable posse anywhere near his confederates in Redeye. But lest the sons of bitches get away, still knowing he was a crook, himself, Will Garner felt it safe to advise his copper majesty that the men he was after might have fled to the Indian country to the north. Knowing you had to have detailed directions to find your way to Natova, Will Garner thought it safe, and smart, to say he'd heard more than one Owlhoot rider had vanished into the Flathead Reservation, possibly bound for some secret route to Canada.

He added that Larson and his men would do well to spend the night at the hotel across the way and push on to Fort Missoula in the morning.

Vance Larson said, "Don't need no hotel. Got a fold-down Pullman berth in my private coach. I can sleep as well or better on my way to Fort Missoula than any fucking hotel!"

Will Garner shrugged and said, "It's none of my business, I know, but have you considered how your riders are supposed to sleep on the way to Fort Missoula?"

His copper majesty sniffed, "I have not. Why should I? I'm paying the hungry bastards good money to ride with me. If any of 'em can't take a night in the saddle it's just as well we separate the men from the boys before we meet up with that fucking wizard I've been chasing after. He's good. Damned good. I don't know how he does it but so far he's shown he's tricky in a gunfight as he is a poker game, and that is one tricky bastard in a poker game!"

As he turned to leave, his *segundo*, Nutmeg, who'd naturally been listening, quietly asked, "Have you considered, sir, the advantages of having someone like this mystery man we're after on our side? I mean, it seems to me there's much to be said for the old saw about joining those we can't whip."

"It seems to me you're about to talk yourself out of a good job!" snapped Vance Larson, adding, "If I thought I could have him on my side I'd invite him to be on my side. You weren't there the night he made a total asshole out of me with his magic card-tricks. Like he *enjoyed* it. Like he didn't *like* me! I don't know why he didn't like me, but I could tell he didn't. I could tell. I can always tell when other men don't like me!"

Nutmeg Waterman just smiled. As the miserable cocksucker had just pointed out, backing his imperious plays paid mighty well, and so who was he to tell a man who said he could tell when other men didn't like him that he was purely full of shit?

As Vance Larson's wolf pack rode out of Peacock, Longarm and Foster could see the lamplights of that Jesuit mission gleaming off to the north and resisted the temptation to push their jaded Appaloosas faster. They'd get there when they got there. They didn't want to founder such good riding stock if it could be avoided and as long as those windows ahead were aglow, somebody inside would still be up and about.

As they rode on, Turk Butler had spotted a lamp-lit window ahead far to their east–south-east as well. It lay due north, under his lucky star. That had to mean something. He staggered on, crashed into an errant aspen sapling in the dark and tried to strangle it, howling mindless slobbering curses at it.

Inside the cabin a furlong north, young Tommy Phalen had been left in charge of the homestead and his younger siblings while their father carried their ailing mother into Fort Missoula to see the doctor. As all three of them heard the wild howling somewhere in the dark outside, Little Sister commenced to cry whilst Little Brother asked in a big-eyed voice, "Is that the boogeyman, Big Brother?"

Tommy replied with a confidence he didn't feel, "There ain't no boogeyman. Got to be some critter."

They heard the same howl, closer. Little Brother asked, "What if it's a wild Indian?"

Tommy didn't answer. He and Dad had talked about wild Indians. He bade his little brother to hang on to their baby sister as he rose to trim the lamp they'd left burning in the window. Little Sister could not have cried any louder. But Little Brother joined her, wailing that he didn't want to get scalped by wild Indians.

Tommy hissed, "Shut up and let me *listen*!" as he made his way over to the mantelpiece to get Dad's old buffalo gun down. The chamber of the big fifty was empty, of course, but Dad had shown him the bodacious shells he had leftover from his buffalo-hunting days. They were in a drawer in Dad's writing table. Tommy felt a thrill of pride as he found he could tell which end was which in the dark, and even load Dad's buffalo gun as, out in the darkness, Turk Butler thought he was demanding to know who'd put out that fucking light.

That's not what his husky jabbering sounded like to a frightened boy with a big fifty in his kid-sized hands. He moved to the widnow by the bolted door and threw open the sash, calling out, "I see you, there, you rascal, and you'd better *git*!"

Turk Bishop howled back at him. Neither had the least notion what the other was howling but Tommy could make out Turk's advancing outline and so he shouted, "I durn it told you to *git*!" as he pulled the trigger.

The recoil staggered the lightly built boy back across the room to deposit him on his lean rump beside his bawling siblings.

But not before he'd made out an unforgettable image in the orange flash of a whole lot of black powder. Tommy gasped, "Oh, my Lord, it *was* a wild Indian! One of them border-jumping Sioux we heard about, I'll vow! Half nekked and coming right at us all wild-eyed and war-whooping and Lord have mercy, where's that horse pistol Dad rid with in the war?"

By the time Tommy Phalen found and managed to load

a couple of cap-and-ball chambers of his father's Colt Dragoon, Turk Butler had staggered on to the north, chasing his lucky star, and this was just as well for all concerned. The kids would not have had a chance had the injured but dangerously pain maddened Turk crashed in on them. But a big fifty letting fly in your face at point-blank range has a way of changing the direction you were staggering, even when you only feel all that hot lead as a whipcrack in one ear, passing by.

So Turk Butler was still out there somewhere in the dark when Tommy Phalen's dad got home, having left his wife with the doctors in town, to hear a mighty wild tale from an excited kid who, come to study on it, had never lied to him before.

"Are you sure it was an Indian, not a wolf or catamount, Tommy?" the man of the house asked.

When his son insisted he'd shot an Indian, or tried to, least ways, his father led the way across the grass with a bulls-eye lantern until, son of a bitch if he didn't spy blood on the pale green bark of that aspen sapling!

"You winged him, Tom!" Jake Phalen almost sobbed with mingled guilt and pride as he pictured what his kids had just been through. Heading back to the cabin, he added, "Gather up your little brother and sister, Tom. It ain't safe out here tonight. We're all going back in to Fort Missoula and wait 'til everybody hears what my son, Tom, did out here tonight!"

His son was glad it was dark. He felt silly with his eyes all filled with tears like so. He wasn't sure what he was crying about. He had no call to be crying. He's save Little Sister and Little Brother and all of a sudden his father had stopped calling him Tommy. He wasn't sure why, but he somehow knew his father would never call him Tommy again, and he wasn't sure if he ought to feel one way or another about that.

Well before the Phalens could buckboard back to Fort Missoula, Longarm and Foster led their now lathered and heaving mounts into the dooryard of the Saint Ignatius misson on foot. As Indian kids came to tend the jaded war ponies, petting and praising both, a tall lean figure in the black robes Indians cited in describing their kind was standing in the welcoming doorway. As they approached he called out, "Come in. Rest yourselves over some warm broth, perhaps a bit of bread and cheese with a glass of wine?"

Longarm said, "We'll be proud to take you up on that, Father. I ain't fixing to insult you or your order by asking you to swear to secrecy, so I'll tell you right out we're both lawmen, working undercover in a secret mission."

"In what way may we help you?" the missionary asked without blinking an eye.

Longarm introduced both of them by their true names and titles. Father Bernard, as he was called, seemed more impressed by a Canadian Mountie down their way than a U.S. deputy marshal. He suggested they take it on in to the refectory. That was what they called the private dining room monks and priests got to eat in, a refectory.

After that it looked a lot like an army mess hall with a big, long table running the length of her. The three of them sat at one end, and a Chinook dressed tribal but sporting a big cross on his chest served them without Father Bernard having to tell him much.

By the time they had bread, wine and cheese in front of them, having said they had no call to wait on broth to heat up, they'd filled Father Bernard in on all they knew.

He repeated his question as to what they expected him to do about such a mess.

Longarm explained, "We still don't know where we're headed or what we may be getting into, Father. In the meantime we've uncovered more than one relay station along their trail to Natova and, like I said, that payroll robbery at Peacock was an inside job. Somebody ought to know about whether we make her back alive or not."

"You think it could be that serious, up ahead?" asked the concerned older man.

Longarm said, "We've no way of knowing what lies ahead until we get there, Father. We've considered wiring what we've already gathered in. But we suspect that Big Al, for one, has an ear to the singing wire as it zigs and zags across the reservation from Forts Missoula to Colville."

"We have no telegraphic connections here, I fear," sighed the priest.

Longarm said, "I know. But you send regular *mail* to the outside world, don't you?"

The priest said, "Of course, but I don't see . . ." and then he proved he did by smiling like a kid swiping apples as he said, "Of course! If you wrote out full reports to both your headquarters, and they left here as our regular reports to our order's central chapter back east, nobody would even think to intercept them until they could be forwarded to the proper addresses with our order's return adress on the envelopes!"

Foster brightened and said, "Rather like diplomatic immunity works!"

Longarm said, "Even better. Secret dispatches moving in a diplomatic pouch is still known to be secret. How in thunder is Will Garner to know an envelope mailed to your home office or mine by the Society of Jesus contains one word about his stage payroll robbery, and he ain't under the only wet rock I mean to turn over, in writing."

Father Bernard said he'd see they both had a writing table, paper and ink to work with in the rooms he meant to put them up in for as long as they liked.

Within the hour he turned out to be a man of his word and both undercover lawman were too keyed up to sleep before they'd filed full reports on the machinations of the plot, so far.

But after a good night's sleep on less-worried minds, followed by a simple but hearty breakfast, they bid a fond farewell to Father Bernard and his shyer fellow missionaries to try for an early start.

They found their two tough Appaloosas willing to move on after such rest as horses manage, standing up in a stall. Like most prey animals, horses slept way lighter than meaner critters such as bears, wolves and humans could get away with.

As the big war ponies carried them north on the Fourth of July, Foster got to speculating on the robber's roost ahead, describing it in some detail in advance.

Longarm warned, "Don't paint castles in the air, pard. It can throw you off when the real deal looks nothing like you've been picturing it. Remember that ghost town that wasn't? All we know, or think we know, is that somewhere out yonder there's this hidey-hole presided over by some cuss they call Saint Lou and . . . what's that going off, up ahead?"

Foster opined, "Sounds like somebody blasting," as they pushed on over a wooded rise. Then they were loping across the logged-off grasslands around the Flathead Agency called Poison, where some cuss atop the roof of a stable was celebrating the Fourth a mite early by tossing quarter sticks of dynamite, one after the other, as he lit the short fuses with the cigar gripped betwixt his grinning teeth.

The Indian Police had roped and hauled him down off the roof by the time Longarm and Foster found Old Sarge in the trading post.

Chapter 28

Old Sarge looked as disreputable as expected with his grizzled beard and Union forage cap topping off his greasy buckskin jacket, hickory shirt and too-tight pants of army-blue striped with artillery red down the sides. After he'd sold them some mighty expensive trade twist—they had no cheroots for sale—Old Sarge directed them up the eastern shores of Flathead Lake to another pal at the Bigfork Agency, this one a blacksmith who'd no doubt shoe their ponies for a nominal fee of twenty-five dollars a hoof.

That left them free to join the crowd along the lakeshore as the fireworks display was set to start. More than one Indian gal had giggled at them by then, of course, but neither undercover lawman had giggled back. So they went over to the agency with clear consciences when a Chinook runner said their agent wanted a word with them.

As they entered a sort of orderly room where a prissy little fuss sat at a desk like a first sergeant, the priss declared with no shilly-shally, "I hope you both know it's a federal offense to trifle with a ward of the government on her own blamed reservation, and in any case I would like to hear what you two think you're up to, up this way!"

Since they could hardly tell him the truth, Longarm said soothingly, "We know the rules, sir. I scouted for the army during Red Cloud's War over to the east. As to what we're doing this deep in Indian country, I already told you I was an old Indian scout. So, seeing we heard Sioux had been spotted out this way, we came looking for that army column we heard tell of, hoping to join it, as civilian scouts, that is."

The agent confided in a friendlier tone, "You're out of luck. That Sioux Scare was a false alarm. The cavalry from Fort Colville is headed back there, even as we speak. It was all a big flap over nothing!"

Siezing the moment, Longarm replied in a worried tone, "Do tell? Fort Colville, you say? Reckon we may as well ride on up yonder and see if they'll sign us on, anyway. Understand the Apache are on the warpath to the south this summer."

The agent shrugged and said, "You can try. Doubt they'll send troops posted near the Canadian border south to chase Victoriao along the *Mexican* border. Apache like to zigzag north and south across the border down yonder, the sneaky rascals. Where are you boys figuring to spend the night here in Poison? I just warned you about what happens if I catch you shacked up with any of my Indians!"

Longarm asked if there was a hotel. The agent laughed and demanded, "In Poison? This far north of our reservation line? You'd best spend the night in our guest quarters. We'll all feel safer in the wee small hours."

They asked if it was all right to go out again and watch the fireworks. The scrawny little cuss, having gotten his way with two bigger men, had mellowed considerably by then and all three of them strolled over to the lakeshore to watch skyrockets and fireballs from Roman candles soar out above the placid moonlit waters.

When it was all over the Poison agent treated them to snacks in his kitchen and had a cook who looked like kin to the one down at the mission show them to one spartan room with one window and two army cots for them to spread their own bedding on. So they went back to the tack room of the stable Old Sarge had directed them to, earlier, to get their bedding, saddles and all.

It was still early, with plenty of oil in the one lamp they shared, so neither was sleepy as Longarm finishing making his bed and got a folded survey chart from a saddlebag to study, spread out across his bedding as he sat sidways on the cot.

When Foster asked what he was looking for, Longarm said, "Common sense. This tangled trail to the wonderland of Natova gets curiouser and curiouser as we get ever closer. If our next relay stop is here at the Bigfork Agency near the north end of that big lake outside, I can't see where that blacksmith could mean to aim us from there."

Foster said, "Well, hell, we knew it was supposed to be a secret. If we knew where that robber's roost was we'd have raided it by now!"

Longarm said, "No argument about that. The question before the house is where along this border line the son of a bitch could *be*!"

Before the Canadian could say it, Longarm said, "I know, I know, it's a given a heap of this western slope ain't properly mapped. But let's not get silly about that. Major features like rivers and serious ranges *have* been mapped, and I'll be whipped with snakes if I can find *that much* uncharted border to work with! If those yarns about escaping over glaciers means shit, Natova has to lie somewhere betwixt this clearly defined, substantial and border-crossing Flathead River, running north into Canada, and the glacier-covered Great Divide running north and south across the same infernal border, let's say in line with and no more than twenty miles east of the well-traveled river valley!"

Foster said, "You can hide a lot in twenty miles of mighty rugged country."

Longarm made a wry face and replied, "You'd surely *have* to and I just can't picture it."

Foster insisted, "You're not *supposed* to. Didn't you tell me one time, how the James-Younger gang hid out for years out back of *known addresses*? I'm betting on an innocent-looking turn off, suggesting no more than a blind alley ending in some settler's door yard, leading just a little farther into a secluded dell where . . ."

"Ain't supposed to have settlers on Indian land," Longarm cut in.

"And what do we call Younger's Bend in the Cherokee Reserve?" asked the Canadian, dryly.

Longarm said, "Touché, but the story going 'round says nothing about white outlaws living in sin with Indians. Natova is said to be a hole in the wall, a secret passage, a place nobody can *get* to from here. We have to be missing something."

Foster said, "Of course we are. We don't know the way. As in the case of that misdirection you keep saying stage magicians use, the crooks running Natova have some simple but effective way to hide the way in or out of their secret hideout. It wouldn't be a secret hideout long if it was easy to find. Why don't we get some sleep and ride on for Big Fork in the morning to ask for some damned directions?"

They did. But it wasn't as easy in the saddle as it looked on paper. Lake Flathead was over twenty miles long and you had to go around some of it to get from Poison to Bigfork. So it was well after noon when they rode in, using the hangdog appearance of their mounts as an excuse to visit the local smithee.

After their Appaloosas had been reshod at twenty-five dollars a hoof they rode on for the Hungry Horse Agency with instructions to avoid Reservation Headquarters north of the lake at Kalispell. Hungry Horse made more sense. But it lay close to fifty miles to the north–north-east when you counted the bends, and their war ponies, expensively shod or not, were commencing to tire. Appaloosa were tougher than most breeds. But as any top hand could tell you, it was best to let a mount rest up a few days betwixt day-long spells under saddle and bridle. Longarm said he didn't see how they'd last all the way north to the damned border and Foster agreed that they'd best swap for fresh mounts at Hungry Horse when they got there.

As they made for Hungry Horse that afternoon, they were far from the only riders on the western slope concerned about how far they could hope to push riding stock.

Off to the west a cavalry column had just dismounted to take a break by the side of another mountain pathway when a dispatch rider from Fort Colville found them at long last.

Dismounting from his own lathered bay, the young dispatch rider saluted the more casually dressed major in command to stiffly say, "Order from Fort Colville, sir!" as he handed over the sealed envelope.

The already saddle-sore major tore open the orders from Headquarters as a couple of junior officers naturally headed his way to ask what was up. They didn't have long to wait. Their squadron commander finished scanning their new orders, balled the paper up in his fist and said with a sigh, "Son of a mother-fucking mongrel and a laughing hyena bitch in heat!"

One of his troop commanders suggested, "I take it we're not going back to Fort Colville after all, sir?"

The major said, "No, Captain, we are not. We are going back the way we came to scout for more shit-eating Sioux!"

"That Sioux Scare is on again, sir?" asked another officer in a dubious tone.

The major nodded curtly and replied, "I'm afraid it is, Mister. This time with more substance to the rumors. According to Headquarters, some homestead family beat off an Indian attack north of Fort Missoula the other night. No doubt about it being Indians because one homesteader saw him well enough to wing him. After that it's safe to assume none of the friendlies on this reservation would have gone on the warpath on his own. So that leaves hostiles, from some other nation."

"But how can Headquarters be so certain they were Sioux, sir?" asked another junior officer who probably had a great future ahead of him.

The major said, "They can't. That's whey they send out patrols and ours is not to reason why. Ours is to track down and capture the savage sons of bitches and *ask* them if they're Sioux or, for all Headquarters cares, South Sea Island cannibals. The point is that *nobody* is supposed to go on the warpath and Headquarters expects us to put an end to it."

"If they turn out to be Sitting Bull's bunch," another captain declared, "I vote they all get shot trying to escape. I had friends in the Seventh the Sioux still owe me for."

The major grimaced and stiffly replied, "Our orders are to track down and round up whoever that war party may be, Captain. This man's army is not a fucking bank. Nobody owes anybody anything. If they want to make a fight of it we'll oblige them. If they want to give up without a fight any officer or man in my command who settles a personal grudge by mistreating a disarmed prisoner had better commend his soul to Jesus because his ass will belong to *me*! Do we understand one another, gentlemen?"

There came a sullen murmur of agreement. The major didn't care if they disliked his orders, as long as they obeyed them.

He didn't like his orders much, himself. Having come upon naked white bodies after Mr. Lo, the poor Indian, had worked them over in his Noble Savage way, the major was inclined to share General Phil Sheridan's views about "Good Indians." But he was a professional soldier and professional soldiers did not play tit for tat. They soldiered.

So he let his men and their mounts finish their ten-minute trail break before he ordered his remounted column back the way it had just come, making it easier on everyone by having only the officers and noncoms ease along the upward slope to position themselves as leaders of the new heads of their troops at what had been the rears of their amused columns. As they rode east again more than one old soldier had to allow the old man knew his ass from his elbow, unlike some who'd have tried to turn a column back like a double-jointed wiggle-worm on such a narrow pathway. They rode back to where passage through a grassy park allowed them to dress up right. As they were doing so, a rider in an army-blue jacket and cavalry hat, but no pants, tore in on his own lathered mount to rein in by the mounted major and exclaim, "Sum of a bitch have you all gone crazy? How come you let poor Turtle Singer ride on west without telling him you fuckers turning back? How come you turn back? You got Chinook sweetheart back at Whitefish Agency?"

The major said, "We knew you'd notice, Turtle Singer. That's what they pay you Chippewa scout to do."

The scout protested, "How many times I tell you? Turtle Singer not Chippewa! Him *Ojibwa*! *Ojibwa*! *Ojibwa*! Now you say it."

The major said, "Chippewa. Rest up a tad and ride out ahead some more. Seems we're after Sioux after all and I'm hoping you'll cut their sign for me."

The Algonquin speaking Ojibwa, or Chippewa to the ears of many a white man, snorted, "Bullshit. No sister fucking *Nadowessioux* this far west. Turtle Singer cut *Nadowessioux* sign if any out there. Hear me. No fuckers track like Turtle Singer!"

"He's modest, too." the major smiled. Then he said in a more sober tone, "If you can't cut Sioux sign cut the sign of anybody out ahead of us. We'll be riding back to Whitefish Lake and from there due east as far as the Hungry Horse Agency."

Turtle Singer asked, "What if I cut Chinook sign, or maybe white man's sign?"

The major said, "Don't be ridiculous. This is a Chinook or a, right, Flathead reservation. Of course you'll cut *their* sign. This is where they *belong*, for Pete's sake."

Then he had another thought and said, "If you cut the sign of white riders, this far north, I'd better have a word with them. We have heard rumors of white renegades, outlaws or whatever in these hills. Makes almost as much sense as wild Indians when you think about it, some."

Chapter 29

When Longarm and Foster finally made it to the Hungry Horse Agency they didn't have to swap their Appaloosas after all. They seem to be stuck in Hungry Horse for the forseeable future.

They'd been directed to the private cabin of a breed who worked in the agency telegraph office. His daughter said she didn't know what he did there. They chose to believe her because she was in her teens and dim-witted besides.

After that she was fat and, unlike some breeds, she'd been born with the less attractive features of both races. Her hair was brown and frizzled. The Scott Irish blood she credited her missing dad with might not have been the only none-Indian ancestry he could boast, judging by the shape of her skull as well. After that she'd inherited the tawny skin and sort of Mongoloid eyes and cheekbones of so many North West nations. She said her dad called her Lexi for Alexis and she had no idea why he'd ridden off to the east but he had, saying he'd be back soon and instructing her to make welcome any white boys who might come asking for him, only not to fuck 'em.

Longarm and Foster both assured Miss Lexi they'd find it easy enough to abide by such rules. So she allowed they could stable their pretty ponies out back and stay with her in the cabin 'til her dad got back.

That evening she proved an able enough cook if one could abide canned Boston beans, sourdough biscuits and planked trout with every meal. She said there were heaps of trout in the Flathead River, and they believed her.

Having rested up, saddle-sore and untempted by the lady of the house as she snored nearby, albeit in pitch darkness, they found the next day more tedious. But that had nothing on the day after that as they waited, and waited, for her fucking father to get back.

They'd missed him at the agency as well. When they learned a pair of white strangers now occupied his cabin with his innocent only child, the agent sent for them.

They fed him the same line about searching for that army column. The agent, this one with more beef and self-confidence, told them they were pointed the wrong way. He explained, "You should have headed west from the Bigfork Agency, not east. But no matter, as they're headed this way, and ought to get here any time, now. You say you gents have scouted Sioux?"

Longarm nodded to reply, "Some. You mostly see where Sioux have been. When you see 'em more personal you could be in trouble. Got pretty good at reading their smoke talk, of course. Like the sign talk all the horse Indians share, smoke talk is based on a limited vocabulary. You seen any smoke talk out this way, sir?"

The agent shook his head and replied, "Indians who *belong* here keep assuring me there are no Sioux on this reservation. On the other hand, Chinook are peaceful traders who get along with most everybody and have less experience with hostiles than we do. Sioux means something like sneaky bastard in the first place, you know."

Longarm said, "No offense, but the literal meaning of *Nadowessioux* is Little Old Snakes. Of course, we have more in mind than the offspring of a hound when we call a cuss a son of a bitch."

The agent said, "Whatever. My point is that the hand sign for Sioux is a throat-slitting gesture, and did Custer know how many of the sneaky bastards were out ahead of him?"

"He thought he was chasing a platoon-sized war party." Longarm explained.

The agent said, "There you go. Sneaky snakes-in-the-grass even fooled an old Indian fighter like Custer, and he was looking *out* for 'em! You two had best stay put with fat Lexi, long as you keep it in mind she's a half-witted ward of the government, and let the army catch up with you, here."

They both agreed that that sounded like a grand notion. Back outside, Foster asked, "What are we to do? We can't stay here! What will we ever do if those cavalry troops overtake us?"

Longarm smiled thinly and said, "Spoken like a true rider of the Owl-hoot Ttrail. If it looks like they're fixing to arrest us we tell 'em who we are, of course."

"Then what about our mission?" asked the Canadian.

Longarm shrugged and answered, "What about it? If that breed don't come back, and it's commencing to look as if he don't intend to, we've nowhere to go from here and, what the hell, you can't win 'em all."

"Maybe we can get your army to help us find Natova," Foster suggested.

Longarm suggested that they cross that bridge when they came to it. So they went back to the cabin, and that night they had canned beans, sourdough biscuits and mud pupples instead of trout. Mud puppies were these green and good-sized salamanders as dwelt in the still water of the high country. Neither Longarm nor Foster would be able to say what mud puppies tasted like, pan fried. Neither one felt up to tasting what surely looked like shriveled up fried puppies, with long thick tails.

And so time passed, like cat shit through a funnel, as they speculated on where Lexi's dear old dad might have gone. Foster suggested and Longarm had no call to disagree, something had come up the wire from Fort Missoula to spook a gang member working in the Hungry Horse telegraph shed. But when Foster asked, "Do you think they could be on to us?" Longarm could only reply, "How? In all our adventures since Great Falls, have you told anybody we were lawmen working under cover?"

Foster said, "No. But what if Will Garner in Peacock spread the word we'd double-crossed him?"

Longarm shook his head and asked, "Why would old Will want to do a dumb thing like that? Would you tell pals you'd pulled off an inside job if you didn't mean to share the profits with 'em? Garner's plot to dry gulch us was to shut us up. His only hope, now, is that crooks up this way don't question us too sharp about that payroll robbery. One thing he may think he has going for him is the simple fact we're strangers to the gang, and who are you going to believe, strangers who claim they have no payroll money on 'em or an old pal who says they robbed him?"

Foster marveled, "*Now* you raise that possibility? Don't you see we're riding headlong into quicksand?"

Longarm shrugged and replied, "You said you wanted to find the place, didn't you? You sure are a caution for crossing bridges you may never come to! I don't know what spooked Lexi's dad but something must have for him to blue streak out on her, abandoning his daughter, his job and tolerable cabin. So I vote we stay here no longer than the end of the week and admit we've lost the scent. We ain't getting anywheres and Lexi is commencing to seem better looking with each passing sundown!"

Foster laughed, said, "I know the feeling!" and they agreed to stick her out just a few more days as, to the west, the U.S. Cav was hardly riding to their rescue whilst, to the south, Vance Larson and what was left of his thinned-down and grimly determined personal posse had made it to the Arlee Agency and lucked out with Indians kids who recalled those swell Appaloosa war ponies.

"They *are* headed for the border, as I thought!" His Copper Majesty declared after a consultation with Nutmeg Waterman in his coach. Nutmeg agreed that that seemed the size of it, but speculated on the *motive*.

He said, "This Armstrong D. Weddington, Buck Crawford or whomsoever has been pulling rabbits out of hats all along the way from there to here, sir. Why should he blue streak for the border when he seems to be able to vanish into thin air at will?"

"I'll ask him in the moments he has left if we capture him alive." snarled the copper king, adding, "I don't know *why* he made a sap out me in Helena. Suffice it say he did, and by God I mean to make him pay! What's the next likely place for them to go to ground, to our north?"

Nutmeg replied, "The Indians say there's a swell town called Poison up on the shores of that Lake Flathead to the north."

His Copper Majesty said, "That's where we're headed, then. Rustle up my coachmen and have our riders mount up."

Nutmeg observed, "It's late in the day and the boys were looking foreward to a warm set-down supper here, sir."

Larson snapped, "We'll stop for the night at sundown. Wherever north of here that might find us. If there's a beanery handy they can set down for their suppers there. If there ain't that's what frying pans, coffeepots and campfires were created for. I said I wanted to move on. What are you waiting for, a kiss good-bye?"

Nutmeg got cracking. He needed the money. So a while later they were on the road again, or in point of fact the well-sprung private coach was running astradle the pony track, with its steel-rimmed wheels leaving wet tracks of crushed grass.

As more than one of his remaining riders bitched—they now numbered a baker's dozen—they could have eaten in Arlee for all the time it saved them. They were only six or eight miles north in the middle of nowheres much when His Copper Majesty called a halt and, alighting from his coach like the copper king he claimed to be, Larson pointed at the sunset to the west, exclaiming, "I'll not risk driving in the dark along a less than perfect trail. Some of those bumps along the way were bodacious. So we'll set up our night camp here. Do I have to tell you how one sets up a night camp, Nutmeg?"

He didn't. He got to laze in his coach whilst others gathered fire-wood and built night fires north, south and in line with the handsome private coach. His Copper Majesty had resisted the temptation to gild it with gold leaf and settled for a two-toned red-and-blue paint job with his own notion of the Larson coat of arms on the door. For if such trimmings were good enough for the royal coach of Queen Victoria it was good enough for a copper king. He'd had no idea, when he'd ordered such trimmings, that they might be the death of him.

For as he held court by the central fire, seated by his fancy coach, with Nutmeg and some of the harder cases from Slickrock, the buckshot Turk Butler, who really needed medical attention if he was to live much longer, had been holing up in the woods by day and slogging north toward his lucky star from sundown to sunrise, night after night, drinking from mountain brooks like a critter, with his face in the water, and not having had a bite to eat since something awful had happendd to him. A man could last four minutes without air, four days without water and forty days without food, if he could find no food or felt too feverish to consider eating when he could just keep following his lucky star.

Hence, even though he was on foot and slowly but surely dying, Turk had lurched north, on to the Flathead Reservation, well behind Longarm and Foster but ahead of Vance Larson's party.

He had no way of knowing this, even had his brain been functioning at its never-too-bright best. So he'd never have spotted his old boss from up on the ridge he was running had not his attention been drawn by all those night fires and then, as he stared downslope like a wary wolf outside the range of human ken, it slowly came to him just what red-and-blue-with-gilt trimmings had to say about that coach down yonder.

"The boss! It's the boss!" Turk Butler half sobbed and half slobbered as he launched himself down the long slope at an ever faster run. For now everything was fixing to be all right. The boss was the copper king of Montana Territory. Anything the boss wanted to happen had to happen. The boss would make the painsome itching go away. The boss would cool his fevered brow. The boss could do anything. The boss was his friend. He loved his boss."

As he came running down the slope at them, bare-chested and howling like a banshee, more than one man there went for his gun. But his copper majesty called out,

"Don't shoot him! He's one of our own and look at that boy run!"

As he rose from his folding chair to wave Turk in, the feverish, half-delrious mass of moving muscle recognized that hatchet-faced man to the Boss's left as one of the bunch who'd murdered poor Kesystone and Clay McCord! As he swung his wild stare the other way he saw the boss had *another* lynching son of a bitch from Slickrock to his right. Turk saw it all, now, as he kept on coming. The boss was not his friend! Keystone and Clay McCord had been his friends and that cock sucking boss had had them *killed*!

"What are you doing? What's got into you?" Vance Larson blurted in sudden concern as Turk Butler kept coming right through the campfire, kicking a frying pan one way and a pot of brewing coffee another as he scattered coals with his boots and just kept coming, with his God damned pants on fire!

"Somebody stop him! He's gone loco! Keep him off me, damn it!" cried His Copper Majesty as Turk Butler just kept coming, arms outstretched as if he meant to give his boss a great big hug.

Nutmeg was the first to come unstuck. He shouted, "Stop right where you are, Turk!" as he drew his six-gun and, when that didn't work, shot to kill.

Nutmeg knew how to kill with a six-gun at point-blank range and his shots went true as he emptied the wheel into the heaving rib cage of the bellowing Turk Butler. All five of his shots hit vital organs. Turk was as good as dead on his feet but too worked-up to notice as he grabbed Vance Larson's throat in both his big paws.

They went down together as by now other hired guns were pumping round after round into Turk's still massive if leaner and hungrier hide. The flames from Turk's burning pants spread to the expensive broadcloth of Vance Larson's suit. But His Copper Majesty didn't seem to mind as one of them emptied a canteen over the both of them while Nutmeg rolled the limp mass of Turk Butler off their mutual boss.

Dropping to one knee for a closer look by firelight, Nutmeg Waterman sighed, "Aw, shit, where will I ever get such a grand job again?"

One of the Slickrock riders who'd killed Keystone and McCord asked if His Copper Majesty was dead.

Nutmeg said, "Dead as a turd in a milk bucket. Turk busted his neck like a hangman's rope would have."

Getting back to his feet, Nutmeg added in a philosophical tone, "I recon there must be a God after all. Lord knows this imperial prick was overdue a hanging."

"What do we do now, Nutmeg?" asked one of the more regular Larson riders.

To which Nutmeg could only reply, "Haul him and his fancy coach back to Helena and see what we have coming from the company in lieu of two weeks notice, I reckon. Lord knows we have no reason to chase on after murderous magicians, now!"

Chapter 30

The morning before they'd been fixing to pack it all in, Longarm and Foster were awakened by the dulcet tones of Lexi, shouting out back by the stable, "Daddy! Oh Daddy! Oh Daddy!"

So they got up and ambled out back to meet up with her long-lost dad, another fat breed who answered to the handle of Jacques Portier. As they had Lexi's usual breakfast of canned beans, sourdough biscuits and in this case suckerfish, Portier explained where he'd been all that time. He confided, "Our string of pearls has been broken. One of our friends down in Redeye came home early, caught his woman in bed with a delivery boy and shot them both. We don't know how much he can tell the law, but when a man faces the hangman it tends to loosen his tongue."

Longarm asked, "How much could any particular relay man know about the whole picture, Jacques? Just getting this far, we got the impression nobody was supposed to know more than who'd sent us and where he meant to send us next."

Portier said, "That's the way it's supposed to work. I just had a hell of a time getting relayed all the way up the line to Natova. I had to get there to warn them what came over the wire, from Redeye. Ain't no telegraph line from here to there."

The two undercover lawmen exchanged glances. Longarm asked if such powers as were, up Natova way, about Owlhoot riders such as him and his pal, Mike, here, adding, "We're sort of stuck in the pipeline like turds in a sewer drain. I hope they don't expect us to back out and face the music in the shithouse!"

Portier shook his head and said, "They know you boys are hotter than a whore's pillow on payday night, and they naturally don't want you caught. They have enough to worry about with that jealous asshole down in Redeye. They're worried about renewed army patrols as well. So I'm to lead the two of you, myself, direct to the end of the line with no further shilly-shally."

"And no further . . . How much are you fixing to charge us a meal at the hands of your daughter, Jacques?"

The fat breed chuckled and said, "I figure five hundred ought to do me. Don't scowl like that. I just said I'd be saving you stop after stop along the line, didn't I? My orders are to shunpike, steering clear of chimney smoke and mostly following game trails lest anyone feel able to tell the U.S. Cav which way we might have gone."

Longarm said, "Sounds sensible. When do we move out?"

Portier said, "Sundown. Passing such cabins as we have to in the dark. We'll travel at night and camp with no fire by day. It's high summer and we don't really need fires. Night riding will keep us warm enough in the cooler shades of evening and beans taste tolerable cold from the can."

Since fat Lexi was serving them, Longarm resisted rude remarks about not having to put up with fried pan-fish, and after breakfast her dear old dad left them alone with her some more as he went about more important matters, he said, around Hungry Horse.

Foster speculated the fat bastard was probably getting laid.

Longarm said it was no bet and added it would serve the fat bastard right if they both had a go at his fat daughter. But in the end they agreed molesting children was disgusting enough when the children were pretty.

So they groomed their war ponies and saw to their saddles and saddle guns and still had a hell of a lot of time to kill before old Portier came home for supper, the canned beans, sourdough biscuits and real trout, this time, cooked with inspired originality by Lexi that evening. She burned the biscuits.

All three submitted to her farewell huggings when they mounted up to ride out after sundown. Portier was good or crazy. He led them at a lively pace ever onward and upward to the east. Starting at a fair altitude at Hungry Horse, daybreak found them at Timberline after their all night climb through spruce giving way to juniper, breaking free of everything taller than stirrup high, and not too much of the same.

Timberline was a clearly defined contour line winding north and south, above which things just got too tough for trees. It was the winter winds that turned more ambitious junipers into what looked like driftwood, tortured to death and cast ashore more than two miles above sea level. Further up the ever-rising slopes, summer grass and forbs served to give an impression of rolling prairie until, even higher, snow stayed put all year to slide slowly down to warmer climes as glaciers.

As they made day camp in the shade of a juniper bower right at the timberline, Foster exclaimed he'd heard Natova lay in glacier country, but added, "We're still well south of the border. I take it we follow game trails north, between Timberline and those snow fields above?"

Portier told Foster to let him worry about where they had to go from where they were, adding, "We can't go anywhere until it's dark again. You can see a rider miles away above Timberline.

Foster started to ask why, in that case, they didn't want to move north *below* Timberline, through tall timber.

Then he smiled sheepishly and said, "Right. Other people hunt or rangle cattle below Timberline. But who are we likely to meet up here after dark?"

Longarm, rejoining them after cutting some summer grass for their tethered ponies, juniper not being worth browsing, hunkered down to quietly inform them, "We got company. Don't turn your heads that way, but there's this full-blood pretending he's a cigar-store Indian a pistol shot north along the tree line."

Foster didn't look that way as he asked, "Can you make out his tribe?"

Longarm said, "U.S. Cav, I reckon. He's wearing army blue from the waist up, breech clout and bare bow legs from yonder to his moccasins. Look like Algonquin-style moccasins. Cavalry hat. Hair braided down either side of his face. No paint. Likely scouting for those cavalry patrols we've heard so much about."

Longarm got out two cheroots, lit one and held the other up as he nooded in the mysterious redskin's direction.

The scout broke cover and drifted in, pausing at conversational range to declare, "Hear me, I am Turtle Singer of the Ojibwa Nation, Who are you?"

Longarm called back, "Nature lovers. Loving nature with this B.I.A. guide, here. He belongs on this reservation. Ain't you a tad west of your wild-rice swamps, old son?"

"Who told you about our ricing grounds? Are you trying to mock me, *shemanese*?"

Longarm repeated his silent offer of tobacco as he soberly replied, "Would any of us long-knives mock any of your kind?" before he recited in a firmer tone, "By the shores of gimme gimme. By a great big muddy puddle . . ."

Turtle Singer laughed despite himself but as soberly recited back, "Stood the wigwag of Baking Soda. Daughter full of wind, Baking Soda!"

Foster asked their fat breed guide what he was missing. Portier said it beat the shit out of him.

As Turtle Singer came on in to hunker down and accept the cheroot with a nod of thanks, Longarm explained, "Inside joke, shared by many a bilingual full-blood raised on any Algonquin dialect."

Foster said, "The two of you were mangling Longfellow's poem about Hiawatha, right?"

Longarm nodded but said, "Mr. Longfellow mangled it first. He aimed to set an Iroquois legend to poetic license. But not speaking any Iroquois he fell back on the more familar Algonquin, in this case the Ojibwa or Chippewa dialect, to describe how the original Iroquois organized their Five Nations, as deadly enemies of all Algonquin speakers. So, to Indians, it's as if one set out to recite the legends of Richard the Lion-Hearted and his Third Crusade as Arabian poetry, with all the crusaders having Arab names."

Singing Turtle lit his own cheroot before he asked, "Have you forgotten Minnihaha?"

"That pretty little thing with that *Nadowessioux* name?

Who could forget her, seeing Hiawatha was so fond of her in spite of what he'd always called her nation in Ajibwa? Of course, according to Mr. Longfellow he was an Iroquois medince man who'd become confused along the way. Growing up in an Algonquin wigwam and all."

Foster said, "In other words you're saying Longfellow was writing a lot of poetic twaddle?"

Longarm shook his head and said, "*I* never said it. *Indians* keep saying it to me. They feel a lot of things we do and say are comical."

Then, lest Turtle Singer feel too smug, he added, "I've always found their habit of stirring white flour into coffee sort of comical and the less said about some of their other culinary customs the better."

Turtle Singer pounted, "Hear me, my peope do not eat dogs. We eat *moose*. That is another Ojibwa word, and your people pay a lot for the black rice we gather in our ricing grounds!"

"He means swamps," Longarm explained.

The Indian scowled and said, "You *are* mocking me! Hear me, our black rice tastes better than anything grown in China or the Carolinas! I wish I had some right now! Why am I wasting time here with rude *shemanese*?"

Suiting actions to his words the scout rose to his feet and padded silently away, cutting into the trees to regather his own pony, Longarm hoped.

Foster said, "I think you hurt his feelings."

Longarm said, "I was trying to, once I'd steered him away from tight questions about us."

Turning to Portier he said, "We'd best be moving on, Jacques. That old boy is sure to report this position to the army."

Portier said, "We'll move down the tree line a piece,

then. My orders are to show you the way to Natova in the dark."

"Meaning we're not supposed to see our way by daylight?" asked the Mountie in mufti.

Portier didn't answer. They didn't press him. They made day camp to the south, a slick choice to Foster's way of thinking, and caught up on some shut-eye before riding on after sundown above Timberline.

Longarm held his own council. It was Foster who pointed up at the clear, starry sky to protest, "We're headed the wrong way! Everyone knows Natova is the other way, up by the border!"

"Were you there, pard?" asked Longarm, dryly, without further comment. Foster started to say something dumb, nodded thoughtfully and said, "Of course! How perishing obvious as soon as you consider how many others sought in vain for Natova along the border to the north!"

Longarm said nothing. He'd long since noticed crooks were by definition big fibbers. Anybody could promise an outlaw on the run a safe hideout beyond the reach of U.S. Jurisdiction. Anyone could say, "Just give us the money and let us worry about where our Island of Lost Boys might be. The more outlaws who thought Natova was where it couldn't be, the more lawmen who'd search for it in vain. It was all a big fat lie that worked because it was so blatant. Folk believed or disbelieved what you told them according to how your unsupported words fit their fancies. They'd all laughed at mountain men who'd made her back to civilization all ababble about lakes filled with washing soda, ghost towns stuck to canyon wall like wasps' nests, hot springs and steaming geysers shooting high as any steeple, or mighty redwood trees soaring even higher. Yet all those tall tales had panned out true, whilst cold sober solid citizens still sent away for patent medicines guaranteed to grow hair on bald heads, melt fat away like candle wax, make you stronger than Ajax without having to exercise a muscle. Cures for incurable illnesses sold even better. Folk bought what they wanted to believe they could buy and an outlaw on the dodge would pay most anything to stay the hell out of jail or escape the hangman's noose.

That night, high in the sky with that ever-waxing moon to offer some helpful hints, Longarm saw Portier was leading in what would have been plain view along the wide-open slope above Timberline. Towards the break of day, way the hell south of where they'd expected, Portier led them up a steeper incline that wound 'round an isolated granite dome, thrusting up like a coral reef or mayhaps a coral island. You couldn't see the top, even as the sky got lighter up above it all.

Then, as day broke over the snow-capped higher peaks to the east they saw they weren't riding *'round* the granite massif. They were riding up a cleft on the eastward cliffs of the same. It was a bright and sunny summer morn as they came up out of the cleft to ride atop a broad flat-top worth, say, eighty acres, with a small but substantial village of stone-walled structures in plain sight to anybody as high in the sky. But who was likely to be higher? Nobody lived on those higher snow-capped peaks to the east. There were not higher peaks of any sort to the west.

"Welcome to Natova," said Jacques Portier, leading them on to the cluster of stone-walled buildings.

Longarm said, "Pretty slick. Hidden in plain sight, like that purloined letter Mr. Edgar Allan Poe wrote about."

Foster shook his head and said, "It's a brazen swindle! There's no hidden valley athwart the border after all!"

Longarm replied, "I noticed. But consider what they've promised to deliver. Anyone can see no lawman in hell would ever track you to this island in the sky. Not looking for a secret canyon way the hell to the north, least ways."

They both knew they'd have to plan their exit later, out of earshot to Portier or anyone else up there.

Portier reined in out front of a more imposing building. So they followed suit, tethered their war ponies along with his paint to the hitching rail out front and followed him inside, they supposed, to talk about their entry fee to this exclusive club.

As they stepped in out of the sun's dazzle it took them a few moments to make out the flashy brunette seated at a desk in the center of the one room in all her glory. As their eyes adjusted she got less pretty and more hard-eyed. She said, "Good morning. They call me Saint Lou and I call the shots here in Natova. The gentlemen to my right and left may strike you as gussied-up dudes. But they can afford to dress so fine because I pay well for the best guns money can hire."

Portier was already leaving. A third gun-hand shut and barred the door after him. Longarm was too polite to observe that all three of her hired guns looked like her pimps. He nodded and said, "Pleased to meet-up with tou at last, Miss Saint Lou. I reckon you know who we are and why we're here?"

Saint Lou purred, "Indeed we do. We've been expecting you, Deputy U.S. Marshal Long and Crown Sergeant Foster. So first we'll have your six-guns and then we can talk."

Chapter 31

If Longarm had said it once he'd said it hundreds of times to junior lawmen he was breaking in, there were times for talk and times for action, and you never told a suspect he was under arrest before you had the drop on him. So that overconfident impulse to gloat was going to cost Saint Lou more than gloating was worth.

Longarm had naturally entered such uncertain surroundings with his double derringer palmed in his big right fist and the fools had shut and barred the only door. Crown Sergeant Foster had been broken in to follow the same rules. So he was already slapping leather, the same as everybody else, and things got mighty confusing for a time.

The palmed derringer made the difference as Longarm fired first on the faster one near the desk, to put a second last shot in the other.

The hard-eyed harridan screamed like a felt-up banshee as Foster beat the one by the door to the draw. She craw-fished clear of the deck still seated in her captain's chair on casters. Longarm shouted, "Window!" as he chased after Saint Lou through thick gunsmoke while the brunette clawed her satin skirts up.

She hadn't been out to tempt him with her private parts, he saw, as she would have drawn that garter gun if he hadn't back-handed the gal over backwards, chair and all, as he drew his .44-40.

He risked the time it took to hunker down and rip her fandango skirts off and into strips, to have her hog-tied and lashed to her chair on the floor before he made it over to the one other window through the stone walls. His stood at right angles to the one Foster manned by the front door.

"See anything?" Longarm called.

Foster called back, "Portier led our ponies away. Got a clear field of fire across a sort of central plaza. Nobody in sight out there. You?"

Longarm called back, "Smaller field of fire. No windows covering this one. Suicide for anybody on the roof across the way. Mighty big boom for anybody moving in blind from either end of the breezeway. May as well chance her now as later, after they've had time to think!"

Stepping over the dazed and moaning woman on the floor, Longarm made it over to the fireplace, found the coals of a night fire had been banked, and soon had fresh juniper cordwood blazing bright.

Foster asked why, pointing out, "It's a sunny summer day outside and I for one feel sweaty enough right now!"

Longarm said, "Ain't warming things up for us in here. Hope to warm things up for them out yonder!"

Once he had a good log-fire going, Longarm balled up the remains of that torn-away fandango skirt and placed it atop the fire. The results were not as disgusting as he'd hoped. Silk burned with a clean flame. That was likely why they used it to bag artilley charges.

He asked Foster if the one he'd downed by the door was dead. Foster glanced down, said, "Not yet."

Then he planted the instep of his boot sideways across his victim's exposed throat and threw all his weight on it. There came a big wet crunch and the Canadian said, "He is now. What's the form?"

Longarm said, "Strip that fancy leather and likely pissed-in *charro* outfit off him and toss it over here."

Foster didn't argue. He nodded and said, "I follow your drift, as you so quaintly put it."

Longarm moved back for another glance out into the breezeway, nodded, and got to work on the soggy blood-and-piss soaked pants of the ones he'd downed.

Saint Lou was coming around, with her long legs exposed and asprawl, now that she'd been tied up with her shredded fandango skirt. She shook her mussed head to clear it as she plaintively asked, "What happened just now? Are you all right, Lem?"

To which Longarm replied, not unkindly, "No, Ma'am, he ain't. Can't say which of these old boys might be your Lem but in either case it was dumb to deal with men you all *knew* to be trained gunfighters as if you were holding up a candy store!"

"Untie me or I'll fix you good, Longarm!" she hissed.

He told her flattery cut no ice with him as he gingerly dragged pissed-up leather pants to the fireplace to toss aboard the burning logs. The whole place suddenly filled with stinking smoke and Longarm chuckled.

As he worked the fireplace damper Foster knew what he was doing. The tied-up Saint Lou coughed and sputtered, "Don't you know how to work a damned fireplace damper, you fool?"

He said, "Sure do. I could use more rags over here, Sarge!"

When the Canadian lobbed the other victim's leather vest and hat to him, Longarm was delighed to see that old boy had left half his wet brains in the crown of the same.

"You're crazy! Make up your mind! Open that fucking damper or shut it and asphixiate us all! See if I care!" snarled Saint Lou. Longarm was commencing to suspect she was not a nice lady.

A distant voice called, "Hello, Saint Lou! You all right, ma'am?"

Longarm moved over by Foster to shout, "Lady can't talk to you now. This is Deputy U.S. Marshal Custis Long, backed up by Crown Sergeant Foster of the Northwest Mounted Police. If you boys don't want to surrender I strongly advise you to saddle up and ride."

"What have you done to Saint Lou, to Lem, Spud and Aaron?" that same voice demanded.

Longarm suggested, "You let us worry about them and you'd best worry about you. I'm only warning you to avoid needless injury to the smaller potatoes. Seing we got Saint Lou and expect her to sing real sweet in the near future."

"Have you been smoking loco weed?" the outlaw outside jeered, adding, "We know more about where *you* are than you know about where *we* are. We know how much food and water you got in there. How long do you figure you can hold out?"

Longarm replied, "Long as we have to. Won't be all that long."

As the gunslicks huddled across the way with staff members and other guests hiding out there, one observed, "They say Longarm's good and he just now, somehow, turned the tables on three good gunfighters and a mighty dangerous gal! What do you figure he's up to? He has to have something in mind!"

The self-elected spokesman, like all such natural windbags, chose to decree, "They're bluffing. *Have* to be bluffing. We got 'em pinned down with no food or water."

A cooler head among them pointed out, "Could get mighty rough on Saint Lou and the boys if they're still alive and . . . look at all that smoke coming out the chimney, now! What could they be burning in there? What could it all mean?"

Their spokesman snorted, "Likely Saint Lou's papers, out of spite. You got to picture how spiteful they must feel right now. They know we got 'em boxed in like rats in a trap. There's nothing they can do about it!"

He was wrong, of course. A good hour's ride to the north, the commander of that patrolling cavalry squadron reined to call out, "What do you make of those smoke signals, Turtle Singer? Could they possibly be Sioux? Can you make out their meaning?"

The Ajibwa whose father and father's father had fought the sister-fucking *Nadowessioux* before him shot the major a look of distain and replied, "Hear me, not possible. Really them! Smoke say they have sighted column of *Washichu*. That what they call you. Of course they sight us, out here on open ground. Turtle Singer know where *they* are, too, show off sons of sneaky little snakes! What about those other *shemaenese* I told you about? I thought you wanted me to cut their trail for you."

The major said, "Forget 'em! We were never ordered to track down suspicious white riders! We were ordered to track down Sioux and by Custer's hair I think we've *got* 'em if those smoke signals are rising from that granite butte down yonder."

He told his scout to take the point as he stood in his stirrups to gather in his junior officers. Once he had, he said, "Some asshole Sioux with a mighty poor grasp of field tactics is perched like a cat up a tree saying dirty things about us in smoke. Captain Brannigan, you'll move in in a column of twos a hundred yards upslope. Captain Dorfler, you do the same a hundred yards lower, along the tree line. I'll move in along *this* contour line. First we surround them. Then we move in afoot through that rock pile. Are there any questions?"

There were none. The plan was simple, direct, and usually worked, as it did that time, save for a little gunplay at the end when astounded deperados, or mayhaps a third of them, elected to fight their way out against hopeless odds. One did not shoot it out across open ground with lighter civilian ammunition against the slower but surer U.S. Cavalry's awesome .50–70 carbine, designed and meant to empty a saddle as much as a mile away.

Most of the eighty-odd souls trapped atop the butte everyone had described as a hidden canyon gave up without a fight and possibly a third of them were no more than camp followers.

The troopers gathered 'round were confused and to some extent a tad chagrined as Longarm explained he and Foster hadn't meant to make fools of anybody. As Longarm explained to the bemused major, "It was like that old joke about the janitor locked in the shithouse. He commenced to holler 'Fire! Fire! Fire!' because how many others were likely to come to the aid of a man yelling, 'Shithouse! Shithouse! Shithouse!' "

"Then you're saying there were never any Sioux around here at all," the major sighed.

It had been a statement rather than a question, but Longarm replied, "I ain't saying shit about the Sioux, Major. I don't know what, if anything somebody saw as a Sioux in these parts. Folk see Sioux as far south as Texas even though Sergeant Foster assures me Canada has 'em under control well north of the border. But looking on the bright side, you soldiers blue are fixing to get a heap of credit for bringing in all these wanteds, with so many of them wanted serious by the Federal Government.

So they shook on that and got to work herding outlaws afoot down to Fort Missoula, which was closer. As the army turned the prisoners over to civilian lawmen so's they could get back to chasing Indians, Longarm and Foster rode together by stage as far as the railhead to the east of the Rockies, where they parted friendly, each to go his own way with a mission completed added to his tally.

Thus it came to pass Longarm got into Denver late of a Saturday night and got to spend that as well as Sunday and Sunday night in the company of a certain society widow who lived down Sherman Street from old Billy and his easily shocked wife.

Chatting about his recent adventures, sometimes dog-style and sometimes missionary, Longarm was able to sort his recent adventures out in bed with a willing listener. He felt no call to relate the dirty details to either his widow with the soft brown hair or old Billy Vail when he reported in, Monday morning.

As he entered the waiting room, old Henry, the young squirt who played the typewriter and kept the files out front, told Longarm the report he'd sent in earlier by way of the Society of Jesus had been received and acted upon. Will Garner had made a full confession about that inside job and all the others from Mother Krieger to the expensive blacksmith at the Bigfork Agency who'd sent them on to Jacques Portier had been picked up.

Henry said a night letter from the marshal's office in Helena had the hard-boiled Saint Lou singling like a canary, naming names nobody had ever known they wanted so bad for so much crookery.

So when Longarm joined the older, shorter and way stubbier Marshal Billy Vail in the oak-paneled back office, he began by plopping down in the leather guest chair and exclaiming, "I don't know why I have to tell you where I've been or what I've been up to. Henry just now told me you paper-pushers have more loose ends tied up than one could shake a stick at."

Vail nodded his bullet head to smugly reply, "That's how come we spend so much time pushing papers."

Vail glanced down at the papers spread atop his desk to remark, "I see nothing as to whom you might suspect of having recognized you and passed the word on ahead of your arrival."

Longarm said, "My Jesuit pals asked to let them handle that. Nobody recognized us. We were too slick. But this Mission Indian was standing there like a big-ass bird whilst Foster and me told Father Bernard at the Saint Ignatius Mission who we were and what we were up. It was easy for him to pass the word on ahead of us. When it got to Jacques Portier he blue streaked all the way to the end of the line to ask what they wanted him to do about us when we showed up at Hungry Horse. The rest you know. Father Bernard says that one big gossip has the makings of a good cook and it ain't as if he has anybody to gossip with, now."

Vail nodded curtly and decided, "You done good. There's this budding cattle baron up in Larimer County who says he's a red-blooded American who goes to church on Sunday and fails to see how the Homestead Act of 1862 could apply to him and all that open prairie he saw first. You'd best get up yonder and see if you can convince him of the error of his ways."

Longarm started to say something dumb. But he knew what Vail would answer and what the hell, it felt good to be back to the same old grind.